The Stage Warriors are women from around the world who use theatre to talk about war, politics, crime, abuse, and violence in nations where these subjects are taboo. The interviews in this book explain how these women came to use theatre to enact change, who they help, and the importance of their work.

Beyond the boundaries of poverty, religion, and intolerance, these women use theatre to broaden citizen participation, bring focus and energy, and reshape national identity. Through the shows and workshops they create, the Warriors are finding ways to help the disenfranchised exert power in education, politics, the economy, and the home.

The Stage Warriors have faced stiff resistance. Some have seen their offices consumed in flames. Others have found their cars destroyed. Still others have been physically assaulted. Yet nothing stops these women from making a space where their voices can be heard. These theatre practitioners display the resourcefulness, strength, and promise that characterize women across the globe who are steadily bringing stability and justice to conflicted regions.

Voices of Women from *Stage Warriors*

"When we went out, all of our cars had been broken."

"If people had known who I was my life would have been in danger."

"I feel safer in the jail than I do walking down the street."

"They could take the car over, kidnap the whole troupe."

"We actually announced that war is coming and that we are the war."

"I turned on the TV and there is David being arrested."

"The only thing that they feared for was my life."

"Luckily no one was badly injured, but we were all affected by the fresh tear gas bomb."

"After the show Zahra was ambushed."

Stage Warriors

Stage Warriors

Women on the Front Lines of Dangerous Drama

Sarah Imes Borden

Cune

Stage Warriors:
Women on the Front Lines of
Dangerous Drama
© 2015 Sarah Imes Borden
Cune Press, Seattle 2015
First Edition
2 4 6 8 9 7 5 3

Hardback	ISBN 978-1-61457-088-2	$34.95
Paperback	ISBN 978-1-61457-089-9	$21.95
Kindle	ISBN 978-1-61457-097-4	$ 9.99
eBook	ISBN 978-1-61457-096-7	$ 9.99

Library of Congress Cataloging-in-Publication Data

Borden, Sarah Imes.
Stage warriors : women on the front lines of dangerous drama / Sarah Imes Borden.
pages cm
Includes bibliographical references.
ISBN 978-1-61457-088-2 (hardback) -- ISBN 978-1-61457-089-9 (pbk.) -- ISBN 978-1-61457-096-7 (ebook)
1. Theater--Production and direction. 2. Women theatrical producers and directors--Interviews. I. Title.
PN2053.B596 2014
792.02'33082--dc23   2014011195

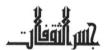

Select titles in the Bridge Between the Cultures Series:
Curse of the Achille Lauro: A Tribute to Lost Souls - by Reem al-Nimer
The Plain of Dead Cities: A Syrian Tale - by Bruce McLaren
Gulen's Dialogue on Education: A Caravanserai of Ideas - by Tom Gage
*Syria - A Decade of Lost Chances: Repression and
Revolution from Damascus Spring to Arab Spring* - by Carsten Wieland
The Ottoman Mosaic: Exploring Models for Peace by Re-exploring the Past
by Kemal Karpat and Yetkin Yıldırım
Steel & Silk: Men and Women Who Shaped Syria 1900 - 2000 - by Sami Moubayed
The Road from Damascus: A Journey Through Syria - by Scott C. Davis

www.cunepress.com | www.cunepress.net | www.cunepress.info

Table of Contents

Introduction 10

Chapter 1: Always in Danger 17
"We were always in danger and we confront
   this danger with our art."
   —Sanja Krsmanovic Tasic and Maja Vujovic (neé Mitic)

Chapter 2: Different Eyes 29
"I want them to see their lives with different eyes."
   —Iman Aoun

Chapter 3: Hate Mail 39
"Do you know you've just gotten the most hate mail
that anyone on this program has ever gotten?"
   —Shauna Kanter

Chapter 4: The Measure of Humanity 46
"My humanity is measured in the way I treat others."
   —Jen Capraru

Chapter 5: Leave Prison Behind 73
"They see our work as an opportunity to leave prison life behind."
   —Penelope Glass

Chapter 6: Healing Wounds 79
"I felt that it may help me to heal my wounds."
   —Sina Chhon

Chapter 7: Chance to Communicate 79
"It was their first chance to communicate to the external world."
   —Zeina Daccache

Chapter 8: Support in Afghanistan 90
"We are working to support the people."
  —Zahra

Chapter 9: A Mirror of Conflict 101
"Theatre wants to help people to help
their society and their country."
  —Monirah Hashemi

Chapter 10: Revolution & Censorship 108
"I just perform and they can come and find me."
  —Dr Dalia Basiouny

Chapter 11: Rise of Fundamentalism 115
"It's about the rise of religious fundamentalism."
  —Madeeha Gauhar

Chapter 12: The Use of Theatre 122
"Most people don't realize that theatre is used for revolution."
  —Phionah Katushabe

Chapter 13: The River & the Mountain 133
"I guess I'm just now finding out how dangerous it is."
  —Angella Emerwon and Esther Bwanika

Chapter 14: No Longer Ashamed 144
"When we found others who were victims
  of the same crimes we were no longer ashamed to speak."
  —FAVILEK and the Bond Street Theatre

Epilogue 172

Resources
Notes 176
Acknowledgements 181
Bibliography 182
Index 183
Author Bio 186

Table of Illustrations

Chapter 2 33
An ASHTAR poster for a public presentation of The Gaza Monologues *on March 17ᵗʰ, 2011 in Ramallah. Photo courtesy of Iman Aoun.*

Chapter 4 53
The poster for The Monument, *performed in 2011 in Toronto. Photo courtesy of Jennifer Capraru.*

Chapter 6 77
Sina Chhon following her performance at La MaMa in 2010. Photo courtesy of the author.

Chapter 7 85
Zeina Daccache directs inmates of Roumieh Prison in 12 Angry Lebanese *in 2008. Photo courtesy of Dalia Khamissy/Catharsis-LCDT.*

Chapter 8 101
Zarha Yagana, member of AHRDO in Kabul. Photo undated, courtesy of Hjalmar-Jorge Joffre-Eichhorn.

Chapter 9 108
Photo from Monirah Hashemi's Masks under Burqa *performed in Turkey in 2012.*

Chapter 13 141
Still from The River and Mountain, *in Kampala in 2013. Photo credit: Jan Cattebeke, courtesy of David Cecil.*

Chapter 14 156
Members of FAVILEK, undated photo courtesy of Anna Zastrow.

Introduction

What would you risk for your life's work? We build significant identities around what we do for a living. We go through school, invest in further education, training, and apprenticeship, and then begin the work itself. Our careers connect us to others like us, feed our families, and fuel growth and opportunities earned through our own labors. We feel invested in what we do. But what is the extent of our investment? How far do we risk our financial freedom? To what extent do we risk our personal relationships? Are our jobs worth citizenship in our nations? Are they worth risking our physical safety? Our families' safety? Our lives?

While there are certainly occupations that we expect to be risky, such as jobs in the military and police force, we don't often think of artists' occupations in this light. We rarely read death-defying accounts involving people who do theatre for a living. While we sometimes see profiles of hardworking, savvy theatre practitioners scrambling to mount a successful show, often artists aren't credited for their perseverance, perspective, and insight unless the show is also a moneymaker. While the glossy and commercial aspects of theatre may receive attention, theatre artists who aren't famous for mainstream film or television projects aren't likely to get coverage at all.

Plays can be many things: provoking, touching, comedic, cathartic, embarrassing, even life-altering. They have not, however, normally been thought of as inherently dangerous. Until now. This book is a celebration of women from around the world who choose to do theatre in dangerous places. The danger may be physical, mental, sexual, political, or social, but for every woman it is real and tangible. Though their work we have a unique chance to witness the strength and commitment these women have shown to their art, their communities, and themselves. They face bombings, death threats, arson, and arrest, and they do it with courage, pride, perseverance, and tremendous humor. These women explain in their own words their artistic processes, the reasons they do what they do, and the legacy they hope to leave through their work. These women are on the front lines of dangerous drama. They are Stage Warriors.

At first glance, the connection between these women isn't obvious. Each woman came to her career (some call it a vocation) in a different fashion. For some, theatre is a defining feature of their lives, while for others it is only a small part of how they see themselves. The women also differ demographically.

Some come from privileged backgrounds and have supportive families. The majority of these women come from modest means, although not poverty. A few do come from outright poverty, and by the standards of the West, are still there. But Stage Warriors are defined by their similarities, not their differences. These women share similar ways of approaching workshop exercises, similar feelings of responsibility to their communities, and unusual ways of defining the word *safety*.

Theatre of the Oppressed

The first similarity between these women is methodological in nature: the Stage Warriors have been taught certain theatre practices and they use these methods in creative and effective ways. One phrase that appears consistently throughout this book is "Theatre of the Oppressed." This is a particular method of remaking theatre so that it's more than just actors performing for an audience. The actors help the audience define their own stories and how to tell them.

It would be impossible to explore the work of the Stage Warriors without discussing Augusto Boal and his Theatre of the Oppressed. Many of the Stage Warriors in this book mention specific aspects of Theatre of the Oppressed in their interviews. What is Theatre of the Oppressed (TO) and how is it applied today?

In 1971, Brazil was ruled by military dictatorship. While its harsh policies affected every citizen, the poorest Brazilians undoubtedly suffered the worst persecution and injustice. These citizens lacked a vehicle to express their anger, sorrow, or hopes. They needed a means to give voice to their experiences and to encourage solidarity against the oppressive regime. A director and playwright named Augusto Boal shaped a series of theatrical interactions that allowed ordinary men and women to use theatre to fight for freedom.

Boal did more than create a bridge between traditional theatre performed on a stage using a fourth wall and theatre done in the streets with participants who did not consider themselves professional actors. He got the audience to define their own oppression, work on ways to stand up against this oppression, and then help others do the same. There was no "audience" as we normally think of it. Instead, there was a room of "actor-participants" or "spect-actors," led by trained artists who used games and exercises to help each person be involved in the creation of the play.

The first technique Boal introduced was Newspaper Theatre. In this technique, a group of trained actors would lead the actor-participants in scenarios taken from a newspaper article from that day. Boal wanted people to explore the newspaper as a theatrical fiction: what did the story say? What could it mean? Could it be wrong? In the era of the military junta, it was necessary to question what was in the newspaper. Unfortunately, it was also dangerous.

Boal was tortured and exiled for his Newspaper Theatre work in Brazil, and could not return until 1985, after the military had been overthrown.

During this exile, Boal found many more ways to use theatre as a tool for social and political change. In 1973, while living in Peru, he developed Forum Theatre. In Forum Theatre, a group of trained actors present a scene concerning a particular problem or injustice. The spect-actors are then invited to help the protagonist of the scene overcome the problem. The spect-actors look at the solutions presented, and can analyze outcomes and apply the ideas to their personal situations. Forum Theatre is sometimes referred to as "rehearsal for real life." Zahra, from the Afghan theatre group AHRDO, talks about these rehearsals for real life when she discusses her work. She notes that Afghan citizens were more willing to accept theatre as relevant to real life (and a socially acceptable pursuit for a woman) when they realized that the actors were working towards something more than frivolous entertainment.

One of the most commonly discussed and utilized forms of TO is Invisible Theatre. The aim of Invisible Theatre is to spark dialogue and initiate actions to address specific problems. Invisible Theatre is different from Forum or Newspaper Theatre because it is not improvisational but is fully rehearsed before it is presented. It's also different from TO because the audience is not aware they are seeing a performance. In Invisible Theatre, actors create a dialogue specific to a problem or injustice in their immediate area that needs to be addressed. They then go into public spaces and perform their script where they know people can hear them. Cafes, health clinics, subways, and busy street corners are all good backdrops for an Invisible Theatre piece.

Invisible Theatre has its own set of risks and rewards. Because the actors are not on a stage, people may freely observe and interact with them. If the "audience" doesn't like what they hear, the actors could be harassed or even assaulted. The flip side of this risk is the opportunity for immediate positive feedback. If two men overhear a piece about mistreatment of women, perhaps one of them will vow to watch his behavior. If a group of women see an Invisible Theatre play about reproductive healthcare, perhaps they will talk among themselves about positive changes they can make. Invisible Theatre is a great way to introduce specific concepts to a small group of people who probably would not go to see an entire play on a volatile subject. The Stage Warriors in Afghanistan, Chile and Serbia all talk about how to approach creating a piece for an audience that may not want to come into a theatre and feel disenfranchised, lectured, or belittled. Invisible Theatre offers a solution to this issue.

There are many other modes of theatre that fall under the category of Theatre of the Oppressed. Some of them are rather abstract, such as Image Theatre, which strives to communicate through "images and space" rather than words. Others are quite concrete: Legislative Theatre, for instance, aims to write down the results of Forum Theatre and then compile a list of laws to be introduced at a local or national level.

All of the branches of Theatre of the Oppressed have a few things in common. They use a disciplined approach to ensure that every participant is heard equally. They encourage spect-actors to respect the ideas and dignity of each participant. People are invited to be brave, silly, even ridiculous, because the theatre is a safe place to try new things. Perhaps most importantly, games and workshop tools are employed to tailor the experience to each group of participants. There are never two shows or workshops that end the same way.

When a TO group meets, they can use games to get to know each other, trust each other, and feel like they belong to the group. These games give the participants a sense of ownership in the project and can lessen tensions. In some parts of the world, these games can allow men and women to interact in ways that their societies usually discourage. Another key feature of a TO game is the creation of an acceptable group dynamic and dialogue. Some of the women in this book speak of the need for women to find their voices. If they have lived in a country where women are not encouraged to speak up, such women need explicit guarantees that the dialogue they create will be honored and shared only with others who will accept the dynamic. There are many steps between saying something out loud for the first time and permitting it to be said in public on a stage. As Zahra explains,

> We are trying to work on trust building, improvisation, and Image Theatre . . . we are trying to create a game that can help them connect to leadership. How can they take the leadership position, how can they be a leader?

Practitioners of Theatre of the Oppressed guide these steps, allowing participants to bow out if they don't want to take a certain step forward.

Responsibility as Artists and Citizens

Each woman I talked to sees herself as part of a tradition she is fortunate to carry forward. Some see drama itself as a great historical undertaking, one that they are proud to introduce to a community that didn't know much about theatre. Other women said that they are excited to use drama for the benefit of a particular cause, such as making legislative changes in Afghanistan or finding solutions to social problems in Uganda. It was very common that their original works came from a need to show the plight of people who could not find a voice for themselves. The creation of that voice (and its amplification) is a responsibility that the Stage Warriors take to heart. All of the women spoke eagerly about the changes they hoped their projects would affect. A few spoke quite humbly about how they learned that change is something that must be asked for and supported in a community. As Shauna Kanter warns in her interview, "You cannot enforce your own view. You need to listen to people and find out what they need." Jen Capraru speaks eloquently of her fears of bringing a show into Rwanda. How could she be sensitive to the needs of others if she wasn't African? As she says,

> It would be different as a Rwandan, directing this play there, because one would be immersed in the culture. Part of the balance of intercultural theatre is that it's very delicate. It's slow. You must do a lot of research and especially, you must listen. A lot. It can be tricky, listening to people, watching their eyes, trying to understand that which is unsaid . . . people are very welcoming there, they might respond with, "Yes, this would be great!" But there's always that little bit of instinct in me that says, "Is it?" So you watch, you listen, you learn.

The Stage Warriors fight for many things. They fight to be heard, to be understood, and to be accepted. They also fight against oppression, poverty, sexism, rape, and violence. One thing they never do is pit the audience against the players. The Stage Warriors are aware that they are part of communities that are constantly evolving, in which people have different needs and different abilities to listen, speak, fight back, or take control. All of these women talk about the process of discovering what the people need to hear, and how best to open that communication. The process is meant to be inclusive instead of confrontational. When Dah Teatar confronted their fellow Serbs about the war crimes being committed in the former Yugoslavian states, they weren't claiming to be better than their fellow Serbs. Instead, they were trying to open a dialogue about Serbia as a whole. They wanted to say: This is what our government, our soldiers, our people are doing. What do we think about this? Is this right or wrong? Who stands up to our government when we believe it is wrong? The theatre decided to stand against the war and to take the side of people promoting peaceful dialogue and compromise. As Maja Vujovic (née Mitic) puts it,

> There was a lot of resistance in newspapers . . . a lot of resistance from students. It was a lot of people from many other environments who supported us. And we chose, also, to go out. We didn't make a performance in a very comfortable environment, in a space where people are paying. We went out in the streets.

Ultimately, the theatre of the Stage Warrior is out on the streets. It's touring, entering non-traditional spaces, going where there is an audience to be served. By taking their message to the front lines of their communities, Stage Warriors convey an immediacy and intimacy that helps their message hit home.

Many of the men and women who produce this type of theatre have formed networking organizations so that they can meet others like themselves, trade ideas, and pool resources. One of the largest such organizations is Theatre Without Borders. TWB was created in 2003 by Roberta Levitow, Catherine Filloux, Deborah Brevoort, and Erik Ehn. It was intentionally designed as an online community so that artists around the globe could share ideas on using theatre as a tool for peace building and cultural exchange. When Theatre Without Borders announced in 2005 that they were going to hold their first-ever "real life" meeting in the New Dramatists Theatre to get ideas on how to expand and utilize their growing email lists, they expected a dozen people to show up. After they had seated over 70 participants they understood that the international theatre community really wanted and needed channels of communication through which people could ask questions, get advice, vent, create, and make contact with colleagues in remote locations. Thus, Theatre Without Borders grew from a handful of people to a multinational organization that today serves thousands of artists. On their webpage, TWB states, "We started with a need, not a plan, and we exist in our actions to respond to that need. Our purpose is 'Conversation', 'Hospitality' and 'Information Sharing'. We welcome professionals, academics, amateurs, artists working in countries where there is no such thing as a 'professional theatre community' and students."[1]

In September of 2010 the Theatre Without Borders community invited me to their New York City convention, *Acting Together On the World Stage: A Conference on Theatre and Peace Building in Conflict Zones*, presented by TWB and La MaMa E.T.C. Although I had no firm plans for this book beyond an urgent desire to seek out women who were doing dangerous theatre, and a mission to tell their story the best way I knew how, they welcomed me. The organizers and participants were world-class practitioners, performers, and writers. Their generosity of spirit and creativity made the TWB conference one of the most satisfying artistic experiences of my life. It was there that I met Sina Chhon, Hjalmar-Jorge Joffre-Eichhorn, Iman Aoun, Catherine Filloux, the members of Dah Teatar, and several other practitioners whom you'll see in these pages. I owe Theatre Without Borders a debt of gratitude. I also owe them for the recurring thought that presented itself to me during my four days in the conference: everyone there was looking at performance as a way to reach people at a human level, no matter how hard it was to see the situation itself as a human situation. Actors, writers, and directors took abuse, rape, famine, war, disease, and terror as given circumstances for themselves and their audiences. The goal was to create a safe space wherever they could.

In the last few moments of the conference we gathered onstage and were instructed to hold hands. We were told to remember that no matter where we are in the world, no matter what we are staging or where we are working, the people in this room are holding our hands. Theatre Without Borders supports performance as a way to foster peace and understanding throughout humankind.

Dangerous Drama

A final thought on these actresses, writers and directors at the front lines of dangerous drama: they have an incredible definition of the word "dangerous." To a woman, everyone I interviewed told me that I was talking to the wrong person, that what they do isn't very dangerous, but they couldn't wait to meet the other women who were really putting it all on the line. Or perhaps they told me that it was slightly dangerous, but the danger would pass soon and then we'd talk. Even Dalia Basiouny, who couldn't immediately schedule her first interview because she was providing first aid supplies to people being hurt outside her door, told me that she didn't fear her productions about the Egyptian Uprising would get her killed.

The women who worked in prisons thought the touring groups sounded dangerous. The women in war zones asked about the safety of women working on domestic violence plays. When one of the women interviewed for this book was assaulted by men who were angry that she did theatre, I got e-mails from three other women asking how they could help. They didn't know her, her work, or her circumstances. They simply knew that she had fallen at the front lines, and as fellow Stage Warriors, they weren't going to leave her behind.

Women who have survived threats, arson, extortion, assault, and exile come to this stage to create art that will change the world. Welcome to the front lines of dangerous drama.

1 - Always in Danger

Dah Teatar in Serbia:
Sanja Krsmanovic Tasic and Maja Vujovic (née Mitic)

"After this performance, we got a threat called into our office. Then there was a robbery. Someone broke into our office and stole our computers, the central computer and the monitors. They took our camera, different technical things, whatever they could. Just one week after that a fire broke out in our office."

One of the most striking images to come out of the Theatre Without Borders conference was the sight of three young women standing in a circle, exchanging clothing. Over and over again the women put on different pieces of each other's outfits until the identity of each character, each woman, was lost. The characters represented thousands of Bosnian, Serbian, and Croatian women who suffered during the war in former Yugoslavia from 1991 to 1995. The war was one of the most bitter and savage in modern history. Women were systematically raped, sometimes in theatres for a paying public or in detention centers where they were housed for the sole purpose of being available for rape by Serbian forces. The International Criminal Tribunal for the Former Yugoslavia determined that Serbian forces were targeting Bosnian Muslims as young as twelve years old to take into designated "rape houses." Ethnic cleansing was perpetrated on a wide scale, and The Hague estimates over 104,000 people died. In September of 1998 the United Nations released a statement saying that, in all, 50,000 women had been raped, 12,000 children had been killed, and 2.2 million people had been displaced from their homes.

Maja Mitic has been with Dah Teatar since its inception in 1991. Dah Teatar, directed by Jadranka Andelic and Dijana Milosevic, set out to bring the front lines right into the heart of Belgrade. Sanja Krsmanovic Tasic joined the group a short while later, after she realized that she needed to use her artistic talents in a deeper, more meaningful way. In a joint interview, Sanja and Maja took time away from their US tour to share with me their politics of theatre and their belief that everyone in a war needs healing, even perpetrators of violence. They took me back to the days when the front lines of Serbian drama were wherever Dah Teatar drew them.

* * *

Sarah: Could you please tell me how you got started in theatre?

Maja: I studied in a conservatory-style program. I was with only my level, eleven people, taking acting classes at the university. I have this very classical education. I was eighteen or nineteen years old and it was very much like Russian school. I did a couple of movies, then I did a couple of works in the National Theatre, but I felt that I wasn't growing and developing for myself and I wasn't so satisfied.

Then in 1991, on a day that was very important, they had these pro-test demonstrations. The first protests against the civil war we were start-ing at that time. It was March 1991. I heard that theatrical director Dijana Milosevic and Jadranka Andelic were thinking about starting a new group. So I went to Dah Teatar in 1991 after, let's say, seven years of performing with a working national theatre, after these movies and everything. There were 20 or 25 people. After three weeks, only four were still with Dah Teatar. In three weeks we had physical training, vocal training, working on improvisations, and I'm thinking "I'm falling in love with this work, and working with Dijana and Jadranka."

Maja described this time in her life as "long rehearsals, silence, training, endless questions and precise physical training." She remembered those early days as days filled with complex rehearsals that were exhausting but emotionally satisfying.

Maja: Since then, 1991, I am with Dah Teatar. I do something more didac-tic now, which we started recently to do, especially Dijana, Sanja and me. I go to universities to teach M.A. students in London. One of the profes-sors from this university asked me to perform, to do solo performances and that's what I'm doing now. For almost twenty years I have been with Dah. That's my story! OK, now Sanja.

Sanja: I have a different story. My background is in dance. When I was four years old I started training, so by 19 years old I was a professional con-temporary dancer. When I got to know Dah in 1993 I was 30 years old. I already had a career as a dancer. I was part of many projects and worked with dance. But in 1991, when the war started, I was feeling very unhappy with my art. I was always really interested in visual art, philosophy, in dif-ferent things. I didn't find—in my friends, in dancers, choreographers, my colleagues, I didn't find something I could intellectually develop with. You know, talk and have conversation, have the same sensibility about "what is dance?" and "what is art?" and how to express yourself. Those were the big-gest needs that I had.

Bio Points

- Sanja and Maja, both Serbian, have been members of Dah Teatar of Belgrade, Serbia since 1991.
- Maja majored in acting at The Academy of Arts, Novi Sad. She is a tutor at Goldsmiths University (UK).
- Sanja majored in dance at the University of Belgrade and the University of Novi Sad. She is President of the Board of CEDEUM (Centre for Drama in Education and Art).

Sarah: You had become dissatisfied with dance. You didn't have many colleagues you could talk to intellectually, so you joined Dah in 1993, is that right?

Sanja: Yes. This was because I was feeling unsatisfied. With dance I could not express myself more actively against the war. I saw this theatre workshop that was being led by Dah in September 1993 and I wanted to join, because I wanted to learn some new skills. I would continue to do performance art, and this performance art would be my own contribution against the war, as an artist. When I went there I just fell in love with the work and I met Dijana, Jadrenka and Maja.

For me it was a very big challenge and what I found was kindred souls, because all at once I felt I had somebody, some people that I could relate to and talk to and who had opinions like mine. Recognizing something, seeing, like they were reading my thoughts. Everything they said, I had been thinking a few years before. We just instantly tuned in. We had the same sensibility and the same ideas about what is happening in the country, about how we should express ourselves.

Sanja recalled a time in her life when dancing had a very literal meaning. She had lived in India, where many of the traditional forms of dance use mudras. Mudras are very specific gestures and expressions that act like a sign language to the audience. These gestures do not change from performance to performance. The traditional dance becomes its own language.

Sanja: This technique, the art they were doing, was very interesting and challenging. I rediscovered something that I found many years before when I was a child. I had studied Indian dance because my parents were diplomats and they lived in India for a while. I'd do any ballet, any dancing, but I loved Indian dance techniques. The Indian dance techniques have this very wonderful way of doing movement that has meaning. Indian dancers are storytellers. So this was, for me, a complete revelation I found in Dah: when we do actions, when we do our scores, it's also movement with meaning. It has sense. I reconnected with something I had been fascinated with as a child and as a dancer.

Slovenia moved to separate from Serbia by adopting laws that severed itself from Yugoslavia on February 23, 1991. It was done very quietly; even the local news only covered it for 15 minutes in a report titled "Now We Have Hope." On June 25th *of that year they declared independence. On December 17, 1991 The* New York Times *reported that Slovenia and Croatia had made official bids to become part of the European Community. This official recognition was in aid of repelling the Serbs, who at that point controlled over a third of Slovenia.*

The Serbian delegation proclaimed that the Declaration of Independence made by Slovenia in June 1991 was actually worsening the civil war in former Yugoslavia. The Serbs had invaded Slovenia and then tried to sever their ties to a larger diplomatic community. At the time the German Foreign Minister, Hans-Dietrich Genscher, said that months of negotiations hadn't stopped what he characterized as "aggression by Serbia." Officially, the Serbs denied anything un-provoked was happening. In September of that year President Slobodan Milosevic stood in front of 150 party officials in Belgrade and proclaimed:

> *If we must fight, then my God, we will fight and I hope they will not be so crazy as to fight against us. Because if we don't know how to work well or to do business, at least we know how to fight well.*[2]

Sarah: Can you please explain to me, what was going on as the war was starting in the early 1990s? What was the environment like for theatre? Were people free to say what they felt about the war, what they thought?

Sanja: Officially there was no war. Officially, when you put on the TV news or you would read the newspapers, they were just saying "how wonderful a country we live in" or "Milosevic is great." Officially there was absolutely no war, nothing is happening. What they were actually doing was they were drafting men, young men, in the night. They would come to homes and draft people in the night. And the theatre world, I think, was quite igno-rant. They were playing the role, just entertaining people, behaving normal-ly. Maja knows better if there was some attempt in official theatre against the war, but I don't know that.

Maja: I would speak about us, about Dah Teatar, because when we started in 1991 it was right before the war. After seven or eight days the war started in Slovenia.[3] We had started to rehearse a performance [one that had been planned before the war] based on the works of a Serbian writer, Momocilo

Nastasijevic. We had planned to stage an indoor performance for a very small audience and we were very dedicated to that. But every break, every single break (and we would work even Saturdays!), every break we would say, "What is going on in Slovenia?" These breaks in the work became rehearsals for another performance.

Dah Teatar decided to present an anti-war piece on a grand scale. The company took over the square in the center of Belgrade, Serbia, to perform their own interpretation of Brecht's poetry and songs in a new work called This Babylonian Confusion. *At a time when it was forbidden to even acknowledge the war that was starting, Dah came out publically to announce that they were rebelling against these "dark times," as Bertholt Brecht famously called war.*

Maja: We went out with two performances as Dah Teatar. This famous performance put us immediately on the side against Milosevic, the war, everything. It's the most famous performance of Dah Teatar. It was called *This Babylonian Confusion,* based on Bertholt Brecht's poems. That performance was done in a gallery in the middle of town for about twenty minutes. We were in Belgrade's main square and we wore costumes of angels in black, with very minimalistic wings.

We were performing Brecht's poems, doing actions and singing songs. We actually announced that war is coming and that we are the war. We were the first ones who did that.

For me, personally, I immediately faced this fact, together with Dijana and Jadranka, and three other actors that were with us in 1990-1991. Immediately, even during [the reign of President Slobodan] Milosevic, we had a lot of journalists who wrote about us. We were a special group, very dedicated and related to the times we lived in.

Dah had been committed to doing its first piece, the Momcilo Nastasijevic play, but it realized that its purpose was something much larger. Maja remembered how she felt when she realized that they hadn't meant for this to happen, it was just that Dah could not possibly ignore this deep and abiding feeling that was moving them.

Maja: As a company, of course we wanted to work on this delicate play [*Gifts of Our Ancestors,* by Momocilo Nastasijevic], so we continued to work on this story, but we *had* to go out. And we did it. That was something that marked us forever. And this, at the very, very beginning, the first moment . . . that was really strange. I remember, we started to go . . . then after a couple of days it was really, really strange. So it was kind of our horoscopes, that we started almost the same time, but the decision to make theatre wasn't to make an anti-war performance. The decision was to be dedicated and to work very profoundly and deeply. But of course, we had to face this fact, so we did two performances almost at the same time. We went out with these performances.

Serbia wasn't "at war." We didn't have civil war on our soil. Later, in the Kosovo war, we had NATO bombs in 1999, but we didn't have war. We were just involved in all these wars with young people drafted to other regions like Croatia, Bosnia, Kosovo.

Sarah: Did anyone tell you that you must stop performing?

Maja: Not in that sense, not in 1991, not in that sense. But they would ignore our art and we could not get money from of the Minister of Culture or the City Council. There was a lot of resistance in newspapers, a lot of resistance from students. There were people from many other environments who supported us. And we chose, also, to go out. We didn't make a performance in a very comfortable environment, in a space where people are paying. We went out in the streets.

Trouble didn't come immediately for Dah. They were becoming known, and had help from prominent international organizations like the Soros Foundation.

Maja: In 1991, 1992, 1993, the government would largely ignore us. Fortunately other intellectual people, writers, they would speak about us. We were very much recognized by 1992, and we'd get to perform in a famous space. Also, we were recognized by radio stations, and the Soros Foundation [now called the Open Society] helped a lot. They recognized by that performance that we have a human capacity to help change society. It was the only artistic foundation in 1991-92 in our country. We were supported, enough to be able to do something, somehow to be able to survive. There were a couple of years in the beginning when we couldn't have fees, or honorariums. We can live on what we make now, but in 1991, no. I had some other sources to survive, like parents.

We shared a laugh at that. Some things in theatre are universal, and asking your parents for help may be one of them. For a while Dah Teatar flew under the radar. They were making important anti-war statements but they weren't making anyone angry enough to retaliate. That changed when they began collaborating with the international activist group Women in Black to do plays about the female viewpoint of war. The entire point of Women in Black is to be a global non-violent coalition of women who protest injustices and crimes against women. But, ironically, there were several frightening violations of Dah's own theatre and office space as a result of that collaboration.

Sarah: Is it true that you were robbed and something was set on fire? Your office was set on fire?

Maja: Yes, I'll let Sanja talk about that.

Sanja. Yes. We were robbed three times, and once we had a fire in the offices. That's back when we started to work with Women in Black on these performances. We were performing excerpts of a book about the female side of the war, published by Women in Black. We started to collaborate with Women in Black around 1996. We were formed the same year, 1991.

Women in Black started in Israel in 1988 and then other countries followed their model of peaceful, vigilant protest. Women gather in large, public protests to remind everyone of the horrible toll war takes on humanity. Women in Black Belgrade (Zene u Crnom) was formed on October 9, 1991. This branch was a Nobel Peace Prize nominee. It still exists, primarily opposing nationalist aggression and promoting education and tolerance. Women in Black Belgrade also has a publishing wing. Dah's 2009 show Crossing the Line *is based on Women in Black's book* Women's Side of War, *a collection of testimonies about the horrors faced by women during the Serbian/Bosnian war.*

Dah also wrote The Legend About the End of the World *in collaboration with Women in Black. It features three women trying to find a way to build a life on a foundation of ruins. A key image from this show is the creation of a mandala, a Hindu or Buddhist geometric design representing the universe.*

Sanja: We knew Women in Black protested against the war every Wednesday in the main square. Their book *Women's Side of War* was the first time we collaborated closely. We had this one very beautiful action on the square in 1996. We drew a huge, beautiful mandala out of salt during our performance of *The Legend About the End of the World*. It was three actresses (Maja, me, and Tina, who is not in the group anymore) and we drew this mandala. There was very, very strong opposition and aggression on the street when we were doing it. People were really shouting; someone tried to spoil the mandala, which was easy because it's salt.

Sanja recalled that Dah Teatar began to be a target of threats, intimidation and violence around the beginning of 1997. At the time, Dah was trying to call attention to atrocities happening in the Serb-Croatian War. One of those atrocities was Srebrenica. In July of 1995, over 8,000 Bosnian Muslims were massacred by Serbian forces. It was one of the worst war crimes of the conflict.

Sanja: We continued to do different actions with Women in Black. A few years ago, Maja did a part in a performance for them. She did a scene that talks about Srebrenica, about the massacre in Srebrenica. It was a beautiful scene where she's putting down loaves of bread and saying the names of the people who were killed in Srebrenica. So, you know, we're working very closely with then and we have a lot of trust, it's a deep relationship. We presented our show based on their book in Bosnia and Croatia, then later of course brought it all around Serbia, just like we still do today.

Women in Black invited us in December of 2010 to do our performance piece that we do in a public bus. It's called *Invisible City.* Its main themes are minority rights, human rights, and we've added parts about gay activists and the people who work with Women in Black.

So, we did this on the 10th of December, Human Rights Day, in collaboration with Women in Black. Right after we did this there was a big security scare. They checked the bus for bombs; we had a police van in front, some police cars behind. We had plainclothes policemen in the bus during the whole trip. After this performance, we got a threat called into our office. Then there was a robbery. Someone broke into our office and stole our computers, the central computer and the monitors. They took our camera, different technical things, whatever they could. Just one week after that a fire broke out in our office.

So we called the police, and it was in the papers. We just wanted to have the media and other people pay attention to what is happening. We considered this to be a reaction to what we were doing. After a while, we also got a very interesting CD about satanic organizations, you know, like a very awful CD, about people who are against Serbia, and people who are into satanic sex acts. I think they meant us. I think they were showing us who they think we are. So, you know, we were always in danger and we confront this danger with our art and with what we do. We just go on with what we do.

Sarah: What was the reaction to your performance when you started to tour in places like Bosnia?

Sanja: Believe it or not, it was a wonderful reaction in Bosnia. The women who shared their stories in the book, some of them were in the audience. The mothers of Srebrenica were in the audience; they were in tears. They were greeting us, kissing us, hugging us. For them it was such a wonderful thing to hear that their stories are being told. That the truth is being told. But then we had a different experience in Serbia. Maybe Maja could say what it was like. How it was to play in Bosnia and Croatia and then go to Serbia. It was coming to terms with what we were doing. It was so important to perform in Bosnia but in Serbia it was a little bit of a different story.

Maja: It was a different story because it was much more dangerous to perform and say this statement, the truth. This book is based on testimony from women in all parts of Yugoslavia; they are also from Serbia. One story that my character tells is about a child that is shot in the head. She's a Serbian woman. But it doesn't really matter if I'm Serbian or not. It's a mother who is losing her baby, it happens to be a Serbian woman. Her name is Radmilla. Through the names, if you are really listening, you can tell who is who.

It's about facing the facts of what actually happened. I mean, I'm sorry, but during the Second World War, Serbs, together with Jewish people and Roma people, they were mostly killed in our region. That's fact. But now, in *this* civil war, Srebrenica happened. So I really think that I am a good citizen of my country because I want to talk about this. Because this is how I'm healing my nation. Because you put the things on the table and then you can continue. This is my belief as a person.

Performing in Serbia, for Serbs, for Serbians in America, of course you sometimes hear the opinion "oh, that didn't happen." But then you also have people who say, "this is really true," and they want to talk about us. This is a kind of reconciliation for them also, because when we made this peace we made it with ourselves when we went to Bosnia. In the beginning all of us felt very guilty, but then we learned from Women in Black and from these beautiful women in Bosnia that if we are responsible, then we also have this responsibility to pass the knowledge to others. We exchange the performance, and after the performance we can talk about it.

Sanja and Maja have had negative and positive reactions to their show as they tour it around the world, including in the United States. Although they have received some unpleasant comments and emails, they are content that this is part of the feedback process and are happy to continue it for their show Crossing the Line.

Maja: For me this is very important. I would say that after these performances it is so good that we do this now; we stay and talk. After some other performances that we do together we aren't so happy to talk. However, after *Crossing the Line* it's really good to come back on the stage, in jeans or whatever, and talk as people. How much are we responsible? Why do we do what we do? Do we want to have a relationship with this time in which we live? How we can heal our society? Can we go on? Do we want to go on? All of those things. I mean, we talk about our society in the first half, this is our local story. But if you look artistically, this can be any society that has any kind of war.

There are many levels of war: the war in the Congo now, or the wars of the Lebanese. But even in a rich country, if you are in the United States, there are many who can relate to what it happening. I mean, raping is raping. Killing is killing. It is important I not only *think* politically, but that I make art. This is, for me, very important. I think my feeling after touring in the States is that we achieved this. There were many young people who came in a couple of nights ago; there was one who said, "Yes, I see the connection and the similarity in what we [the United States] are doing." He had to question himself, and I think this is great.

Sarah: And that is relevant now, because as an American I can be ashamed of American soldiers who behave badly in war the same way you can be a Serbian person ashamed of Serbian soldiers behaving badly. Raping is raping, no matter where you are.

Maja: Absolutely.

Sanja: One of the times that I felt a special atmosphere in the audience in Serbia, was when we performed in the south of Serbia. There were many men who were veterans. They were fighting in Kosovo. They came to see the performance because this woman had made them. You know, a women's right activist who was organizing the performance. It was very cold, bad conditions, hard for us to perform. But just to know that these men came, that they were listening.

Some of them had tears in their eyes. And for them, just to confirm this story, that was very important. For Americans I think this is a way for the stories of the Iraqis, or the stories of the warriors, to be spoken of. That people who were in the war could also come and see these performances. It is difficult. I know it's difficult. It's difficult for the mothers, it's difficult for the sisters, it's difficult for the wives. To acknowledge that you have a criminal, that you do not have a war hero.

There is no such thing as a war hero. To me, a war hero is the deserter, the person who refuses to shoot. This is, for me, a war hero. Just to find out that this is terrible, and that you are affected, that it's not right, it shouldn't be done. This is so important.

We have had many reactions. We have had people who didn't know what was happening, and through our art they really got in contact with what was happening in the 1990s. Because we had this terrible amnesia, not knowing . . . we had this terrible censorship on the television and in the news. We didn't know what was happening in Srebrenica, it was forbidden to talk of it. You could find out from word of mouth from a friend, if at all. The government was keeping secrets from the people. It was terrible, because of course the people would react. It's a very long and hard story, and we would really love to perform it as much as possible in Serbia because we find people who are really thankful for us doing it. Saying "thank you so much," and "you are helping me heal, feel less guilty and feel good." The thing for me is also catharsis and cleansing, finding the way out and washing the wound. Cleaning it so that it can heal. This is, for me, the symbol.

Maja: I am thinking, listening to Sanja, it's so rare, everywhere, that you have testimony of the war from women. We know these numbers. We know numbers of what happened in Iraq or in Afghanistan. In Germany we know about concentration camps in the Second World War and all this stuff. But when you have this testimony, you hear the name, the name of a woman. It's not a number, it's not a man's history, you go on the stage and instead of saying *Antigone* or *Medea* or whatever, you're presenting this contemporary text and it's so powerful.

People are really shocked because it's what we see in the movies. It's what we see in *The Deer Hunter*. That's why we all love *The Deer Hunter*, because we related. Not only to the war, but to losing the youth, losing your friends, changing people, changing lives, changing love. All this stuff. So now with these performances we make something very strong. And they are shocked because of it. Through the actresses they hear the story and it's not just the numbers. I think this is where Dah Teatar is very strong.

Sarah: Has there ever been a time that you felt so threatened or so exhausted, so sad, that you did not want to continue performing it?

Both women: Never. Never, no. Never.

Maja: The impulse is so strong I think we find strength. We are used to it, you know. We are tough. We survived through so many hard things. The NATO bombing in Belgrade. Everything. And you know, we are very strong now. We can't be weak so we have to be strong. It's not only about us. We want to put this discussion on a higher level, not to only talk about our war. It's a basic decision about how to want to live this life. I didn't make the decision to create this performance because I want to change the world.

I made the decision ten years ago when I decided how I want to make art. Because of this decision, how I want to make art, and which kind of craft I want to have, I became strong. Because I am strong I can make a performance about these things and I will be completely safe.

This is a decision that many artists are doing in the USA: Bread and Puppet Theatre, La MaMa in New York. There are so many types of wars, terrible wars. As a person, you can make decisions. Like a doctor, you can decide what kind of doctor you really want to be. Do you want to cure people, or to make money? In the arts you make decisions much earlier. Where you live, you live what you see, and then you go from the personal to the general. Somehow we have so many similar things on this planet between us, and we should open those doors to see this.

Sanja: If I did not do this, if I did not do this work, I would do something very radical. I would go out in the streets, you know. It's just about my great need to do something. To do something with my art is the best way. It's so important. It's about being active, in a way . . . being an architect in fulfilling your complete role as a human being in your own way, in your own ethic, how you think is right. I was feeling so helpless before I started to do this work and now I'm very happy.

*   *   *

Dah Teatar is continuing the work both in Serbia and abroad. In 2012 the group returned to La MaMa Theatre in New York City to perform as part of Soulographie, a cycle of plays that looked at America's relationship to the concept of genocide. They also traveled to Italy, to Rome and Trentino, to showcase *Networking Memories,* a play about the history of Yugoslavia as imagined by young children who have not actually lived there. It was a critical success.

2 - Different Eyes

Iman Aoun: ASHTAR Theatre in Palestine

"They started to shout, 'Death for Arabs! Death for Arabs!'"

There are few places in the world that present more political or geographic barriers to live theatre than Palestine. In that part of the world, traveling a few miles to another city can take all day if you must pass through a checkpoint. It can take even longer if you are denied entry at the checkpoint. What does a director do when she can't bring her show to the audience, and the audience literally cannot get to her?

Logistical problems have been part of theatre in Israel and occupied Palestine for decades. A Declaration of Principles signed in 1993, known as Oslo I, established a Palestinian Interim Self-Government Authority in areas of the West Bank and Gaza Strip. Under the agreement, the Israeli military was to withdraw from Gaza and from the Jericho area of the West Bank. A further set of agreements in 1995, known as Oslo II, brought 3% of the West Bank under Palestinian Authority jurisdiction and divided the West Bank into three areas: one under exclusive Palestinian control; one where Palestinians would exercise civilian control while Israel controlled security; and one area to be controlled exclusively by Israel. This fragmentation of the West Bank into zones meant that Palestinian freedom of movement was curtailed by checkpoints.

Israelis and Palestinians alike were caught in a chaotic shifting of borders, agreements, and rules. In 2000, the Palestinian al-Aqsa Intifada, or uprising, erupted. This was the second uprising of its kind; the first occurred in 1987. The al-Aqsa uprising was sparked when Israeli politician Ariel Sharon visited a site, known to Muslims as Haram al-Sharif and to Jews as the Temple Mount, in a portion of East Jerusalem that should, according to the peace accords, be under Palestinian control. Over 6,600 people died during the Uprising. The majority of casualties were Palestinian,[1] and these casualty figures do not account for Palestinians who died because they were unable to cross a checkpoint to reach medical care.

Since the start of the Oslo Accords, Israelis and Palestinians have been negotiating boundaries, territories, water access rights, construction permits, even international aid. Both the United Nations and the International Court of Justice have proclaimed that Israel is occupying Palestinian land. The entire area remains deeply divided and volatile. On September 23, 2011 current Palestinian president Mahmoud Abbas formally requested that the United Nations grant Palestine admission to the UN as a full member state, and on November 29, 2012, the United Nations General Assembly voted to upgrade the status of Palestine to that of a "non-member observer state." The personal and political struggles of Palestinians were thus brought to the world stage in a way that wasn't possible before. Iman Aoun of ASHTAR Theatre has been waiting for that chance since the 1980's. She is ready to be heard.

*   *   *

Sarah: What was your beginning in theatre?

Iman: Oh . . . that was very long ago!

Iman has a great throaty laugh, and she giggled frequently while talking about the early days. She seemed to enjoy talking about her start.

Iman: I started when I was a kid at school. I was still in my seventh grade, which means that I am eleven, twelve years old, and I . . . at that time, of course, we're talking about the seventies, and so very seldom would a young girl be involved in theatre, in that time. What I used to do is to go from one school to another. So I was lucky because I also met some of the teachers who used to give theatre lessons in private schools. And they liked my acting, so they were working with me, even off school time.

From the minute I discovered that I have a love relationship with the stage, I never left it. It was like a perfect marriage! So, I'd been doing that since grade seventh. At university I did my first degree in social work and psychology. I wanted to combine my passion for theatre with my social studies, because up until we started ASHTAR Theatre in the nineties, Palestine did not have a theatre school. Before that, whoever wanted to work in theatre either had to do it through experience, or to go abroad and study. I wasn't one of the lucky ones who were able to leave the country and go abroad to study theatre, so I did something else. I majored in social studies. I started to do workshops in psycho-drama, in order to make a bridge between the subjects.

Sarah: A bridge to professional theatre?

Iman: In 1984 I met the only professional theatre group at the time, which used to be very active in Palestine—they were called El Hakawati Theatre

Bio Points

- Iman, a Palestinian, began her theatre training in the 7th grade.
- Iman founded ASHTAR Theatre in 1991in Ramallah, Palestine.
- ASHTAR Theatre has published an Arabic translation of the works of Augusto Boal, the creator of Theatre of the Oppressed.

Company. I joined them and I started to work with them, and kept doing my education as well as my theatre work. Like a snowball, it started to grow, bit by bit. I started to go abroad and do workshops with them or perform and tour, and meet other theatre people around Europe, the States, in the Arab world. So that's how the whole idea of drama became my background.

Sarah: When you started doing theatre professionally, did you feel like you had a lot of artistic freedom in Palestine? Were you free to say and do what you wanted in the theatre?

Iman: Well, we're talking about the 1980s, so there was censorship from the Israeli Army governor, because at the time Jerusalem and the West Bank were under military control. It was governed by the military. There was very high political censorship of our work. We were not really able to move from one place to another, to perform for our audience, especially in the West Bank. We were able to perform in Jerusalem and in historical Palestine, which means Galilee and the Triangle [a combination of villages in the middle of the country] but we were not able to reach our community in Gaza or in Ramallah or in Nablus.

To be able to perform any performance we had to have permissions. And to have permission, we had to submit our text to the censor. There was a different type of censorship for the Israeli theatre companies. For them it was moral censorship. They were not able to talk badly about religion. But, for us, it was a political censorship. That had driven us, as a company, to work more indirectly, to focus more on our body-work and on the visual aspect rather than on the words. Somehow, it also encouraged a new form of visual aspects. Improvisational-based works that are less based on the text and more on the images of what we are presenting.

There are loads of stories about the censor, but I don't know if you want to hear about that or not. I mean . . .

Iman laughed again. Who could resist hearing that story? Rebelling against this type of censorship is something most have never even had to think about as a Western practitioner.

Sarah: Well, yes, I would like to hear more about the censorship! Give me an example.

Iman: Okay . . . one of the very famous examples. We had a play called *Ali the Galilean*. Ali is a character who's Palestinian and lives in the Galilee, but he moves from his village into Tel Aviv, because he needs work. He's there selling falafel, and then there is a bombing in Tel Aviv. Who do they accuse? Ali, because he is Palestinian and he's living there!

So, Ali starts to deny his identity, because now he's lost between who he is and who he wants to be. The fear, also, of what would become of him if they imprison him for nothing. So the whole play is about this. Anyway, we submitted the text to the censor; the censor didn't allow it. They allowed it in the Galilee, but they did not allow it in the West Bank, of course. We kept asking them. We had an attorney who was following all of the censorship closely. We said, "Well, we have to reach our audiences everywhere, because we are an outreach group. We are a touring group."

At the time we had a deal with French TV, who wanted to come and do a story on Hakawati. So, the perfect story would be if the censor would allow us to perform in Jericho, let's say. Then we went to Jericho, we started to promote the idea that we are coming to perform in Jericho, but the censor wouldn't allow us the permission. We took the camera people and we went to the censor with the lawyer and we said, "We want this performance to happen and we have the French TV to film us. You should give us permission, it's not harmful, and, we're talking to our people." Of course, they don't want that. But back and forth, we set everything.

We set up the stage and everything, and at the last minute they relented. Because of the French presence and the French TV, the censors came to the theatre, they issued the permission! Then they said, "Well, listen, this is the last time we want you here," because the permit had come from the Israeli military governor. He said, "This is the first and the last time I want you here. You get the permission only because you have the French TV, but you, you do more harm than a stone. I want you to perform and be out and never to see you again." So that was my story. We did the performance, of course.

Sarah: Were there times where you were directly threatened? Were you in danger because you were performing Palestinian works for Palestinians?

Iman: Yes. We were. That's another story, about our relationship with the censor, the Israeli Occupation and the Israeli settlers. Once we were invited in '86 to perform in Acre, or Akko, or Akka . . . I don't know which name you know. They're three names for the same place!

Iman started to give some back-ground on this particular festi-val. The town she is talking about has quite a complicated back-ground. Acre (Hebrew: Akko; *in Arabic,* 'Akkā*) is a city in the Western Galilee region of northern Israel at the northern extremity of Haifa Bay. Acre is one of the old-est continuously inhabited sites in the country. It hosts a theatre fes-tival known for its liberal view-point. In 1986 there had not yet been what Palestinians call the Intifada. The first Intifada was an uprising against Israeli occupa-tion that lasted from 1987 until 1993. The uprising included civil disobedience, strikes, boycotts, re-fusal to pay taxes; it also included violence towards Israelis (especial-ly in the form of stone-throwing) and towards Palestinians per-ceived as collaborating with Israel. According to the United Nations, Palestinians were victimized dur-ing this period, yet did not surren-*

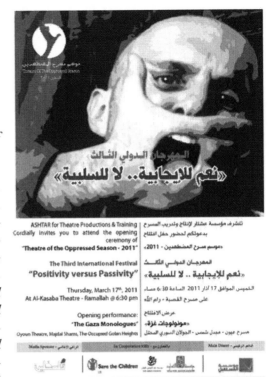

An ASHTAR poster for a public presentation of The Gaza Monologues *on March 17th, 2011 in Ramallah. Photo courtesy of Iman Aoun.*

der. A UN report stated, "Palestinians attempted against all odds to overcome se-vere economic hardship through reliance on their community-based economy.[2]"

This uprising marks a turning point in Palestinian history. Before 1993 it was illegal even to call oneself Palestinian; after 1993, people were able to declare themselves as such.

Iman: We were invited for the festival that happens every year there. It's called the Alternative Festival, which means that they are all progressive Israelis and open-minded people. They invited us. We went to perform, it was 1986 already and before the Intifada, so it was a big deal for anyone to say that he's a Palestinian. We presented ourselves as the Palestinian group. Of course, this irritated the municipality of Akka. They came and they put the Israeli flag on top of the place where we were, and we were in open air in a big square. They put an Israeli flag facing the stage. They put the Israeli flag just on top of the wall facing the stage. So we said, "Whoa . . . that's quite hot."

Sarah: It was inciting.

Iman: Yeah. Very provocative. And so we said, "Okay, fine." We went to the organization and said, "Listen, you have three options. You take this flag down, or we put the Palestinian flag next to it, or we're out. We don't perform." Of course, at the time, to fly the Palestinian flag, you go to jail. You weren't able to say that you're Palestinian. You weren't able to say that you have a flag, and if you use it then it's a crime. We were stateless, nationless, whatever "-less" you want to use. It can fit us.

These were the three options that we gave to our hosts. The organizers said, "We absolutely want you to stay! It's a crime to use your Palestinian flag so we're going to take down the Israeli flag." We went up, we took the Israeli flag down and in a split second we started the performance. There were hundreds and hundreds of press people, even on the stage with us, trying to ask us questions in the middle of the performance! Reporting, "This Palestinian group is coming from Jerusalem and took this Israeli flag down in Akka." It was, like, the biggest scandal ever.

We shared a laugh at that. I can picture a young Iman, standing on stage with her troupe, amazed that a simple flag has caused "the biggest scandal ever."

Iman: All the press was, "Why did you do it? How come? What happened?" We explained what happened, and, well . . . everybody wrote, and it was a big, big issue.

The second year, the same organizers invited us to the same festival. We said, "Well . . . we should go!" We went. But that year there was a fascist Israeli group growing, and the whole theatre where we were supposed to perform was filled with hundreds of Israeli flags!

Sarah: Ohhh . . .

Iman: Okay? They knew what we did the year before. We went in and we started to perform. In the middle of the performance, or even before the middle, after ten minutes, Kahana people who were sitting in the audience started to shout, "Death for Arabs! Death for Arabs!" and started showing the symbol of the Kahana group [a radical Israeli group that has a fist in front of a star as its symbol]. They said, "There is a bomb here!" Everybody is freaking out, shouting, "Everybody out! Everybody out!" We all went out.

We knew there were no bombs. Nothing was there. They didn't want the performance to continue. They didn't want us to be there in the first place.

They kept us all for one hour, waiting. Everybody from the audience stayed. Everyone stayed with us; then, after the search that took one hour for nothing, we came back and we restarted the show. They were very excited that we were there and that we performed. They stayed the whole evening. But then, when we went out, all of our cars had been broken. Smashed and painted, with slogans on them like, "Death for Arabs all the way." That's another example of the irritation, the provocation we faced.

Now, on another level, recently, between 2001 and 2004, we used to have checkpoints all over the West Bank. We had 740 checkpoints. We had . . .

Sarah: I'm sorry, did you say 740?

Iman: Yes, I said 740 checkpoints. 740 in the West Bank. Now, we have much less, but this is not because the Israelis are making life easier. On the contrary, because now we have the wall, there's no need for checkpoints in every single point. Now we are all closed in a big prison.

Between 2000 and 2003, Israel began construction of a wall along portions of the West Bank, reportedly to keep Israelis safe from Palestinian suicide bombers. The concrete wall (it is a fence in a few places), sometimes called a security fence or an apartheid wall, depending on the political leanings of the speaker, is built on occupied territory. In 2004, the International Court of Justice issued an opinion that the wall was "contrary to International Law." The wall is controlled at gates by Israeli soldiers. An article published in 2007 by the Official Journal of the National Association of EMS Physicians and the World Association for Emergency and Disaster Medicine, in association with the Acute Care Foundation, concluded that Palestinians were prohibited by the wall from accessing educational or medical resources.

Iman: So, at times, where there were all these checkpoints, we needed to go from one place to another to perform for our audience in the West Bank, but we could not reach them. For example, if we would go from Zone A to Zone B, that should take, in normal life, 20 minutes, 30 minutes, or one hour. It would take us the whole day. Because we have to do a detour that is enormous, and to wait in lines that are endless. From one line to another, waiting for the soldiers to check you at checkpoints, and then from one checkpoint to another. Of course, all longer roads are closed because the settlements are built in between the Palestinian villages in the West Bank. So all roads are cut for Palestinians, to save the [Jewish] settlers. So we had to go in some instances on donkeys and use carts.

Sarah: On donkeys?

Iman: Donkeys. Or we'd walk and hold heavy bags with our sets and iron poles or whatever we had to set up. For miles and miles in order to reach a place and perform. So, then, of course, if you irritate the soldier, it's very easy that the soldier would shoot you.

Sarah: How is it now? What is it like to travel and perform for you, now?

Iman: Now, certain places are very closed up, either because the wall needs to be crossed in a bizarre route to get to them, or because you have to take very long roads in order to reach them. Like, to go from one end to another, which is just across the street. You spend hours and hours for nothing! Hours of agony, when you could do the work very easily. But we still do, we still carry our things, we still go from one place to another to perform for our audience.

It depends where we are. I know that not far from my home in Jerusalem, six kilometers away from where I live, they built the wall, and that really breaks certain neighborhoods. Not even neighborhoods! The road that we used to take, the main road that lead into Ramallah, is cut in half. People who live on one side cannot really cross the sidewalk to the left, because there is a wall in the middle of the street. It's insane. It's completely insane. It doesn't follow any order, and it cuts the village in half. Sometimes, it cuts the school or hospital off from the village. Especially when you have a school that is outside of the gates of the wall, kids would wait hours and hours to be able to cross. People go to see the doctor, and many of them die or go into labor at checkpoints. Babies die, mothers die, because they weren't able to go to the hospital. The soldiers who are at the gate of the wall wouldn't let them in or out.

Sarah: How do you put that into your work? How do you use that or show that?

Iman: [After a heavy sigh] How did I use that? . . . Well, I did not use that, very frankly, because in my work the focus wasn't about the action that is on the ground, because I cannot change it. What I focus my work on is what I can change. What I really impact! How can I leave an impact?

Sarah: And how you make a difference?

Iman: Yes. So, knowing this, feeling this, instead of just showing it another time to the people because they know it, I use it mainly in Invisible Theatre or in street theatre. The work is so much, sometimes you forget what you're doing.

Last year, for example, we invited [the New York company] Bread and Puppet Theatre to come to Palestine. They came and because it was the year of Jerusalem, capital of the Arab culture, everybody should be in Jerusalem to celebrate the city! Of course, no one from the West Bank or Gaza who had special work could enter Jerusalem. None of us were able to enter.

Sarah: So it was impossible to enter the city everyone had gathered to celebrate.

Iman: For years, because they are imprisoned, inside this wall, or from 1993 inside the checkpoints. This big prison had started back in 1993. What we did is a poetic kind of breaking through into Jerusalem. We broke through with puppets. They made gigantic puppets that should represent the sea, the gates, the checkpoints, the police, the dream behind this wall, what we would find in Jerusalem. Why do we want to go to Jerusalem? And we marched from Ramallah into the street of Jerusalem, which is a long street that takes the cars into Jerusalem. We did not do all of it, because it reaches the checkpoint, which we cannot reach as they might shoot at us.

We did another play that is Forum Theatre, based on what happens at the checkpoint and how the Israelis are training the young Palestinians who are around the checkpoint at Kalandia refugee camp—how to become collaborators with the Israeli secret services. We worked on this, because our main focus is our society. We want to give to our society the possibility to discuss their problems, to be able to look at their issues in a new way in order to be able to resist the occupation.

In order to have our national freedom, we have to be free ourselves first. Thus we have to free ourselves from our taboos and social inhibitions.

Sarah: You talk about giving your society that "dream of the sea." That you know there are checkpoints, but what happens at those checkpoints? What is your dream for theatre in Palestine from this point forward?

Iman: Ahh . . . that's a good question, my goodness! Dreams are nice, but I'd rather dream in the night, not in the morning. I want to make a real leap within my community. I want my people to understand that, to be able to achieve a different life.

A life without the occupier. A life that is not under oppression. I want them to see their lives with different eyes. And I want them to understand, to comprehend. To analyze, to change this duality of oppressed/oppressor. First of all, they should not be oppressive themselves.

They should understand that they have to need help, and the help should come from themselves. Agree that they are able to help themselves, that the oppression has two ends. They must see both ends and know that they are entangled into oppression's vicious circle.

I believe that my people should really understand how to become action-oriented more than reaction-oriented or reactionist. They should start to think how to really act rather than react.

* * *

There is no doubt that ASHTAR Theatre is leading the way in theatre and social awareness in Palestine. ASHTAR offers intensive theatre training programs for local students throughout the year, equipping young Palestinians with essential skills that go beyond acting. In addition to an increased level of self-awareness and confidence, the training methodology gives students leadership, communication, and teamwork skills. ASHTAR is also an educational publishing powerhouse. It has released nine books about theatre, the uses of drama, and the sociological impact of theatre on society.

ASHTAR's most visible effort, the global launch of *The Gaza Monologues,* is an unqualified success. *The Gaza Monologues,* personal stories written by the children in ASHTAR-led workshops, were sent out to the world and performed simultaneously on October 17, 2010 by over 1500 young people in 36 countries. They were heard everywhere, from the Freedom Theatre of Jenin, Palestine to Zambuko Izibuko in Zimbabwe. American, British, Chinese, Australian, Swiss, Egyptian, and Greek stages helped make the release a truly global event. The week before the "International Day of Solidarity with the Inalienable Rights of the Palestinian People" on November 29, 2010, *The Gaza Monologues* reached the harbor of the United Nations headquarters in New York City. WBEZ 91.5 called the performance, "sincere, compelling, and heartfelt" and described *The Gaza Monologues* as "reveal[ing] the human face of Palestinian youth who have virtually no outlet to the outside world."

3 - Hate Mail

Shauna Kanter, New York

"Your reasons for doing something can't address self-promotion, can't address what you want, you have to be open and honest. In other words, it's not to serve you. It's to serve peace."

Shauna Kanter and I first met in New York City in 2005. I was new to the city and needed an artistic base to call home. VOICETheatre became that base, and I appeared as an ensemble member in their Off-Broadway production of Retzach at 59e59 Street Theatre in 2006. Through the rehearsal process it became clear that Shauna's vision for the show was heavily influenced by the time she had spent in the Middle East. Each scene was crafted with nuanced references to political, emotional, or psychological injustices seen every day in Israel and Palestine. When researching practitioners for this book, Shauna was at the top of my personal wish list. We sat on a staircase in the La MaMa Theatre in 2010 and I finally got an answer to this intriguing mystery: how did the New York Jew with a refined English husband become possibly the first person to ever put Israelis and Palestinians together onstage?

*   *   *

Sarah: To recap some background that I would like to cover, could you please explain the history with your mom and how that has informed you as an artist and as someone working in the Middle East?

Shauna: The history is that after WWII my mother smuggled guns as part of a terrorist organization founded to create the state of Israel. She lived in Paris, she got sent money from the United States, went to Switzerland, bought the guns and packed them up in wooden boxes and sent them to Palestine. So when I was growing up everything I was told about Palestinians was, you know, complete brainwashing. It's not unlike what most Jews are told, only I was being told it from an ex-terrorist point of view!

To Shauna's credit, we were able to share a good laugh over that. Laughing off the idea of a parent in a terrorist organization is probably not a universal reaction.

Shauna: I was being told what to believe about Arabs from someone who actually packed the guns. When I first went to Israel and spent time, really meaningful time there, I discovered, much to the chagrin of all the Israelis I was around, the Palestinians that I met were completely . . . they were all . . .

Shauna hesitated for a second, and what's coming next is obvious. To tell this story fully, we have to hear the story known as "the guy pissing story."

Shauna: Do you want that story of the guy pissing? I don't know . . .

Sarah: Oh, yes.

Shauna: Oh god, when was it, it was in 19 . . . 87, 1988. 1987, it was in '87. I was in Jerusalem with my husband and we got lost trying to get back into the old city of Jerusalem. We were in the aqueduct outside of Jerusalem, very far down, and you know, basically like in a hole, you know, in a pit, and we went up and found this guy pissing in his backyard, and he invited us into his house. We went into his house and we spent hours there, and this guy's family told us their story. This was the very first time that I had heard this kind of talk. I mean, very few Jews at that time went into Palestinian homes, and I was in one. And their story was, their two sons had been part of PLO meetings. The IDF, the Israeli Defense Force, came in the middle of the night and threw out all the appliances in their house . . . which was actually above where we were. They were living in their garden shed below their real house that they still owned, but . . . were forbidden to go into. They opened up the windows, said, "you see that?" We looked at a big house with boarded up windows, he said, "that's our house but we're forbidden to live there."

   All the appliances that were quite costly for them to buy were thrown out of the windows. All because their two sons had gone to the meetings of the PLO. Their two sons were still in jail.

Shauna is married to renowned British actor Robert Langdon Lloyd. Used to performing in cosmopolitan theatres and before supposedly worldly people, Shauna and Robert were very surprised that when they shared their story it was not always appreciated.

Bio Points

- Shauna, an American, trained in acting at Carnegie Mellon and SUNY Purchase.
- She founded VOICETheatre in Paris in 1988.
- Shauna's father was a Broadway stage manager. Her mother was an actress.

Shauna: So this was a very intense introduction . . . we went back to the people that we were with and we told them this amazing adventure that we had had. This one actor who was sharing a dressing room with Robert took his stuff out of the dressing room and refused to share a dressing room with Robert. Because we had had this experience and we had been in a Palestinian home. So that was my sort of introduction into this whole world. Other than my mother's beginning, right?

Sarah: That informed your work when you created VOICETheatre?

Shauna: Yep. I knew that I wanted to write about this, and so I was given my very first directing job in Paris in 1988, and I knew that I wanted to write about oppression. So I wrote a piece about oppression from within, oppression from within a family, oppression from within the state. Oppression the state places on an individual. And part of that piece was a Palestinian character, very small, one page. From that piece I created *Pushing Through* (1988) and it may have been the first piece that put Palestinians and Israelis on the same stage. That piece ended up touring for five years, and from that I got to know ASHTAR Theatre in 1997. (See the interview with Iman Aoun.)

Sarah: When you were first doing *Pushing Through* on tour you weren't even in the Middle East. You were on tour in places like Maryland. There were numerous protests but it wasn't Palestinian people protesting you, it was Jewish organizations.

Shauna: It was . . . the times that there were demonstrations against us, it was always the Jewish organizations. I was interviewed on National Public Radio on Weekend Edition and at that time the producer, Ned Wharton, called me and said, "Do you know you've just gotten the most hate mail that anyone on this program has ever gotten?" Because I stood up and said, "I don't think that the Palestinians can be lumped together, all into terrorists," much like is happening right now with the [controversial building of a] mosque in downtown New York, where all of sudden all Muslims are terrorists.[1]

Sarah: What did you do when you found out you had gotten the most hate mail of anyone ever on the program?

Shauna: I cried. You know, you feel awful. I mean, there are a few things you can do to be safe but you also have to take on board that a lot of people are gonna hate you, a lot of people are going to call you traitor. If you go online and type in my name I'll come up a "Jew hater."

Sarah: Still today?

Shauna: Yes, still today. You have to go down the numbers, but it's all on there.

After the critical success but social unrest surrounding Pushing Through, *Shauna created a second piece called* Warriors of Fate. *This time the conflict would be seen in situ: the piece, written and directed by Shauna, would be performed in Israel and in Ramallah, Palestine. Shauna partnered with the Peres Centre for Peace in Tel Aviv and the Palestinian Regional Authority to produce the show with actors from both countries.*

Sarah: Instead of fading into the woodwork you've chosen to extend those associations with Palestinians.

Shauna: I suppose I have. I think it's very important when people go into another country to work that they let go of their expectations, their desires, their goals. Because your goals in, let's call it America, can be very different from what is possible, what the people in that other country want to achieve. I had to do that over a series of years. I had certain goals and expectations, desires, wants, and needs that were not realistic. They were the goals of the conqueror and it's very important to understand that it's very cheap for me as a Jew to say, "We want peace, we want dialogue." The conqueror has that luxury of saying, "I want this, I want that."

Being the daughter of somebody who packed those guns that conquered . . . what I'm trying to say is that when you go into another country don't colonize with your theatre. Don't use your theatre or your art to achieve what you first thought you might want to achieve. In other words, let it grow, develop and change because you're working, and if it's going to be a deep association, and I'm talking years, then you too will grow and change and your goals will hopefully change. That's a very healthy association.

Sarah: Tell me about the association with ASHTAR Theatre.

Shauna: The association with ASHTAR began when I was asked to first do voice workshops, and vocal training. That was the first thing we did and that was a big eye opener.

Sarah: I bet. Where were you?

Shauna: In Ramallah, working in the West Bank. And the big eye opener was that very few people in the company knew that I was Jewish. At that time we took the stance that maybe it wouldn't be such a good idea [to let everyone know] because they wanted the training more than the politics. So we kind of said, "You know what, that's not important now, we need the training." So we did that. And a few people knew and that was that. For me personally, it was very interesting, too. I was privy to all kinds of conversations that . . . if they had known I was Jewish it would have been a completely different scenario. You know, I was Shauna from London, and so a lot of people thought I was Irish! Anyway, so that was the first. The second time I worked with ASHTAR I did acting workshops. That was a year later and then it was known that I was Jewish. That was a whole different bag of beans.

Sarah: Were you anxious about that?

Shauna: It was . . . um . . . yeah. Yeah. Yeah. I mean, that placed me in a lot of situations where I shouldn't have been where I was. If people had known who I was my life was in danger.

   The third time at ASHTAR was when I directed, in Arabic, *Brecht on Brecht*. It's a play, a set of poems that Brecht wrote pretty much after 1933 when he and his family left Germany as Hitler came to power. It was all about the restrictions of the Jews, very specifically in Berlin. And wouldn't you know it, that the same restrictions that the Jews had in Berlin were the very same restrictions Palestinians have to this day in Jerusalem? Things like, you can't go from one side of the city to the other side of the city without being thrown into jail and that city happens to be the city of your birth. Things like, I know someone, an actress that worked with me, whose father died in an ambulance because there was a border. The border was closed. Her father died in the ambulance because he couldn't be let through. He died.

   I have all kinds of stories. My lighting designer couldn't come to a tech [technical rehearsal, where lights and sound cues are added] of this very show because he wanted to go dancing on the other side of Jerusalem, the city that he was born in. He went to a disco. It was meaningless. Just was a young guy who wanted to go dancing and he was thrown into jail because they did a passport check and he was thrown in an Israeli jail. So he couldn't come to our tech. You know, things like that. There are many, many, many other stories.

Shauna and Iman Aoun have been working together to bring these stories out of Palestine and onto a world stage. In particular they wanted to tell stories from the years of the land, air, and sea blockade of Gaza (still going on at the time of writing) during which various material goods were not allowed to enter Gaza and people were denied freedom of movement to leave or enter. Palestinians call it "the siege of Gaza." An Israeli military attack in December of 2008 left at least 1,300 Palestinians dead and 100,000 more displaced from their homes. The impact of the siege is chronicled in a play called The Gaza Monologues. *I spoke to both women about this project and what they hope to achieve through it.*

Sarah: *The Gaza Monologues* are trying to tell some of those stories. Please tell me about that show.

Shauna: ASHTAR does trainings and has for a long time now. They train people to go out and create theatre in Palestine and in Gaza. And during the siege of Gaza, there was a trainer from ASHTAR in Gaza, and Iman (Aoun) was sitting in Ramallah, and they couldn't move. So Iman was sitting in Ramallah, saying, "What the hell can we do?" They remembered that they had this trainee, and they asked him to get together a group of young people and start a writing workshop. The writing workshop started and monologues were written. What's going to happen at the United Nations is that the 33 monologues will be performed by young adults representing 30 countries.

Sarah: Shauna, is there anything else that you want to add about the process that you have gone through with your identity as a writer, as a director, as a Jewish person?

Shauna: Let me back track a little bit. I would say from 1988 to 1993 I was very interested in creating dialogue. But as I said earlier, dialogue where the conqueror is the one who's in charge is a whole other bag of beans and is a great luxury, and the motives are very different. The motives of guilt and shame are of no interest to the ones who have been conquered. So that whole 5 years of work and touring . . . all that led me to work with ASHTAR. I lived with Iman and her family and worked in their theatre and saw firsthand what it was like to live under occupation. What it does to you psychologically, spiritually, intellectually, in every area. Then I went and did this other project, *Warriors of Fate*, mostly because I was given the money to do it.

And you know what, in answer to your question, I think that as artists a lot of us get pigeon-holed sometimes, or typecast, if you will, into niches where we've done work and we're known. Really, we shouldn't be doing that. We've moved on and you don't know it until you know it. You know sometimes when you're in the middle of the project.

In answer to your questions, Sarah, I would say, "Always check your motives." I'm suggesting that the motives have to be pure. Your reasons for doing something can't address self-promotion, can't address what you want, you have to be open and honest. Take on board who and why you're doing this for. In other words, it's not to serve you. It's to serve peace. And that peace may not be the quality of peace that you originally wanted to serve.

In my own case I wanted to have Jews and Palestinians talking to each other. Now I know that, and this was true twenty-five years ago when I began in this and it's even more true now because those people are older, that they can't really talk honestly to each other. At this moment in time, they can agree to disagree, that's about it. But you're going to be really honest, you're not gonna agree. Really honest. So for now, we talk separately and that's the peace. That's the quality of the peace. It's not what I wanted, it's not my result that I was looking for. But we move on.

*   *   *

Shauna is continuing to write and direct. Her Dust Bowl-era drama *Birds on a Wire* was featured in TheatreSpeak and became a 2012 Regional Finalist in the Kennedy Center Theatre Competition for Best Play. The 2013 production of *Birds on a Wire* in New York City was a critical success. We recently had a conversation about projects for 2014. Shauna says her role as a wedding officiant may provide material for an upcoming piece.

4 - The Measure of Humanity

Jennifer H. Capraru of ISÔKO Theatre, working in Rwanda

"I haven't had a death threat, but I have been threatened with not having a visa."

In 1994, the news of a horrific genocide focused world attention on a small nation situated in the center of the African continent. The brutality that occurred in the Republic of Rwanda was not what many would conceive as a civil war in the traditional sense. Instead, the events were the culmination of decades of animosity and violence between the Hutu and Tutsi tribes. The tribal conflicts were complicated by the ethnic favoritism of the colonial Belgian government, which granted independence to Rwanda in 1962. While never reaching the scale or horror of the violence that occurred in 1994, ethnic hostility and genocide had been common for many years previously.

Pogroms against the Tutsi began as early as 1959, and were highlighted by an especially vicious period of violence in 1973 that corresponded with what is often described as the start of the Second Republic. Tutsi refugees from all over east Africa responded with the formation of the RPF (Rwandan Patriotic Front or Rwandese Patriotic Front), and in 1990 a period of armed conflict with Hutu authorities began in Rwanda.

The Hutus and the Tutsis fought for three years, with few major concessions made by either side. The conflict was thought to have ended with the 1993 Arusha Peace Agreement. However, the civil war took on a horrible new dimension on April 6, 1994, when Rwandan President Juvenal Habyarimana was assassinated. From the day Habyarimana died until mid-July 1994, extremist Hutus committed genocide on a scale that has rarely been seen outside of the Holocaust. For one hundred days members of the Tutsi tribe were raped and slaughtered by Hutus.[1] The Human Rights Watch organization estimated that 800,000 people were killed before the genocide abated.

In 1999 over 120,000 citizens accused of abetting the genocide were jailed. Over three million Rwandan refugees had to decide whether or not to return to a broken country. Rwanda has worked tirelessly to rebuild itself as a safe, peaceful nation committed to the prosperity of the citizens. Since 2005 the nation has made enormous strides in offering its citizens electricity, clean water, and education. The country's literacy rate was fifty-eight percent during the civil war. It is now seventy-one percent. Despite the growth, however, there are still deep scars that remain from the Rwandan 100 Days of Genocide. April 7th is Genocide Remembrance Day, and is followed by a week of official mourning.

In 2011, I had the chance to talk to Jennifer Herszman Capraru, a Canadian-born director who has been working in Rwanda since 2006. Her aim is to create theatre that promotes global peace and equality for women and girls. Jen's theatre company, ISÔKO Theatre Rwanda, is based in the capital of Rwanda, Kigali. Their production of Colleen Wagner's play *The Monument* brought international attention to the plight of genocide survivors and how theatre can help people continue their healing process. *The Monument*, a play about ethnic blood feuds, rape, and killing, is not written as being particularly about Rwandans . . . but it could be.

I wondered if a place where such horrific violence had happened was safe for female theatre artists directing a piece about the brutality of war. As Jen explained to me, my thinking was outdated: physical violence isn't the problem in the new Rwanda: now you have to protect yourself financially. Non-Governmental Organizations (NGOs) can be more flexible and free with funds than large government enterprises. Unfortunately, they can also economically exploit ambitious and well-meaning artists. Since theatre cannot be easily facilitated in Rwanda, NGOs are a make-or-break relationship for most companies. The new front lines being drawn are about the power of relationships, influence, and money.

*   *   *

Sarah: Jen, how did you become involved with these artists in Rwanda? How did you decide to start a theatre company there and work with these Rwandan actors?

Jen: I didn't set out to go there, I went by accident, in 2006 as a replacement crew member on the Canadian film feature *Shake Hands with the Devil*. I moonlight as a script girl, I do film continuity. A girl had that job and she got pregnant, and the union called me, saying, "Can you speak French? Have you had your shots for Africa? Can you leave in a week?" I said, "Yes." So we shot the film, and I was there for three months in the summer of 2006.

Sarah: At that point did you make contact with people who wanted to start a theatre group? Did you decide that you were going to put one together on your own? How did that come about?

Jen: At that point, I worked on the film, a tough shoot, yet at the same time so astonishing, to discover this extraordinary country. Amongst the Rwandan crew members, there were some who also worked in theatre. Not many. The casting director had a theatre company, some of the actors were theatre actors, and I realized that there are theatre artists who came back to Rwanda, though there aren't a lot of them, they are creating contemporary theatre. They're struggling to build a scene, and a renaissance began to bloom, which is flowering now. In 2006 I had the idea of just mounting one play, not launching a theatre company in Africa. That play was to be *The Monument* by Colleen Wagner.

Sarah: So it really wasn't, "I want to start a company; here's a play;" it was, "This is the play I want to do"?

Jen: Yes. I was innocent. I didn't realize it would be so hard to direct a play there and to bring it to a professional level. I was full of hope and energy, from seeing the rebuilding of the country, and noting how theatre lagged behind, when it can accomplish so much. There were three other women, Rwandans from the diaspora, who were creating theatre. I thought I would like to contribute by directing one production. In 2007, I was invited back to give workshops at the Rwandan Cinema Center by Eric Kabera, which was a fantastic experience.

I was able to tour the country with their festival, HillyWood; they have an inflatable screen and tour all the little communities and show them films in their own language. It's extraordinary. I began to meet more local artists, and became more encouraged, and then I received a lot of different contracts. I worked for the UN, with Mashirka Arts, where I made small collective plays with street children, ex-sex workers, housewives, and radio actors. Plus, I was invited to direct a workshop at the University of Rwanda, and lead writing workshops at Kivu Writers. In 2007 it was all just one big, affirmative, "Yes!"

Towards the end of that second trip I field-tested *The Monument*. We did public readings in French and in English at the Gisozi Memorial Centre, and during the talkback we asked the audience, "What do you think of this play? Do you think it's too much?" People said, "No, you should do it. And you should do it in Kinyarwanda—our national language."

Sarah: Why were you asking, "Is it too much?" Do you mean it would be too emotional, would it be too complicated? What did you mean by that?

Jen: I have zero interest in re-traumatizing people or opening up healing wounds. Catharsis is a delicate process in Rwanda and I needed to study Rwanda and speak with Rwandan colleagues and friends to begin to start to

Bio Points

- Jen, a Canadian, founded ISÔKO in Kigali, Rwanda in 2008.
- She earned an MA from York University. She studied directing in Germany at Landestheater Tübingen and the Volksbühne, Berlin.
- Jen is head of Theatre Asylum in Canada.

---

understand, as a foreigner, the basics about the history, the culture and the people before launching into a production at all. It would be different as a Rwandan, directing this play there, because one would be immersed in the culture. Part of the balance of intercultural theatre is that it's very delicate. It's slow. You must do a lot of research and especially, you must listen. A lot. It can be tricky, listening to people, watching their eyes, trying to understand that which is unsaid . . . people are very welcoming there, they might respond with "Yes, this would be great!" But there's always that little bit of instinct in me that says, "Is it?" So you watch, you listen, you learn. That's the most important advice I can pass on to anyone interested in this type of theatre: you must learn as well. I've learned so much, working in Rwanda, about a great many things . . . about the nature of theatre too . . . assumptions I've had for years have been reexamined, questions about reconciliation, forgiveness, questions that relate to my own biography. And, I thought it might all be too much, because the play is haunted, it is set in metaphorically in a grave, in a post-conflict zone that hints at Bosnia.

Wagner didn't set it in the former Yugoslavia, but it does, through its materiality, reference the genocide in Bosnia. It's a story of a woman seeking to find her daughter who may or may not have been raped and killed along with twenty-two other women during genocide. She's somehow gotten custody of a young soldier who may or may not be the perpetrator, and they embark together on an epic journey towards truth and some idea of forgiveness. It's a very, very difficult process. They don't reach a point of resolution, but they reach a place where they move near and far to one another, and by the end begin to see each other simply as human beings.

There are in my mind twenty-five dead, not twenty-three, as the two lead characters are spiritually dead at the beginning of the story, and become human once more as they witness each another's humanity. That is the first step. That's a challenge for both sides. In Rwanda, though the process of colonization, what was represented as an ethnic divide . . . was traditionally a class divide. The stringent divisions of Hutu, Tutsi, and Twa were manufactured by the Belgian colonial powers in order to divide and conquer. So the audience back in 2007 at the first readings were far beyond where I was, thinking it could be too much, it would be too intense . . . (she laughs).

I've seen Rwandan theatre since then, and studied scholarship on it, for instance by Ananda Breed, and some of it can be intense—some references the genocide directly. Hope Azeda is creating theatre in some of her work that, I think, relates an atmosphere of genocide in certain productions, and asks its audience the tough questions. I think that is quite intense, and powerful, for the public. I admire her, she's Rwandan, she's coming from a different place, Uganda, where she grew up in exile. She is a trained theatre artist, from Makerere University.

Sarah: A different viewpoint?

Jen: You know? She's got a cultural passport. What passport might I have? It is a question I've often asked myself. What right do I have to make theatre in Rwanda? Hopefully as a trained and experienced artist, possibly as a woman, with a focus on human rights, looking with fresh eyes at the complex situation there, that provides some currency.

I received an amazing cultural, historical, and spiritual training on *Shake Hands with the Devil,* working for months side by side with Rwandans. We shot in 2006, yet most days we were existing in a liminal space that was 1994, and it was very challenging, especially for the Rwandans. I made a young friend during filming who was a camera assistant, Fabrice; I'm friends with his family. They invited me to always stay in their home when I'm directing there. Unlike an expat, I'm integrated into this lovely warm family, which helps me to land and take root, it's a lot of fun. We all come home from a hard day's work, kick off our shoes, have a beer and watch the World Cup. Fabrice is studying film in Paris now. The first day of filming, he sat next to me and said, "I'm gonna practice my English with you. Can I sit beside you every day?" and I said, "Sure, what's the exchange?" Teasing—I would have done it anyway. He said, "I'll teach you Rwanda. Wherever we go, I'll tell you about the history, the geography. The legacy." And he did. So along with him and other friends, and the experience of shooting, day-in, day-out, for months, I was lucky to get some beginnings of an understanding of Rwanda. I felt informed enough, to try to put on *The Monument* there in 2008.

Sarah: When you did *The Monument* you had an acting ensemble of four people. How did you find them? How did you approach working with them? Was it difficult to say, "I have this intense piece I want to do"?

Jen: To cast the play I talked to Hope Azeda who was the Rwandan casting director on *Shake Hands with the Devil* and to Kiki Gakire Katese at the University of Rwanda. Carole Karemera I only met in the fall of 2008, when she invited us to perform at Ishyo Arts Centre once we had toured. Kiki was to play Mejra, but in the end did me a huge favor by introducing me to the extraordinary Jaqueline, who plays her now. I also asked everyone I knew, "Do you know anyone with performing experience?" In 2008 it was a challenge to find actors in Rwanda. That was due to the lack of training programs. A radio actress came in who was great and quite famous. But her work didn't translate to the stage. There are actors that I've trained, but they always have to have that stage spark. That theatrical intelligence that exists before training.

I searched high and low, held auditions, had folks read the script, had conversations with them, held classes—a really challenging process as there's little infrastructure. If you want actors, often you have to train them. If you want lights, you have to make them. If you want a theatre, you have to help create one. It's insane but also fun for someone like myself who's worked all over Canada in some beautiful high-tech theatres. It's a return to the roots of theatre and why we do it. Theatre at its most essential. To excavate a play about forgiveness through theatre and its rawest form, that really focused the meaning of the work for me.

The Monument *was directed with three actresses and one actor. The three actresses were Jaqueline Umubyeyi, Sonia Uwimbabazi and Solange Liza Umuhire. Each of these actresses has had success in the arts through music or film. Jaqueline Umubyeyi, in the leading role of Mejra, is a survivor who lost family members to the genocide. Casting a young man to play the perpetrator in the show was going to be a delicate task.*

Sarah: Talk to me about casting the male actor, Jean-Paul Uwayezu.

Jen: Sure. I should say that I created the roles of Ana, Mejra's daughter, and Ini, Stetko's girlfriend, they don't exist in the original script. Jean-Paul was an actor I met in 2007. One of the jobs I had then was giving collective creation workshops for a local NGO whom we later partnered with for a short while. They had great young people just starting university who were in genocide-awareness youth groups. They wanted to use theatre as a tool for social change and learn more about it. I volunteered and gave ongoing workshops to provide them with some methodology. I worked with them in French mostly, and the ones who spoke French would translate for the ones who spoke Kinyarwanda or had come from an Anglophone country to Rwanda.

There are always some people who stand out, you notice there's another level going on inside. Jean-Paul stood out because he was talented, he was confident, he was a leader, and he was a great communicator, a great listener. At the time he was a management student at ULK [ULK is the Kigali Independent University] but he'd never acted in a play before (laughs).

No . . . not even in his high school. So I was kind of frightened. He was my first choice, instinctively. Yet I knew that if he couldn't make it, I'd need a back-up. I went on an odyssey in search of actors. I found all kinds, anybody who had ever acted, anyone who had ever tried. A friend would tell me, "This guy was in a play in high school and he rocked." I would say, "Let's find him."

It was a serious challenge to find a young man to play the role of Stetko. It's a brutal role. The role of a killer, of a genocidaire, who is nineteen and on trial. I set it a couple of years after the genocide, during which Stetko would have been seventeen. There's a word in Swahili, *kadago*, it means small. It's the word that they use for child soldiers.

At sixteen or seventeen Stetko is almost a child soldier. The play dissects the roles of perpetrator and victim on either side of the conflict. Who is this youth, why and how was he motivated to do such acts? Wagner delves profoundly into that. The question of choice—did he have a choice? I researched Bosnia, and found that some of the play's references, names of women being gang raped, then buried collectively in a forest, came from articles on the March 1993 trial of two young Serbs, Borislav Herak and Sretko (like Stetko) Damjanovic. Not an easy role. After seeing many other actors, I came back to Jean-Paul, I think he did four auditions for me, which he teases me about now, you know? But he got the role.

Jen laughed at the memories of calling Jean-Paul back those four times. Jean-Paul was the right for choice for many reasons. When Jen cast him she was unaware that he, like so many others, had lost family during the genocide. His family was on the run for three months. Jean-Paul was only 11 years old when his brother died. His brother's body was later found. In a 2008 interview with the Toronto Star, Jean-Paul revealed that his family was against him taking the role until they actually saw him perform.

Jen: Now we tease each other, and he's all, "I had to audition four times for her!" But he managed to prove it to me and to himself, so I took a risk on him. I had an instinct. Considering his biography and his lack of training, he did an extraordinary job. Basically, combined with his natural talent, in two months he learned how to become an actor. He owns the role. The same can be said for Jaqueline, who plays Mejra. She owns her role. They're completely in these roles now. I think part of the reason is due to the fact that it's in their own language. I didn't want to play it in the languages of the West. I needed it to be in their language, Kinyarwanda. So much has been appropriated from what happened in Rwanda in 1994. If it is a foreign play, let it at least be in their own tongue, their own bodies and consciousness.

Sarah: Tell me the process about the tour itself. Where exactly did you go, who was your audience, how did the audience react to your play? Tell me about the performance.

Jen: The first time we played *The Monument* was on July 4, 2008. July 4th is the American liberation day, and it's funny, it's the same for Rwanda because it marks the end of the 100 days of the Tutsi genocide. The 4th of July is a huge party and celebration. I chose that day exactly for our first performance. And I can tell you it was the worst rehearsal process of my life . . . but the best opening night of my life. It was the worst rehearsal due to the lack of infrastructure. There were so many things that happened,

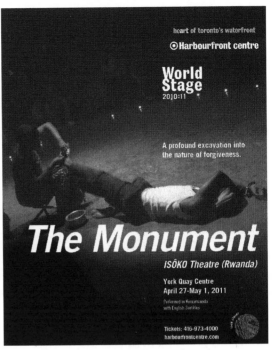

The poster for The Monument, *performed in 2011 in Toronto. Photo courtesy of Jennifer Capraru.*

from investing in our rehearsal space, which we couldn't use because it was situated next to what became a noisy café; then they were redoing the roof and hammering all day. I lost rehearsal space, I lost money, I lost actors, I lost partners, we had to move around. All the worst things for creative process. As well, in the end I designed the show myself, it was my first time. The production really tested my stamina, creativity and faith.

In Rwanda, you can't just phone up a theatre and say "I'd like an AK-47 please." In the play, Stetko sits in an electric chair and recites a five-page monologue on his actions during the genocide. But in Africa, people are not executed in electric chairs. Maybe in South Africa, but in Rwanda people are executed by firing squad. I can't bring in a firing squad, but I could have an extra, in a RPF uniform, with an AK-47. The gun would be blank of course, with no firing pin. This resulted in a circus of Kafka-esque rounds of administration. I'm just mentioning a single prop here. One costume. To be able to get it from The Rwandan Defense Forces, this was difficult for the army. But finally when I said *Shake Hands with the Devil* they relented; as production companies have made many films about the genocide they understood the need for a representation of a gun.

But on stage was different for the army. They were like, "What if someone grabs it and runs away?" "None of this has ever happened. What if people are traumatized by a gun?" In the end, what we agreed on is that they would have a soldier come, he would bring the uniform, the blank gun, sit and watch the show, and take away the gun every night.

Sarah: Wow.

Jen: And he would be paid.

Sarah: Of course.

Jen: If we went on tour he would need a per diem, transport and hotel. So that prop cost quite a bit. Whereas in Canada, or other countries, you would just borrow a prop AK-47. That was one incident. The great thing was, different soldiers came each show, and saw our work. They had questions afterwards. One wanted to be an actor!

Another worry was design. In the end I made my own moral and aesthetic choices about how far to go with representations of the 23 bodies that are called for in the script. Before I direct a play I don't see videos or images of it. But since I've finished this show I can look at [other productions of the script]. Those I saw used some form of representation of corpses. Puppets, life-like dead bodies. You can see them online. I had never planned to bring that kind of documentary theatre to Rwanda, it's too literal.

I took a symbolic approach, in order to create a critical distance. Part of the issue for Rwandans is bodies. They have lost their loved ones, who are perhaps in a mass grave. Just as Ana and Ini are missing in the play, their loved ones are missing. Somewhere. They find bodies each year. April is Remembrance Month, the içyunamo (mourning). The genocide started on the 7th of April 1994, and bodies that are found throughout the year are laid to rest during that month. Most of one's friends are melancholy; they are attending bone burials.

I think theatre can be useful during that time, we always try and perform then. But I never planned to have realistic representations of bodies; the place we go in theatre is the abstract. Yet small, personal mementoes could be witnessed as marking a life. I remembered visiting Auschwitz. I took my lead from there. In my production, each woman is represented by a small, but personal, object. The aftermath of trauma, embodied in fragments. More of an anti-monument, meant to provoke thought.

During the entire play, the twenty-three girls Stetko finds and digs up at the climax are an unseen yet constant presence. Everyone in the audience is wondering where they are. In fact, they're hidden behind a large drum, as they're tiny, and wrapped in fabric that looks like swaddling for a baby. It's silky, transparent. Inside, everything is waiting. Patiently. There is a pen that represents a student, a school uniform for a young girl, a cross for a girl who was religious, a bit of laced-up boot, a notebook, an identity card, a baby blanket. Personal things. A pair of broken glasses. All are painted to look caked in the red earth of Rwanda. They are the remnants, the fragments of memory, of the past. They are brought out and handled as precious, with love, with deep mourning, in a ritualistic sense. They have traumatized no one. No one has ever gotten up, nor rushed out of the theatre. We've had reactions from laughing to crying, to people simply sitting in profound silence.

We have talkback sessions after each performance. We had always planned talkbacks, about the themes in the play—genocide, reconciliation, memorial, the possibility of forgiveness. This is something that Rwandans, and the actors I work with—who are all educated, and speak four or five languages—as Rwandans, they deal with such dialogue as an integral part of their lives. Even if we hadn't planned talkbacks, we would have created a space for them, as the audience just doesn't leave after *The Monument*.

It's seventy minutes, no intermission, it's intense. Then they sit there afterwards. Quietly. They need to talk. They may not have clapped, as it may have been the first play they have seen. We have discussions, which sometimes take hours. They go very quickly into Kinyarwanda. One of the actors would translate for me. One time, Wagner was with us, she spoke and people said, "You didn't write this play, you snuck into Rwanda, this is a Rwandan play." "How can you, a Canadian woman, write a play based on Yugoslavia in 1993—because for us it's like forecasting the genocide." Many people, especially in smaller towns, were shocked to learn there had been other genocides.

After hours of talkback, we'd realize that we were tired and hungry and on tour. We couldn't talk for over three hours. But we can talk for an hour and a half. It's intense for the actors, for all of us. To rehearse it, perform it, feel then share the grief that lives in it. When we performed in Kigali we played hotels, festivals, schools, wherever we could, it was all site specific. We never used to perform with surtitles. Yet non-Rwandans and non-Kinyarwanda speakers would come back and see it more than once. This was astonishing and empowering for me as director, because it meant my work was getting beyond language and to the universal human language of theatre. It reached out to people who couldn't understand a word of what they were hearing.

Of course that's going to change, because we're slated to start touring internationally. To Canada, in 2011: to Toronto at the World Stage Festival, then Montreal and Ottawa. We'll be playing with surtitles for the first time. That will be interesting. Prior to that I'm going back to Rwanda for six weeks and we will rehearse then perform during the 100 days. I am going to interest more of the ex-pat community, the embassies. We'll perform with surtitles in

English and French. That brings up a whole other set of questions in terms of audience reception due to the surtitles: will they be in our way, how will I deal with them? I have to direct it with an eye to an international audience, yet preserve the integrity of what was found in 2008. All of these questions we're going to work on together.

When I first went to Rwanda and made the production in 2008 I was the director, I was coming in, finding actors and creating the show. I was training them, working with them, doing most of the producing in addition to directing. I had such an extraordinary experience with these actors that we wanted to work together again. We decided to form an NGO. We're not administrators, but these guys are super—it's cool because now it's a local NGO. We have a number,[2] so we can raise funds in Rwanda from embassies and NGOs as well as through our sister organization, Theatre Asylum, my company in Canada.

Sustainability is always an issue. Is it sustainable? We're not building a sports field or planting farmers' fields. Arts, and generally culture, doesn't pay for itself unless it finds support from an audience. In the West that's the model, yet in Rwanda people don't have money to pay for a show, so we perform for free or pay-what-you-can. We don't want this new public to perceive culture as an elitist activity. Art is not a luxury. We don't want people to have to pay the equivalent of an average week's wages [$10.00 USD] to see this work. In Kigali we pass the hat, or people pay what they want when they enter. But when we play in the hills, villages and towns we never ask for money.

The other way you find funding is via the government. The government in Rwanda has to deal with building basic infrastructure and supplying clean water, education, housing, public health. Peace and security. So culture . . . activists and artists and social movements know it can be a powerful tool for social change, and I think the government believes that, yet they only have so much they can support.

The Ministry of Culture helps through writing letters. There are corporations. We had support with water: boxes and boxes of free water for our last show, *Littoral* by Wajdi Mouawad in 2010. That was nice. We get goods in kind, such as donated rehearsal space from the Belgian embassy, donated lighting from the defunct French Cultural Centre. And we're supported by individuals. Rwandans don't have the system that we have in the West, of raising money that you can write off on taxes.

Philanthropists, that's new. It's something that could evolve in Rwanda. So how do you make it sustainable? If it's a combination of money I raise here and there, it will always need to be supported. Supported through the government, from some kind of revenue, which might be box office sales or T-shirts, though that won't bring much. Through corporations, individual donations. Those are the ways any cultural organization supports itself. So that paradigm is a different one in Rwanda than it is in Canada, and part of what cultural production does is to discover what it can be in today's Rwanda.

Sarah: When you go on tour, and your actors are with you, do you ever worry about "where will we stay?" Are people very welcoming, and you always have a place?

Jen: We plan before we go. It's a tour. We stay in hotels, travel on public buses, take our props and costumes with us—they are minimal. When we played in Cyangugu, everyone started laughing during the scene when Mejra finds her daughter, which is deeply tragic. I don't know why they did that. We asked them and they laughed more. Sometimes people are embarrassed. It's difficult for them. Yet they are fascinated. Often at the end, people won't leave, they want to come and have dinner with us, get addresses, get involved. They say, "You have to come back." They're seeing their own stories up on a stage. A lot of foreign films about Rwanda center around a white savior. A man, usually. Now there are films that have their own folk in them, indigenous production such as from the Rwanda Cinema Centre, or *Sometimes in April* by Raoul Peck, the first film looking at Rwanda by a black filmmaker. They see their Rwandan actors speaking their own language; it is transformative for them. We always have a positive and profound response. I think profound is more the feeling. They're so grateful. So are we.

Sarah: You asked what could go wrong. I've talked to people for this book who had their cars destroyed, their offices firebombed, I've talked to people who had death threats, been arrested.

Jen: I've had some bad experiences, but not with audiences or artists.

Sarah: So who were your bad experiences with?

Jen: A local NGO I won't name. It's hard for me to talk about this because it's going to underscore a lot of clichés, Sarah. That you work with a local NGO in Rwanda, a country which is very ethical and low-corruption—but you get ripped off. That's all I'm going to say. That was in 2008 and we haven't worked with them since. And I get represented in a bad light, because I complain, and for complaining too much, I could get into trouble. There are people out there running NGOs as a business to make a nice living. Ethics come last.

So I'm silent. Sometimes, what people represent themselves to be is only a part of what goes on. At our NGO ISÔKO Theatre Rwanda, those of us who are signatories in the NGO are the artists involved in making the work. We have meetings. "Can we trust this person as a production manager? Can he sign the checks, or should we?" We are very, very careful. Because they are

Rwandans, they know the scene on the ground, and I've gotten to know it to a certain extent. Sometimes it's, "Who should go to this meeting, we need a foreign person." So it's me that goes to meet this embassy. "But this embassy it would be better if it was a Rwandan person, maybe a woman, maybe an older one."

We have a good team and we can see who is good for the mission and we can accomplish it. I have also had negative experiences with a couple of Canadians, and another foreigner, a lovely graduate who was to assist, but wasn't around much when the going got tough, and I got tough. Yes I pushed people; they took it personally when it was about the work.

Jen paused for a second and it became apparent that this type of negative experience, a feeling of betrayal, affected her.

Jen: They didn't do their job in the end, and left the project. The show was better off without them, but I was shocked. When I asked for concrete design concepts, or reprimanded them for not being in the process with us, I was made to feel like I was the problem. I pushed myself hardest, and had nothing but admiration for the courage of the actors and what they were achieving every day in rehearsal. I was often in pain making the show, I admit. It is such tough subject matter. I got little support from the foreigners, I felt alienated.

One came to just two rehearsals and she had never designed [the technical aspects of a play]. It's my fault, I should have known better. They held onto the idea of the tent—the one we never got—and defended an assistant I had found for them, someone local who stole production money. None of the Rwandans trusted that woman. I felt I had no choice but to distance myself from the foreigners, and listened more to my Rwandan colleagues, whom I continue to work with.

It's a trust issue. It's on both sides, on the Rwandan side and the foreign side. This is something I don't really talk about, Sarah. I don't know how much you're going to talk about this. But it is an issue. It's good that you're kind of lifting up that stone and showing that ugliness, because it is a part of theatre everywhere, not just in Rwanda. There's always blood on the tracks, there's always guts, there's always love, there's always passion. It's sometimes about people getting messed up by each other. So you find the people you can work with. Those are the people I work with over and over again. I've done that for years in Canada. I work with new people also, you get an instinct about people, you know? The work is so difficult, especially the kind of plays that I'm often attracted to, which are about the mysteries of the human soul. You don't need people on the team to be creating more drama. Let the drama be on stage.

As an experienced director in Canada I have that sixth sense, but in Rwanda it's all new. You have to figure it out again. You may have had a good experience working with someone back home, then they hit Rwanda and become kind of a different person. You can't deal with them anymore. And they can't deal with you, with how focused you have to be to get anything near professional onto a stage over there. Hemingway once said, "Africa burns the fat from your soul." I think whatever you're doing there, if you're really engaged, if you really care and have the ethics to work with the local people—that is the only way you can all have true success . . . (she begins to giggle) and you will burn the fat from your soul, I guarantee it!

Some of the things I learn there I bring back. Like, when I come back to Canada people seem so stressed out. I'm like, "It'll happen when it happens." I have to readjust. Culture shock is, "Oh, I can't be ten minutes late for that meeting, they will not accept it." I go back to my efficient self. I have a Rwandan self and a Canadian self, maybe. My ideas about what defines success as an artist have evolved, and grown beyond Toronto. I have certainly learned a lot from Rwandans, and their idea of ubuntu, which means, "My humanity is measured by the way I treat others."

They see how you treat others. Of course you're working with a post-colonial legacy, you're a foreigner, a foreigner could be a white, black or south Asian person. If you're not from Rwanda you're a foreigner and if you have attitude or place power trips on people, they will go along because they're being paid. But you'll never have the trust that is needed by all, to make this kind of work. That's what I learned in the beginning: stop, look, and most of all, listen. We're still here. We're having a lot of fun and we're preparing to do a big production this summer, *Littoral.*

I start to say "To be clear . . ." and then Jen blurted out . . .

Jen: I haven't had a death threat, but I have been threatened with not having a visa. I've been threatened with not being able to operate in the country. That was all with one NGO. I've never talked about this before. We all know there is corruption here in the West too. Regarding the work in Rwanda, those difficulties aren't talked about. People want to know about the crazy stuff like the challenges of finding actors—that's fascinating, I'm happy to talk about it. But the scary stuff was something else.

Sarah: The corruption?

Jen: To me it's a betrayal. You're trying to do good projects and people love it, but then it's, "Oh, I didn't sign up for this." I had never experienced anything like that. Rwandans don't just come out and say, "I've been ripped off." They have to be diplomatic. So I just dropped it. (Jen's voice got quieter here.) I never tried to get any kind of justice. I just chalked it up to experience and moved on. I became extremely careful after that. I have had far more good experiences than bad, or I wouldn't go back.

Sarah: That's terrible though, for you to feel threatened because you tried to have an arts organization, or did a show there.

Jen: Yes, we were threatened. I was threatened because I worked with an NGO that was not honest. I tried to get the money back, which came from fundraising I implemented, but it didn't come back. If I had just sort of, taken it (not resisted) nothing would have happened. But I pushed. There was a tent involved, that we ordered . . . they have it now. It was meant for touring theatre, to be shared by cultural groups, and for ISÔKO, as an income-generating device to fund the work. But the truth has a way of emerging. Time will tell.

Sarah: I don't want to cause problems for you in the future. We can strike this part if you'd like.

Jen: I don't think there will be problems because they won't read an academic journal. I don't want to give a voice to clichés about corruption, but that is what happened. Corruption happens here [in Canada] too, it's just hidden. Rwanda is for the most part an excellent place to work, and it is growing all the time.

In spite of the challenges, letdowns and lack of basic Rwandan infrastructure, Jen and her group have decided that The Monument *was such a success that ISÔKO will continue to work in Rwanda and internationally. The company that couldn't even get a prop gun for a single scene in* The Monument *is now invited to tour to a prestigious festival in Canada, The World Stage, Harbourfront Centre, Toronto.*

Jen: We put on a second show, *Littoral*. In French, it's intercultural, it involves artists from Rwanda, Canada, Benin, Belgium, an artist from Lebanon who lives in Kigali, France. We're going strong. As the Greeks put it, theatre is a "seeing-place," one that can help heal our world. I have seen how it can impact on people's lives—audience and artists alike. We've proved that, in Rwanda in 2008 with our first production, performing with candles should the lights go out, barely any props, all live sound, transcendent acting, gorgeous a cappela singing and drumming—it can be performed anywhere. This essential work takes us back to the ancient roots of theatre as a ritual, ritual as catharsis, and catharsis as healing.

*   *   *

Jen stressed to me that the theatre scene in which she moves is constantly evolving. While she enjoys the constant movement, she emphasized that following the troupe itself can be difficult for the casual fan. She urges everyone who is interested in the work of ISÔKO or other African troupe) to follow them on Facebook or visit their websites. In the progressive theatre scenes where she operates, cyberspace is the fastest and most accurate way to keep track of an ensemble.

5 - Leave Prison Behind

Penelope Glass of Teatro PASMI in Chile

"They are prisoners but they are also fathers, sons, husbands and they are giving something positive to another group of people. People who are just like them, suffering the same social injustice."

Penelope Glass is an Australian woman who began working with issue-based and community-oriented theatre in the 1970's. Since 1998 she has lived in Santiago, Chile, where she worked for Teatro PASMI, a theatre with a focus on issue-based, community-oriented programs. Teatro PASMI has worked at a grassroots level to promote dialogue about gender violence, especially the high rate of femicide in Santiago and throughout the country. The theatre's version of Ibsen's *Lady From the Sea* is a look at why and how women live in fear. It is presented in a "flexible format," meaning it can travel and perform in a variety of environments, including schools, squares, streets, and community centers.

Teatro PASMI often works in collaboration with shelters, community and women's organizations, and churches—essentially any group wanting to start a dialogue about violence towards women. Teatro PASMI responds to the difficulty women face in empowering themselves in a machismo-driven country such as Chile, using theatre to bring women together into a supportive and responsive community. For instance, Penelope created a one-woman show about women taking back ownership of the birthing process: *Birth . . . We Are Modern Women, Aren't We?* In it, she explores the ways in which science and modern medicine have dehumanized the process of bringing life into the world. Teatro PASMI also focuses on using theatre in populations that do not have access to traditional means of producing art, and on people who are perhaps alienated by or distanced from the arts circuit. In particular, the theatre has run programs for adolescents with mental illness and for incarcerated people. These programs took place at the San Miguel Preventive Detention from 2005 to 2011, and at Colina One Prison since 2002.

It was Penelope's work in prisons that first caught my attention. American TV and movies have conditioned us to regard prisons as inherently dangerous places where art is frivolous and wasted. I wondered, from the perspective of a theatre practitioner: Is it true? If it does some good, is it worth the danger? Or conversely, if it is dangerous, how can the value outweigh the risk? I interviewed Penelope twice, with nearly a year between sessions. I learned that there is tremendous reward for the practitioners and the inmates . . . but that practicing theatre in such contexts is not without cost.

*   *   *

Sarah: When you are not doing your work about male-female communication, when you are at the prison, does it feel different to you? Are you nervous walking into a penitentiary famous for its overcrowded conditions?

Penelope: First of all, I really don't consider my work dangerous. So, the basic characteristic of what you're talking about, I don't consider, and the persons working with me here, none of us working in prisons consider our work dangerous.

Sarah: OK, so that's fascinating to me—let's start off with that. Because my view of working with people who are incarcerated would be that it could be very dangerous. How do you feel about that?

Penelope: Well, from my point of view, every community has its particularities, you know; working in prisons, or working in the outskirts of cities, in supposedly "dangerous situations" . . . it's not really dangerous because you're working on the human level. You just cut through all of those supposed, "Oh, this is a high risk situation." I feel safer in the jail than I do walking down the street at 2:00 in the morning in Santiago, you know?

Sarah: What prisons have you done work in?

Penelope: In a war zone it's very different, but this is not a war zone. I've been working in two prisons in Santiago, Chile: Colina and San Miguel, with Teatro PASMI. We direct and sometimes perform with the groups in Colina. Maybe it just seems normal to us, but I have never considered it dangerous. If you think of it as being dangerous, you start cutting yourself off from personal contact between human beings.

I think the prisoners are constantly threatened with possible situations, you know, possible violence, that could kill you, but I've never felt that in the prisons I worked in. I have been subjected to verbal aggression by guards, I have seen prisoners treat each other badly, and I have seen a lot of abuse of power, but never physical violence.

Sarah: In the US there is a definite threat of violence in prisons. It's very real. Is it different in Chile?

Penelope: If you live there, there's a lot of violence, but if you're going in and out, for theatre work or other things, you are providing something different in that setting, something positive. But obviously, if you're there as a prisoner, it's violent. Prisons are perverted. If you're there all the time, it's dehumanizing, because you have to live there. There are many factors: physical violence, abuse, overcrowding, psychological stress.

To survive, and build relations with people in that place, it's violent, it's dangerous. But that's nothing to do with the workshops. That has never impinged on our work, at all. In fact they see our work as an opportunity to leave prison life behind for the time they are in the workshop; the space we create in the workshop is a sense of freedom. In fact, they call the space created in the workshop "a space of freedom." If you live there, that's a different thing.

There are many obstacles facing the people of this part of Santiago. Santiago prisons can be extremely overcrowded. In 2009 San Miguel prison had 1,654 prisoners when the stated capacity was 892. In the past decade Chile's prison population has spiked, up seventy percent to nearly 54,000. In fact, Chile now has the highest incarceration rate (318 per 100,000 residents) of any country in Latin America. The Santiago Times *reported on October 13, 2009 that the Supreme Court had issued a report "confirming . . . that Chile's prison system is bursting at the seams, more or less incapable of rehabilitating its inmates and extremely dangerous."[1]*

Chile is a very polarized society, and prison is an intensely unjust environment. Almost all of the Chilean general prison population comes from impoverished backgrounds. Those with money may pay for rooms with nicer facilities, and therefore prisoners have an experiential awareness of social injustice. The Colina One prison is in the small town of Colina, on the impoverished rural outskirts of Santiago. As many prisoners' families have moved to Colina to be closer to the prisoners, the demographic of the town has changed dramatically. The Colina Two prison next door is a maximum-security prison, one of the most violent in the Metropolitan Region. Colina One is for long-serving prisoners, and although touted as a "model" prison, it is overcrowded and lacks basic decent living conditions. In March 2012, the 2,500 inmates of Colina One went on a hunger strike as a protest against these conditions.

The theatre groups that PASMI work with have always made a conscious decision to focus on social issues. Both theatre groups have reflected on how men can relate to one another without hierarchy. They also embrace the ideas of leadership, commitment to the community, self-motivation, and respect for the rights of all

Bio Points

- Penny, an Australian, trained in applied theatre at Griffith University, Australia.
- She worked with Teatro PASMI of Santiago, Chile.
- Penny is passionate about sustainable living projects.

---

humans. Through the process of creating a show, the men receive tools to process and discuss emotion. This may be hard for men used to the tough life on the streets of impoverished parts of Santiago.

Sarah: How do you foster that feeling of "leaving it behind" so that they can become artists?

Penelope: Well, we put a lot of emphasis on group work. Listening, trusting, deciding together, and assuring participants that whatever happens in the room, stays in the room. It doesn't go any further than the room. Example: we bring in a whole range of ways of relating that are absolutely different to the ways of relating inside the prison. Having to trust somebody, and it's so monumental when you live having to not trust anybody in order to survive.

Sarah: Are they eager to try or is that difficult?

Penelope: You have to work on the trust, obviously that's not necessarily there. And you don't necessarily know the other people and they don't know you. But the essence of theatre is trust, you know. You have to work on activities that break down the normal way of behaving in the prison. Involving your whole body, appearing to be vulnerable, open to new experiences that you probably don't have within the walls of the prison. That we can have arguments, heated arguments, about different issues, but that they never become violent. Because of the trust and respect that has been developed, arguments never get out of hand. It is sometimes possible that someone is not in a good place. Sometimes people don't come because something has come up and they prefer not to be there that day. That shows their respect for the group process. Then again, sometimes they come even if they are down and because of the workshop this tension can be dissolved.

Sarah: How do they find out about the workshops? Are participants chosen by you, or do they find out through a flier?

Penelope: When we worked in the San Miguel prison, the social worker that works in the prison decided who comes. In Colina One, when PASMI director Iván Iparraguirre first went in, he found out that there was actually a theatre group operating in the prison on its own. There was nobody to support it from the outside.

Sarah: They started it on their own?

Penelope: Yes, and Iván started helping to direct one of their shows, and that became the first workshop group; it was in the Work Sector of Colina One. Then two months later I went in to play a role in the play and we kept going every Saturday, and then eventually it was officially authorized by the prison authority. Therefore we started off in a very different way in the Colina One prison, because we came in independently and not as part of the Prison Service Art Education program. That's a whole different dynamic. No one told us who was going to come into that group.

Then a few months later the official Colina One theatre teacher was sacked, and we started to work with her group in the other sector of the prison. This group renamed itself Fénix. So then we were working with two different groups, and later on, in 2005, a new group called Ilusiones was formed in the Work Sector. The prison theatre groups started to get seen. So did we, because we were there twelve months a year, working and creating something positive.

In Colina One, theatre itself has a high status because it's been going for so many years. The productions have been high quality and socially relevant, and we have been able to perform outside the prison at festivals, universities and cultural centers. Sometimes men want to be in the workshop because they hope to perform outside the prison. But that's not the main aim. The main aim is if you want to work on something for yourself. Not because you want to get a benefit out of it in terms of the prison system, but you want to actually use it to reflect on your way of living and relating to society. I guess it's taken a while to develop this; it took maybe two or three years to develop this in Colina. It is the prisoners in the group who choose the workshop members. They talk to the guys who want to join us and they lay it on the line for them:

It's like this. You gotta come in, do the work, no one cares about your prison status, it's not important in the workshop what you've done because you're already in prison, what's important is what we're all going to create together from now on.

In November of 2011 I had a second opportunity to interview Penelope Glass. As I came back with more questions about her day-to-day operations in the prison it became clear that her work in Santiago had taken on a harsh new reality.

Sarah: So were you at Colina today?

Penelope: Yes we went up to the prison today. We're doing some extra days in the prison because we want to finish two new productions. We're starting to work on the idea of energy. You know, Chile is having a lot of protests at the moment, student protests. The schools have been occupied for six months. They are fighting the government to make a lot of changes in education and it's not easy. The guys wanted to write something about education and the whole trouble with everything being more commercialized. In Chilean society everything is being driven by a financial imperative.

Sarah: Commercialized?

Penelope: Yes. Everything is for profit. Education, health, all of that. So last week we began to go a bit deeper into the subject. They want to say something about youthful energy, the young energy in Chile that is bursting out everywhere. Not only as protests, but the people who add on to the protests, the people who just go because they want to destroy something or they are angry. They are frustrated and they want to hit out at the system to destroy it. The guys relate a lot to that because they've all been through that, and as a result of that, of not being able to control that, they are in prison. It's about looking at that energy, the way you channel that energy, how the system channels your energy, too. So today we did a bit of work about that energy and that inner anger that they often have to express. We improvised around those themes.

Sarah: When you're working with that energy, in that improvisation, can you explain what exercises you do? Who leads it? What does it involve?

Penelope: I try to have part of every session led by them. We start with a physical warm up and then there are members who remember doing warm-up exercises with Jean Marc Munaretti (a Belgian theatre worker we collaborate with) or Ivan. "Okay so who remembers that? Pancho? Okay then you lead it. Anyone else? Then you lead it." And when we do the improvisations, when they comment, we build off of what they say. I don't go in with a plan, I go in with an idea, an objective. I say, "This is what we talked about last time, we talked about energy, we improvised about what happens when we channel bad energy.

What is the difference between that and positive energy?" So I start from that idea, have one idea for an improvisation, and then begin building from what they improvise and comments on that improvisation. So very much it builds between us, and I kind of go with it. There is no fixed workshop plan. . . . . I go in with an idea based on what has been created in the previous sessions. In between sessions, my co-worker Sebastián and I reflect on what has been done and propose possible next steps. It's organic, the unknown is always a factor.

Sarah: For productions that you are creating, how long do they work on each play and where will the productions be held?

Penelope: This year the process is different. It has been more difficult because of difficulties in the prison. We are doing a more condensed process because we weren't allowed into the prison for a few months. Usually we can work on a show for a whole year because we're only there one day a week. At the moment we are there three days a week, we are condensing the process to try and have a performance ready in January. Last year they did a long period of work on improvisation so they are comfortable and strong with that. They build quickly. There is a festival in January, called ENTEPOLA, where we hope to perform. It's in an open-air amphitheater, in one of the most peripheral suburbs of Santiago, it's held at night and they perform in front of 3,000 people. So it's very much a goal to go. They've been five times.

In 2012 ENTEPOLA, an enormous international community theatre festival held in Chile, had performance, conference or workshop entries from theatre companies originating in Brazil, Argentina, Italy, Chile, Belgium, Mexico, the United States and Switzerland.

Sarah: How are they received there? How is their work received?

Penelope: Fantastic. I mean, very often they get a standing ovation. We don't present them as a prison theatre group. We just present them as a theatre group from Colina. We just say they are Fenix & Ilusiones theatre group, and after the applause, we tell them that they are actually from Colina One prison.

Sarah: And what happens then?

Penelope: That's when they often get the second round of applause. It's extraordinary. Because the audience, in this area, it's where a lot of the prisoners come from. It's a suburb of Santiago where there's a lot of crime, but basically it's very poor. A lot of people there have relatives, family members in prison. So it works both ways. It's very positive feedback for them. Receiving applause is a positive thing, it's attention for a positive thing, it's not a negative thing. And it's also about getting out of the stigmatization of what prisoners are like. They are prisoners but they are also fathers, sons, husbands and they are giving something positive to another group of people. People who are just like them, and suffering the same social injustice.

Sarah: Have you seen that change the way they behave in prison?

Penelope: It's important to keep in mind that these men have already done a lot of changing on their own. Often, they are leaders inside their prison community. It's a big, big stimulus for them to go outside the prison and perform. Although firstly, they always want to perform for the prisoners, inside the prison itself, and their families come inside the prison to see that. If they are authorized to go depends on their level of conduct. The prison director and other professionals who work there (social workers, psychologists, etc.) decide. So, sometimes they don't go, which is difficult from a theatrical point of view. How do you replace two or three actors?

Sarah: Have you had anyone in the past year who had to leave the group because their conduct wasn't good enough?

Penelope: They don't leave the group. They just don't go out. They still perform inside the prison, they just don't get permission to go out. No one has left the group for bad conduct, but unfortunately we have had a death this year. It was just a couple of months ago—one of the guys who had been with the group for three years. He was killed in prison. It just reminds you that you are in a prison. It's terrible.

Sarah: How did that affect everyone?

Penelope: Oh, it was terrible. The energy goes down, but worse . . . you feel so impotent. He performed at ENTEPOLA last year. He was actually a member of the San Miguel Prison group for a couple of years, but he was transferred to Colina One, so he became part of Fénix & Ilusiones. He was very optimistic, very positive, very committed. One of the ones who always said "Come on, let's work! Let's not be distracted, let's work!" So it was a blow, a big blow. It's like you forget. I always say you forget you're in a prison until something like that happens. Then you realize they're only with you five percent of the time they're in the prison. Then the rest of the time they have to deal with everything else inside, which is dangerous and violent. It's the second death we've had in Colina and it's always such a blow.

There is a short pause during our conversation. All I could think to say was "I'm sorry."

Penelope: Yes.

Sarah: Was there a grieving process within the group?

Penelope: Yeah, we do something, whatever happens. It's different each time. But there has to be some sort of process. This time was a bit difficult because the first time a member was killed one of the prison social workers rang us and told us the day that it happened. I went there the next day and we did a grieving process where we spoke about Juan and each person talked and then they cried. We were in a room, separate from anybody else, so we were able to do that. But this time, those outside the prison didn't find out about it for about five days, so by that time they had already gotten together themselves. They had already gone through the process. They got together themselves, inside the blocks. So it wasn't as immediate. That was a bit difficult for Sebastián and I, but they had had their grieving process as a group.

It just stays with you, you know? It becomes "oh, we have to do this for Christian! We have to do this for Juan!" But that's in Colina. In San Miguel it's actually quite the opposite. They're very different groups, and often in San Miguel someone will get frustrated and leave as a result of that. Whereas in Colina they are strengthened, in a sense, by the more continuous shared experience.

Sarah: What's the difference in San Miguel? Explain why it's different.

Penelope: In San Miguel we didn't decide who was in the group. The fact that this [Fénix & Ilusiones] is an autonomous group, where they decide who's in the group, it means new people come in with a certain level of commitment. In San Miguel it's possible that they are in the workshop not because they want to be but because their social worker said they had to be. See what I mean? "If you want to get benefits, you have to do this course." Whereas in Colina One, they in a sense invite people. Or they recommend people. So there's a different sense of commitment. There's a different level of human interaction. They spend a lot of time together inside the prison, they become like family. In San Miguel they often only see each other the two hours of the workshop.

Penelope has told me before that she feels it's very important to recognize the contributions of the entire Teatro PASMI team. As a troupe, they are committed to using theatre for social change, and feel that everyone on the team is an indispensible part of that work. For Penelope, Teatro PASMI is her autonomous group: the people are there with a certain level of commitment, a different level of human interaction.

Penelope: I was talking with a colleague in Ireland, she also works in prisons, and she's convinced that it's most interesting to work as a team in a prison, not on your own. And I totally agree with her. It's definitely a much richer process when you're working with somebody else and you can evaluate after each time you finish the workshop. For example, I worked for ten years as Assistant Director together with Iván [Iparraguirre, the Founder of Teatro PASMI and the person who initiated the PASMI work in the prisons], but he's not in Chile anymore, so now I'm working with Sebastián Squella, a young theatre graduate who is being trained by us in working in prison theatre. We're working as a team and it's great. It works really well. So, you're not actually alone.

Sarah: That's got to be very eye-opening for the new person.

Penelope: It's great. He started last year by performing with the guys and now he's taken on this new role of co-directing and doing workshops. It's really fascinating to be in the process, to pass on stuff. I'm interested in that at the moment—how you train people through a practice-based method, not through a formal educational process. Not only the university, or whatever. He's doing "on the job" training.

Sarah: It's an apprenticeship?

Penelope: Exactly! Historically, theatre did work like that. Theatre schools are the last fifty years, really. And with theatre work in a specific community like a prison, how can you learn it if you don't live the experience?

*   *   *

As Penelope and I conclude the interview, we chat about the other people I have interviewed for this book. Like so many of them, Penelope was fascinated to hear what other people were working on and then insisted that their work sounded dangerous. As I've come to expect from these interviews, Penelope then insisted that what she does just isn't that dangerous. "You forget you're in a prison," she reminds me. Just as typically, we end by talking about all of the people who make this work possible. Penelope is anxious that everyone at Teatro PASMI be given equal credit for the work they make possible.

Teatro PASMI's ensemble members include: Iván Iparraguirre, a Peruvian-born actor and director who founded Teatro PASMI in 1994, and who was Director of the Colina One theatre groups from 2001-2011 and Director of San Miguel theatre group 2005-2011; Claudio Cancino, an actor, musician and technician who has been with Teatro PASMI since 1998; Víctor Robles, a documentary filmmaker who has covered the work both in prisons and with women since 2007; Paulina Ledesma, assistant director and apprentice with the Colina One theatre groups from 2008-2010, who supported the work again in 2012; and Sebastián Squella, an apprentice and co-director of the Colina 1 theatre groups since the end of 2011. Other PASMI members working in prisons include Rodrigo Hernández, a photographer who directs photography workshops, and Claudio Geisse, who has run writing workshops in prisons since the 1990's. Among the Teatro PASMI's members working with women is Diane Catani, who has been associated with ENTEPOLA.

And of course, credit is due to the more than 200 prisoners whom PASMI has worked with in the Colina One and San Miguel theatre groups. The prisoner theatre groups include:

"Actualidad Now" (1998-2004)—Colina 1 Work Sector

"Fénix" (2002 to present)—Colina 1 general prison population

"Ilusiones" (2005 to present)—Colina 1 Work Sector

"Sueños de Libertad" (2005-2009)—San Miguel

"Revolution" (2009-2011)—San Miguel

Although the theatre groups in Colina 1 develop separate productions, they mutually support each other's work, working together as Fénix & Ilusiones. They dedicate their work to Juan, Mario and Cristián, the three theatre compañeros lost to the perverse and violent prison world, who continue to inspire us to "make a difference."

6 - Healing Wounds

Sina Chhon in Cambodia

"I was doing it because I felt that it may help me to heal my wounds from the past. Not only that, it may help the listener, the viewer to heal as well."

From 1975 to 1979 over 2,000,000 Cambodians perished under the oppression of the Khmer Rouge. Under the regime of dictator Pol Pot, Cambodians were evacuated from their urban homes and forced to work in farms for the benefit of the regime. Pol Pot wanted to turn Cambodia— now renamed the Democratic Republic of Kampuchea—back to "Year Zero." "Year Zero" meant there would be no banks, intellectual institutions, religion, or modern technology.

The country would be an agrarian, Communist enclave answering to no one but its own despot.[1] Any citizen refusing to toil on a farm would be executed or left to die by starvation.

The tyranny of the Khmer Rouge scarred the country and its people for decades after the regime was toppled. The Vietnamese Army removed the Khmer from power in 1979, but the group remained as an insurgent tribe, occasionally resurfacing from the jungle. Pol Pot never faced charges for the deaths he caused. In fact, he lived until 1998. The only punishment he ever received was by his own Khmer Rouge comrades, who put him under house arrest after he killed a popular officer.

There was no formal closure to the reign of Pol Pot or the devastation caused under his rule. Many families never learned the exact fate of loved ones who died. Some individuals never regained their health after the disease and famine they endured in the labor camps. Once the country was able to meet its basic needs, there was still the matter of healing. How could Cambodia address the suffering of individuals as well as a collective sense of mourning and fear?

Theatre has been a powerful tool to explore that fear and mourning. By confronting the past and honoring the dead, Cambodian theatre has become integral to helping both performers and audience members attain release and, sometimes, closure. Theatre is also a way for citizens to tell their own stories and examine the degree of freedom (or lack thereof) they perceive in their lives today. Playwrights and performers are mixing ancient practices and dances with modern stories to develop a new identity for Cambodian theatre.

In September of 2010, I met three Cambodian artists who were brought to New York City by their American colleague/collaborator, Catherine Filloux. In the morning each performer participated in a Theatre Without Borders panel discussing what happens to citizens in the direct aftermath of violent conflict. That evening I had the opportunity to watch Chhon Sina, Ieng Sithuland and Rithisal Kang perform for the TWB attendees. Their piece, a compilation of some of their more famous works, was called *Voices From Cambodia*. The performance started with "The Birth of Sam and Bopha" and "Our Land's Compassion," from the contemporary opera *Where Elephants Weep*, by Cambodian composer Him Sophy. Chhon Sina then joined Ieng Sithuland to perform the play *The Tooth of Buddha*, a new work by Morm Sokly.

Each part of the presentation was poetic, flowing and slightly sad. *The Tooth of Buddha* is an example of Lakhaon Kamnap (which translates to Poetry Theatre). These three artists have been traveling the world, performing pieces at conferences and speaking out against the oppression that artists feel in Cambodia. They relate vivid examples of the Khmer Rouge's tyranny and explain how Cambodia is struggling to regain artistic and institutional memory after so many artists perished or fled the country. Through their plays, Sina, Ieng Sithuland and Rithisal Kang hope to simultaneously address the horrors of the Khmer Rouge and the modern, universal questions the average Cambodian has today. After the show, Sina (with Rithisal Kang translating[2]) sat with me in the lobby of La MaMa to share her views as an artist and as a survivor of Pol Pot's regime.

*   *   *

Sarah: Would you please tell me how you got started in theatre?

Sina: After the Khmer Rouge genocide regime in 1979, I went to school. In 1984 I had to go to the next level, which would mean I had to get admission from the school to continue with my high school. Or, I had another option, to go to the teacher-training center. I did not get accepted by either institution and I saw the announcement at the theatre school. I was interested. I went back home, I asked my sister, "What about it? I want to go to theatre school." And then I just applied for the theatre school and I got accepted.

Sarah: In the Theatre Without Borders panel discussion you talked about your father, the Khmer Rouge, and the violence that happened. I was

Bio Points

- Sina, a Cambodian, began her acting training in 1984.
- She is a playwright.
- She also teaches at the Royal University of Fine Arts in Phnom Penh, Cambodia.

---

wondering how that has affected your performance. How that has changed the way you act?

Sina: I had a chance to work with this Dutch director whose approach was to talk to the actors so that we can share our true story that happened during the Khmer Rouge. I felt very, very uncomfortable. It was very painful to talk about it. I did not at all want to talk about it.

And so, in dialogue between the director and me, I decided finally to talk about it, to tell my story about my father during the Khmer Rouge. I was doing it because I felt that it may help me to heal my wounds from the past. Not only that, it may help the listener, the viewer to heal as well.

Sarah: Some people in the United States don't know details about the Khmer Rouge and how they treated people. They may not understand what happened to your father.

Sina: My father always had a disease. His stomach hurt. It's called *clahn* in Cambodia. I don't know what it is really called in English. But it just hurt. It just hurt his belly so much and especially it would get worse when the weather was cold or when he got in the water and got wet. The Khmer Rouge soldiers in the village where they were, where we were evacuated to, knew that he had that disease, but they kind of wanted to punish him.

My parents are the people that come from Phnom Penh, called the "April 17 people" or the "city people."[3] They were considered to be the people who were the enemy of the regime. Usually those people got tortured. They wanted to punish him, they wanted to torture him. They knew he had the disease but they forced him into very hard labor. He hurt his stomach, his belly hurt so much. When he got home from the hard labor to our family, we would try Cambodian massage, we used a coin on the skin. It's traditional healing and that's how people felt a disease would get better. We practice that in Cambodia even in the present day. And that's what we did when his wound hurt, his illness was really bad at that time. Then he was sent to the hospital in the village and I couldn't accompany him because only one person was allowed. My mother accompanied him to the hospital. Three days later he was dead.

When I learned that he was dead I was very upset, I was very depressed. In the village they had a group and a supervisor to see you, to always watch you all the time. When you went somewhere you had to ask permission from the group leader. So I asked the guy to let me go to see my father and he did not allow me and I knelt down and I . . . um, begged him again and again that he allow us. The group was always kind of causing troubles and you know they just, they just did some things to make your life trouble. I got beaten. Finally I managed to come and see my father, whose body was wrapped in an old rotten mat and that's all he had for his death.

My mother was there, she was not moving and speechless. She did not say anything. She was in a great shock and she didn't want to say anything. This was 30 years ago. I was young and even now when I hear about my father or my father's name these pictures are in front of me. It's in front of me, I never forget. In front of me.

We pray now before we perform. We pray to God and perform a blessing, like a tradition for Cambodian performing arts. I always pray that in the next life, "Please my father not be born in this time of terrible situation." (Sina took a moment to compose herself after telling me of that very private prayer. Then she continued). He was a good father for me.

Sarah: Please tell me about how you began to use theatre to help heal yourself and other Cambodians.

Sina: So the work, the opportunity to work with the Dutch director allowed me to gain strength.

Sarah: What was the Dutch director's name?

Sina: Her name is Annemarie Prins, a known Dutch director who came to Cambodia to work with us. She chose to work only with the actresses, a few actresses, very well established actresses of Cambodia and she created the work. She allowed me. The work gave me a new knowledge of using theatre to heal and how it is important to do that. I now have a firmer belief in that kind of theatre, in educating the people in the society.

Sina had a breakthrough role when she was asked to play a killer in a drama. The name of the play was Breaking the Silence *and it was produced in Cambodia in early 2009. One of the performances was done in collaboration with the Documents Center of Cambodia, an institution dedicating to documenting the truth of what happened during the Khmer Rouge. They specifically strive to document precisely how many people died and keep a list of their names. Ultimately,* Breaking the Silence *was toured to a number of provinces across the country. Wherever a performance took place people would sit on the ground watching the show very closely. When it was over there would be post-performance discussions. The play was successfully remounted in Singapore the next year. In April of 2010,* Breaking the Silence *was turned into a radio play that could be broadcast over the internet, thereby opening the show to a global audience.*

Sarah: Please tell me about the play where you were the killer and/ or the villain and people threatened you.

Sina: In one play I was the killer, I acted as a killer. When I was given the role by the director I was feeling that a killer was a bad character and it can be very, very dramatic. Even

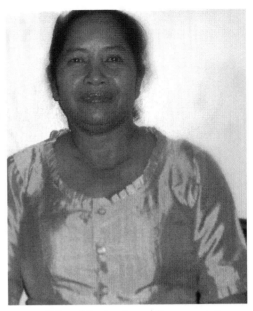

Sina Chhon following her performance at La MaMa in 2010. Photo courtesy of the author.

so, I did it. And this is the theme, the plot—they put the killer onstage and there is an interrogator who asked the killer the question, "Why did you kill? What are the reasons behind it? How did you feel?" And I performed as a killer who is also trying to defend himself. Defend the reason why he kills, why he do all the evil things, and all of that.

The whole time I was acting, I was acting as a guy who was brutal and, I believe, not misunderstood. I clearly said I did it and I defended myself as a killer. Well, there were some people in the audience trying to yell back saying . . . "Kill the guy, kill, kill. He's the killer, kill the guy, throw something at him!" This kind of anger was created within the heart of some of the audience.

Sina's cast mate during that scene, who was attending our interview, was onstage when the crowd yelled at Sina. He told me he recalled that they both felt distracted and worried, because they thought someone might really become violent.

Sina: Then they didn't do it fortunately and I am safe, I was safe. So right after the show I went to the director and I talked to the director. I said, "This is so dangerous what happened, because we are going to do one more show. What happened, it really pulled a trigger, and what if they really get up on stage and hit me?" So it was very dangerous. The director said, "You are going to be fine and this is called healing by theatre, because after that they also have a chance to listen to the other dialogue that makes them understand further on this issue. This is a good thing because it created proximity, the connection between the performer and the audience. This is a success as an artist."

Sarah: Have there been any other times that you felt threatened or that there might be punishment or repercussion for what you do?

Sina: That was the only time that I felt that it may be dangerous. I believe there is a kind of anger during the performance but it's not really that high. But I believe that every time we do the performance there is always a tension, and kind of anger happening, a moment.

Sarah: Do you think Cambodia is a safe place to be expressive? To have an opinion? To be political?

There is a long pause while my question gets translated. I can feel that a decision is being made. For the first time, I see a tear in Sina's eye.

Sina: Not yet. Not yet.

Sarah: Would it be OK if I say that in the book? I don't want you to suffer for having said that.

There is another very long pause and then Sina answers me in English.

Sina: Yes. OK. Thank you.

*   *   *

Since this interview Sina Chhon has continued her work as a playwright and actress. A film adaptation of *Breaking the Silence* was made as part of a series of short films about genocide. A play she wrote about children and prostitution, called *Phka Champei (Frangipani)*, has been directed by notable artists such as Francesca Zambello and Dawn Saito.

7 - Chance to Communicate

Zeina Daccache of Catharsis in Lebanon

"12 Angry Men is in my essence. I love this play and I feel it reflects the reality of society in Lebanon."

There are many populations inside of Beirut's Roumieh prison. Those serving the longest sentences are kept in Building A. The general population is housed in Building B. Building C houses at-risk and younger offenders. Altogether Roumieh prison holds more than 5,500 people at a time. A person with money may buy some private space, while the poor are packed 90 into a hall. An enormous underground market allows people to bring in drugs, food, even televisions. Because they don't have money or cigarettes to spend the black market is useless to some prisoners. Many of the prisoners lack working toilets, drinkable water, or adequate clothing. Some must be servants to other inmates to get basic necessities.[1] It is a grim place with little to hope for.

Yet there is one population that is not in despair. In 2009 a longitudinal study of certain prisoners incarcerated at Roumieh Prison[2] showed astounding results in the improvement of prisoner behavior. Feelings of self-importance and power had been reduced, and the inmates had more insight and had reconsidered their behaviors and attitudes. The surveyed inmates' ideas of injustice diminished. They started working on themselves instead of putting the blame on the faceless scapegoat of "society." Murder was no longer a featured topic in conversation. These men even showed a desire to re-adapt to the outside world. Men, some of whom were sitting on Death Row, were expressing compassion, empathy and joy.

What extraordinary thing did the Roumieh Prison do? What was responsible for such a profound turnaround in the lives of men living in some of the worst conditions on earth?

The prisoners who were interviewed were participants in a drama therapy group inside the prison walls. One woman, Zeina Daccache, brought inmates together in a phenomenal project designed to show these men humanity in themselves and their worth to the outside world. This is the story of *12 Angry Men* and its transformation into *12 Angry Lebanese.* It is the story of the woman who pioneered drama therapy in the Arab world.

* * *

Sarah: Obviously I wanted to interview you because of your experience working in prison and working with *12 Angry Lebanese,* but I want to go back a little bit before that. Can you tell me your history on stage and TV?

Zeina: I have a BA in Theatre Studies. Then I traveled to the private theatre school of Phillipe Gaulier [noted professor of theatre and clown master] in London in 2000-2001. I came back to Lebanon, started working at a rehab center doing theatre with the residents, and I started my drama therapy studies in Kansas, USA in 2006.

Sarah: Did you find that satisfying? What made you decide to go to Kansas?

Zeina: My aim was always like, I didn't want to just do pure theatre, Art for the sake of Art, and be the actress or director of a play. And I always felt that theatre could be the best therapy if used in the purpose of therapy . . . so I was thinking of people who had something to say, something to express, you understand what I mean? This is why, very spontaneously, I said "Oh, why don't I offer theatre courses in a rehab center?" Especially, I was so amazed, because in 2001 there were lots of drugs going on in Lebanon, you know?

Sarah: Drugs affected the culture there?

Zeina: It was kind of a surprise also to me, like, what happened, you know? What happened to the world, what happened to all the young people? Most of them were taking drugs. So, I decided to volunteer first. The rehab center where I worked is called Oum El Nour [Rehabilitation Center from Drug Addiction]. They said, "Okay, we can try," but you knew they were doubting theatre might be helpful in any way.

Sarah: It must have seemed farfetched to them.

Zeina: When we started it was a volunteering thing for the first three months. Then I was employed there for six years.

Sarah: When you began working and doing theatre there, was it with boys and girls, or men and women? How many people did you have?

Zeina: It was a rehab center that had separate centers, like two for the men and one for the women. I was meeting with men and women, but separately. They were not mixed together.

Bio Points

- Zeina, a Lebanese woman, is an award-winning actress and documentary filmmaker.
- She trained in scenic and dramatic art at Saint Joseph University, Lebanon, in clinical psychology at Haigazian University, Lebanon, and in drama therapy at the University of Kansas.
- Her drama therapy center, Catharsis, was started in 2007.

Sarah: Did that make you a little bit nervous, to go into a rehabilitation center for men, and try and teach theatre from a female perspective?

Zeina: In the beginning, yes, and definitely I was also young, you know what I mean? Most of them were coming from aftermath results of the war, like from the militias. They were older than me so they were looking at me and saying, "Ah, what is this little girl coming to do now?"

Sarah: How long did it take for them to warm up to the idea of doing theatre with you? How did you build their trust?

Zeina: The rehab center decided to employ me after the first three months of volunteering, because they saw that the residents built confidence in the group, in themselves, and in me as a trainer. The first year though, I was learning much and did a lot of research and work on myself. As soon as they understood that they were benefiting, and they saw something changing within them, trust was there. With each group you'd be working for a year, seeing them two times per week, and the change was there, you know? So this is when the whole attitude changed. Then it became like the old group already was telling the new group, "Oh my god, it's really helpful, these theatre sessions we're taking," and things like that.

Now in parallel, and I was doing my personal, how do you say, I have done ten years psychoanalysis, it was very helpful also in my approach because I wasn't doing purely theatre. And this is when I came to research, "How can we mix theatre and therapy?" And gladly enough, I found out that in the States there was something called drama therapy.

Sarah: Yes! It's actually kind of a big thing here. Theatre practitioners and counselors are given the training they need to hold therapeutic drama sessions. Exercises like role playing and telling a personal story are done in a clinical way that helps the performers resolve a past trauma.

Zeina: Yeah, I was practicing it, but I didn't know which title to put on that word, you understand? In 2004 I heard there is drama therapy in the United States. In 2005 I applied for the Fulbright Scholarship and I got it. I was one of the six people who were accepted in Lebanon to benefit from the Fulbright Scholarship.

However, my work at the rehab kept on developing, and things were doing really great, and I couldn't leave for two years in a row to go and do my studies. So what I did, I started traveling to the States in the summer, and came back to Lebanon. All the courses of drama therapy, I was taking them there, as an alternative training student. Graduate studies. But at the same time, I kept my job in Lebanon as a drama therapist and enrolled in an MA in clinical psychology at Haigazian University in Beirut.

Sarah: How did that switch into you going to Roumieh Prison?

Zeina: I felt it was the normal path of things. I'd been there for six years in the rehab center, six years and a half. I knew there was this experience in Italy in Volterra Prison in 1999, and I went to Volterra in 2002 as an intern to see Armando Punzo at work there. Armando is the theatre director that has been doing theatre in Volterra prison for more than 25 years now.

Volterra Prison, located in Tuscany, made worldwide headlines when it opened a public restaurant in the prison. Chefs preparing gourmet vegetarian fare were trained inside the jail as part of a rehabilitation program. The Volterra Theatre Festival is built on the plays taking place inside that prison. It is part of an ongoing effort to maintain a healthy social connection and occupational training for the inmates.

Zeina: I started wondering, "Wow, would you think that this would be possible in prison?" I mean, it should be similar to rehab but it's totally different, because you are dealing with more cases and more difficult cases, and for me this was the next step in my work. I decided to see if we can start something in prison. It wasn't easy at all, because it took us a year to get the clearance from the prison authority after having received the funding by the EU, with two refusals of the project at the beginning. And finally we got the clearance. Since the first day, I knew that drama therapy can be really, really beneficial for everyone in there.

Sarah: Tell me about the first time that you went in to teach theatre in this giant prison.

Zeina: I can't say my first time was in 2008, because in 2002 I was in Italy, in Volterra, for a two-month internship. So my first "first time" was in 2002, and there it was like "wow," you know, and there's this, um, how do you say, when you're like amazed seeing something—it's like you're on another planet . . .

Sarah: You're overwhelmed.

Zeina: . . . another dimension.
In Lebanon you need to multiply it by one thousand, I mean you're not talking about a very modern prison, no, you're talking about a prison that is so overcrowded, to me prison is overcrowded. It's not like anything you've seen before, it doesn't look like the Italian prison in Volterra that I've seen where each inmate has his own room, his own activities, etc.

I was wondering, oh my god, definitely, these people will say, "What are you coming to do with your theatre? We need blankets, we need sheets, we need food, we need to go to the tribunal," because most of them are awaiting their sentences for years, you know? But soon enough, I discovered that theatre was a great tool for them to understand that they can, how do you say? Get over, sorry for the word, but get over the shit that they are in, start dreaming, and start working on themselves. Start saying, "No, we can be stronger than what we are in."

Sarah: When you went into the prison, were you alone?

Zeina: I was totally alone.

Sarah: Did you ever think about the crimes these people had committed? Were you scared?

Zeina: Scared? No, but I mean they were there, they were for real, you know? It's not like you're watching a film. They had to talk about it because in the end we're doing therapy. If they wanted to talk about their crimes, they had the total freedom to say it. I was also allowed to see the file, the personnel file of each one. So I read about their crimes, I heard the crime from them, and this helps you in a way, you know which roles should be given to who. Because in the end it's also therapeutic to know what role you are giving to which person.

Sarah: How did you end up with forty-five men?

Zeina: Well, as naive as it was . . . because the project was funded by the USA, the European Union, we were already late one year because the clearance was not there from the prison authority. The fastest way was to take the microphone. There are microphones in the building. So I took the microphone and I said, "Hello, if you are interested in partaking in theatre, please join us in the room downstairs."

We shared a good laugh as I pictured young Zeina picking up the microphone and announcing that theatre had come to Roumieh Prison.

Sarah: And that was it?

Zeina: And there you go. It was like that! I mean, now, I don't do that anymore. Now, you know, we send letters to the room and we say, "If you'd like to apply just write your name and give it to the prison officer." But back then, I was one year late with this project and there was no way I was waiting anymore!

Sarah: It's the boldness of youth, it's, "I don't know that this won't work, so I'll try it!"

Zeina: And it worked! It really did work, you understand? I received three hundred applications, like three hundred persons came to that room.

I couldn't decide just like that, so I said, "Okay, why don't we do an intensive training of drama therapy, and you'll see if you guys want to do this project or no." This is what happened. For the first two months it was intensive sessions, we'd meet a minimum of three times per week. In the end, you'd see people saying, "No, I prefer to stay in the room," others to whom we said, "You are leaving prison soon and it is a fifteen month project." We ended up with seventy names. Names I saw would commit for this long project—because it was a fifteen-month project. We presented this list to the prison authority and the prison authority took out some who were forbidden to participate in any project due to some problems they had up there.

Sarah: Did you get the sense that if men were cut from the program, some of them would be angry or sad about not being able to do it?

Zeina: God was with us. It was like an auto-selection. Even the people who could not be there, you can tell they are not ready to discover themselves, you know? They just don't want to be there. I tried the impossible, to keep everyone, and indeed some names that were banned by the authority were accepted again, as my observation of their behavior was taken into consideration. But for some it wasn't really essential even for them to come back, as they were more fond of other illegal activities inside prison. It's not like I had to say at any time, "No, I don't want you." No, it came very naturally.

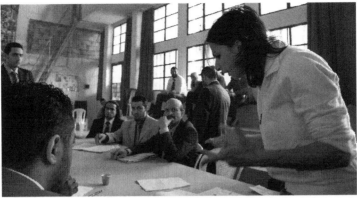

Zeina Daccache directs inmates of Roumieh Prison in 12 Angry Lebanese *in 2008. Photo courtesy of Dalia Khamissy/Catharsis-LCDT.*

Sarah: How did you decide on Reginald Rose's script when you were dealing with *12 Angry Men?* What was the process of turning that play into *12 Angry Lebanese?*

Zeina: Well, *12 Angry Men* is in my essence. I love this play and I feel it really reflects the reality of society in Lebanon. The miscommunication and judgment of "the other." The injustice, the prejudice. I wanted to do this role reversal, that they would play the role of the judges, in order for them to understand how people perceive them. They should understand where people are coming from, "Why would this judge say that, no, this kid should get the death penalty, because maybe he was hurt himself, maybe he had issues with his son."

Sarah: Is it true that the men helped to rewrite the script?

Zeina: Yes of course, we didn't do *12 Angry Men* as is, we changed it, we adapted it a lot. Don't forget that these men, it was their first chance to communicate with the external world. So, for them it was so necessary to add their own monologues, convey their own messages. They added scenes about human rights, their own human rights, about some laws that do not exist in Lebanon and they are shouting out loud to have them. They created songs that lobby for the laws, songs that lobby against death penalty, a dance telling about their own routine in this prison.

Zeina received tremendous acclaim for her production of 12 Angry Lebanese. *Not only did the men grow personally from their drama therapy, the legal community of Beirut had a chance to see what stories and pleas were coming out of*

Roumieh prison. Top government, military and security officials were invited to see 12 Angry Lebanese. *Their attendance meant that the prisoners were being heard by people at the highest levels of Lebanese government. The full story of their process was captured as a documentary film. The film, called* 12 Angry Lebanese: the Documentary, *won Best Documentary at the Dubai Film Festival 2009 as well as several awards in festivals around the world in 2010 and 2011. From this successful production at Roumieh, Zeina was inspired to reach out to many other disenfranchised people in Lebanon.*

Sarah: What is "Catharsis?"

Zeina: Catharsis is the Lebanese center for drama therapy. It was established in 2007 in Lebanon. It's an NPO, Non-Profit Organization. It's the first center, really, in the Arab world that offers services in drama therapy, and we work in different settings. We work in prisons, in psychiatric hospitals, rehab centers, other NGOs dealing with kids, women, etc. We've worked with women in the South after the July War.

The July War was a massive brief but devastating conflict that took place primarily in the southern part of Lebanon (Beirut was bombed as well) in July 2006. The Lebanese call it the July War; it is also known as the 2006 Israel-Hezbollah War or the Second Lebanon War, depending upon the nationality of the person speaking. (Hezbollah is a Shi'a Islamic political party based in Lebanon with a militant faction that has engaged in armed skirmishes across the border between Lebanon and Israel.) During the conflict, Amnesty International called upon each side to stop targeting civilians. In September 2006 Reuters News Agency estimated that 1,300 Lebanese had been killed during the July War. Catharsis used drama therapy to help the female survivors of physical, sexual, and emotional trauma begin to process their feelings and find healing.

Sarah: What were you doing after the July War?

Zeina: After the July War, we were contacted by an organization working in the south, to do drama therapy with women who lived in two villages that were completely devastated by the war. They have lost family members, they have lost their houses. So we went there for six months. We were meeting twice per week with these women and doing drama therapy sessions.

Sarah: What were some of the things that you would do in these sessions?

Zeina: Drama therapy has many techniques. You can move from Phase 1, which are warm-up exercises, it can be warm-up of the body, of the emotions, of the imagination. Then participants move to deeper exercises, such as remembering and enacting the moments that they've been through, talking about their loss, embodying the hope they have, if there is still any hope, structuring the future.

It's where to start from—although not through talking, they really picture the scene and they would do it. They would embody the whole dream they have, or they would embody the future scenes they want to live.

Sarah: How many women did you have participating?

Zeina: We had seventy women split in two groups.

Sarah: What is that like for you to go in and take on six months of someone else's pain and suffering?

Zeina: It's my job in the end; since 2001, this is what I deal with and this is the choice I made. Because of there is a lot of suffering. Everywhere in the world there is a lot of suffering.

Sarah: In addition to working with the women after the July War, you work with domestic abuse victims?

Zeina: We offer services for other NGOs [non-governmental organizations] who work with the women who suffer from domestic violence. We also have a private clinic if an individual is seeking help, therapy, so we offer drama therapy for individuals.

Sarah: Are these exercises? Are they ever turned into a performance piece, or is this something that is strictly for the people in the class?

Zeina: It depends. Drama therapy can lead to a performance if the population wants a performance, or also it can be great as well if you want to just keep it in the sessions. It depends what you want and what the population wants. For example, in prison, both are good. Because we never left prison while we had *Twelve Angry Lebanese;* we stayed there for a year and just kept offering drama therapy sessions to as many inmates as were willing to do it, you know? Now we're preparing the second play inside prison. We'd find new inmates, and many of the old groups.

Sarah: What's the second play?

Zeina: It's *The Hanged Man (Le Pendu)*. It is an adaptation we're doing of a play from a Canadian writer, his name is Robert Gurik.

Sadly, Zeina's dream of staging Le Pendu *could not be realized. Shortly after we spoke, in April of 2011, there was a riot in Roumieh Prison. The theatre burned and there was no hope for it to be rebuilt in time for a new show. Instead, Zeina focused her efforts on a group she had been planning to start—a group for the female inmates of Baabda Prison. Here is what Zeina and her group accomplished there.*

Zeina: In July of 2011 I started the new drama therapy program with the women inmates in Baabda prison, which is also in Beirut suburb. After ten months of drama therapy sessions, the play *Scheherazade in Baabda* saw the light. Twelve performances took place inside Baabda Prison in April and May, 2012. As six inmates finished their sentences we moved the play to a venue in Beirut in July, 2012. It was a real success. The play is a collection of monologues, self-revelatory performances, that deal with women issues in a patriarchal society, about the "adultery crime," domestic violence (DV), and how there is no law to protect women from DV.

Lebanese women in prison face the same difficulties and tribulations as prisoners anywhere. They struggle to accept the loss of their freedom, the dangers of life in prison, and how to maintain an identity in an unforgiving environment. Women in Lebanon face additional issues. Often they have suffered under a patriarchal society that openly practices a double standard. The most common example is punishment for adultery. In theory it's against the law, but in practice it's only against the law for women. Perhaps most egregious is the Lebanese law concerning rape or sexual abuse. Spousal rape is not considered a crime in Lebanon, and women have no legal recourse if they are attacked.

They may, however, be put in prison for defending themselves. There are also legal agreements that protect a rapist if he agrees to marry his victim. In 2012 a bill was presented that would have made spousal rape illegal, but it was amended to the point that it is now essentially up to religious clerics to decide if a rape occurred or not.

As part of the mission statement for Catharsis, Zeina declared, "We offer drama therapy services to the community in accordance with the highest ethical standards, providing a powerful tool to explore and deal effectively with the issues identified by a wide range of clients, including some of the most isolated and disadvantaged members of the society."

Although Catharsis has been very successful and continues to grow, I had one last question about the project that started it all, her work in Roumieh.

Sarah: Did the riot scare you out of working with men?

Zeina: Not at all . . . The call they did by doing a riot was not targeting the civil society, only the government and prison authorities that need to give further attention to prisoners. Indeed, we never left the prison; instead we got funding to refurbish the theatre room that got burned, and we refurbished two other rooms as arts and crafts rooms where the inmates work on products such as candles, and Catharsis sells them for the guys so they have an income generating activity.

*   *   *

In the end, that's exactly Zeina's style. She took the ruins of a burnt room and turned it into a better theatre, added additional artistic spaces, then built a business to benefit the men and women she serves. Catharsis is continuing a program of outreach to the public. In December of 2013 it held an evening of celebration at the UNESCO Palace in Beirut to announce that Zeina's new documentary, *Scheherazade's Diary,* was a critical success. The documentary features the play *Scheherazade in Baabda,* as presented by the female inmates of Baabda prison in 2012. The film won the International Critics Prize (FIPRESCI Prize) in the Muhr Arab Documentary competition at the 10th Annual Dubai International Film Festival (Dec 6-14, 2013) in Dubai, United Arab Emirates.

8 - Support in Afghanistan

Zahra of AHRDO Theatre in Afghanistan

"I hope Afghan women will be introduced to others as they are.
I think that if the facilitation would be given to Afghan women
they could control the world."

On May 3rd, 2012 I received this email: "Dear friends: our AHRDO friend and colleague Zahra, Afghanistan's only female "Joker," was violently attacked on her way to work the other day. She had received threats from unknown men in the days prior to the attack telling her not to go to work anymore. When she continued to do so, she was ambushed and now has to move into a new place with her two kids in order to avoid further harm." The email was signed "HJ JE."

I had typed up my interview with Zahra just four months before. What on earth had happened?

At the Theatre Without Borders conference in 2010, I had an opportunity to watch a panel of artists speaking on the topic of theatre as a tool of recovery and healing. In the aftermath of human rights atrocities during war, theatre can provide catharsis for both the audience and the actors. Hjalmar-Jorge Joffre-Eichhorn, one of the founders of the Afghanistan Human Rights and Democracy Organization, spoke about using techniques of Boal's Theatre of the Oppressed and elements of Playback Theatre to help the people of Afghanistan mobilize and empower themselves. AHRDO has collaborated with ordinary citizens to produce plays that speak to the nation's need for justice, expression of personal truth, and empowerment.

In 2009 AHRDO adapted Irish playwright Dave Duggan's work *AH 6905*, which they renamed *AH 7808*. *AH 7808*, the story of a man who is going to have "truth" surgically removed from his body, was used as a tool to talk about justice in the region and to bring the world's attention to the oppression in Afghanistan. AHRDO has both male and female staff members and participants, but greater focus is placed on the experiences of the women and girls. When looking at oppression in the region, it is impossible to ignore the civil rights violations that have been perpetrated against the women of that country.

The 2009 productions of *AH 7808* caught the eye of major international investors, and with their backing, AHRDO was able to expand its programs. Workshops using techniques such as Forum Theatre and Playback Theatre could be used to help Afghan women explore their own feelings about the war, personal abuse, family struggles, and a multitude of other deeply painful issues. 2010 was a year of expansion and goal fulfillment for the organization. With financial backing and an increasing international profile, the group could continue working in Kabul while solidifying programs in other parts of the country. In their own words: "A wide range of different initiatives were carried out, focusing on working with different victims' groups as well as widows' and women's organizations.

In terms of the former, theatre was used to contribute to ongoing human rights abuse documentation and truth-telling efforts, while the latter were involved in Afghanistan's first Legislative Theatre project, in which women from different parts of the country used interactive theatre techniques to elaborate suggestions for legislation on women's issues. Besides, AHRDO wrote and produced its first scripted theatre play, *Infinite Incompleteness,* based on victims' personal stories of loss during the past three decades of conflict."

The suggestions for legislation on women's issues evolved into legal referenda. As Joffre-Eichhorn explains, "The legal referenda were conducted with ordinary women and representatives of women's organizations as well as political representatives in order to give more democratic legitimacy to the suggestions for legislation that emerged from the Forum Theatre performances. We [created] a final legal report, in which the recommendations were presented. These will now be discussed in the Afghan parliament."

The idea that theatre can make a difference in this way is called Legislative Theatre. It is one way that Theatre of the Oppressed methodology can take theatre into the realm of concrete action that will affect everyday people.

Afghan women are at a particular crossroads in their identity as theatre practitioners. So many women have stories to share, but are traditionally forbidden (either implicitly or directly) to share them through the medium of theatre. At Theatre Without Borders, Joffre-Eichhorn spoke of an Afghan woman who was severely beaten by her husband for attending the theatre workshops. After she recovered from the beating she chose to return. The personal and social pressure to abstain from the theatre can be overwhelming. I asked if there were any women working in these theatre groups that would be willing to speak with me for this book.

This woman's name is Zahra. After hearing and reading about AHRDO's mission, I thought myself prepared to interview this beautiful and brave young woman about how she began attending acting workshops in Kabul. My preparation didn't do the situation, or her, justice. At the time, her personal life was largely that—known only to those closest to her. I didn't know she had been married at thirteen to a man that abused her. I didn't know she had two children by him. I didn't know she had survived his attempt to kill her and burn their house down. Almost no one knew.

During the interview Zahra and I were joined by a young man named Salim who did his best to interpret a mish-mash of overlapping languages, ideas, and gestures. The text that appears here is the literal interpretation Salim provided as we spoke.

The interview was coordinated (and greatly aided) by Hjalmar-Jorge, who served as a sort of cultural ambassador when questions became difficult to translate. The four of us came together in cyberspace and eventually a story emerged. A woman who could not safely see her last name in print introduced me the front lines of drama in Afghanistan.

*   *   *

Sarah: The first thing that I'd like to tell you is that if at any time I ask you a question that you aren't comfortable answering or you don't want to say anything, please tell me and we'll skip it. Okay?

Zahra: Okay.

Sarah: Would you please tell me your full name?

Zahra: My name is Zahra.

Sarah: Should I use a last name or would you like for only your first name to be used?

Salim and Zahra have a brief conference. It's apparent that Zahra is nervous about being identified. For her comfort, the decision is made on the spot that her last name and any other personally identifying information will be withheld.

Sarah: Can you please describe what kind of theatre you do and what your experience with theatre is?

Zahra: Participatory theatre has many facets. One is Oppressed Theatre, one is Playback Theatre. There is Newspaper Theatre. We also have foreign theatre. There is a project that we are involved in, *AH 7808.*

Sarah: Who is involved with these projects?

Zahra: Most of the people that we are working with, most of them are (there is a brief struggle to come up with the suitable English word) house . . . wife? Grassroots-level people, you know, some of them are maybe in

Bio Points

- Zahra, an Afghan, works with the Afghan Human Rights and Democracy Organization.
- Her first theatre training came through participating in workshops in Kabul.
- In her theatre work she plays a Joker—a facilitator who can help the audience understand how to intervene onstage.

---

another area but most of them are in the house. They are, we can say, grass-roots-level people.

Sarah: Okay, and when you are doing theatre with housewives or other people like that, explain what you are doing. Are they workshops? Are they performances? Are they classes?

Zahra: First we try to find the grassroots-level people or housewives. Then we have six-day or five-day workshops with them. We are trying to collect their stories; after that we make a performance for them that shows how in the future they can solve their problems.

Sarah: Give me a specific example. What kind of problem will you use participatory theatre to solve?

Zahra: We are trying to make clear the problems which are mostly regional and what Afghan women are facing with their problems. Problems they are facing in real life, we process those.
    For example, whenever the woman is oppressed, maybe by domestic violence, or they are war victims. The problems that they experienced in their own life, we are working on that.

Sarah: How do you find women to come to your workshops?

Zahra: At the beginning we have organizations which are involved with that kind of problem. They're our partner, we are trying to be in touch with other organizations. Then we go to that area which there was some violence going on. We are trying to find the women that are facing these kinds of problems. We ask organizations to find women with problems and then make a workshop to work with them.

Sarah: When the women join your workshop, how do they feel? Are they excited? Are they anxious? Are they willing or unwilling?

Zahra: When they join or attend the workshop, at the beginning, they look a little scared or like they are not sure what is going on. We may try to play a game or do exercises and it's very difficult for them to understand what is going on. But, step by step, at the end, it becomes more and more interesting for them. They work fully hard and they participate fully. At the end it's very difficult for them to say "goodbye." Many are sad to leave the workshop at the end.

Sarah: I understand. When the women participate in this workshop, do their families usually support this? Or are they against it?

Zahra: We have parts of our people with a different ideology or different mind. Some of them who come, maybe the family will support them a little bit at the beginning. But some of them, when they participate in our workshop they do not say it to their family. They say, "We are going to attend the workshop," but they don't say, "We are participating here in a theatre workshop." Often when they participate in our workshop and they join us at the end, some of the families support them at the end, because the old ladies see the reason for it and they see the changes. They say that after the workshop they can share their ideas and they can talk well. Many times they have asked us to have this kind of a workshop again for them in the future.

Sarah: How did you get started working on this? Why is this so important to you, Zahra?

Zahra: My historical participation in this methodology is very interesting, because when I participated at the beginning I was involved in only in the workshop. I joined the workshop at the beginning; really for me it was too difficult, because I was so different from now. I was thinking to myself that it is not good for me as an Afghan woman, culturally, to participate in this kind of workshop and to work together with men.

But day by day, at the end of workshop, it became more and more interesting for me. I prayed to God that this workshop should not be finished this time—just like, "Be two or three days more!" Because of that, when I saw this kind of changing in myself I understood something was going on, that in myself, I was changed. That is why I believed in the methodology. After that I was entrusted to work with this methodology in the future. As you know, when we believe ourselves in a method that can bring some changes, that is what we will do in the future. So I was going to work with other groups.

Sarah: What changes did you see in yourself?

Zahra: I had six years' work experience and a boss in a different organization. For me it was too difficult to stand in front of the people and to say whatever I want. I knew a part of myself needed to solve some problems with myself. By the end of the workshop I could come on this stage and act in front of the people and perform a performance there.

I asked Zahra if she remembered her first workshop as a participant. She remembered that the workshop was in 2010, but not the names of everyone who taught. Salim and Hjalmar-Jorge tried to backtrack the history of the workshops and Zahra's gradual involvement. What followed was a quick list of names between the three of them punctuated by smiles, some apparent reminiscing and, at one point, giggling. It finally emerged that the leaders of the workshop were Hjalmar-Jorge, Marc Weinblatt, Hector Aristizabal, and Karin Gisler.

Sarah: After you took the workshop and you realized that it was important to you, and it was changing you, you said that you were afraid that it might be culturally a bad idea? I don't know if many Westerners will understand that. Can you explain that please?

Zahra: In Afghanistan, the theatre here was not so good because the theatre was misused by the people. You know, some ladies were dancing, the behavior of certain people was not so good, even before the workshop. This kind of thinking came in my mind also, that maybe that people go and they stay to dance and just see shows without any message. But when I got actually involved in the theatre, I understood, no, it is different.

On behalf of every game and exercise is some philosophical thing that we should understand. Then day by day it's becoming more interesting for me. When the people hear the word "theatre" only, they may think some bad things, you know. When they see me as myself, they may think, "She has a bad character." But when the people are involved, when the people join the Participatory Theatre—after that, they understand that how important it is.

Sarah: So there are people that think you might have a bad character simply because you are involved in theatre?

Zahra nodded her head slightly, "yes," but then continued with this thought.

Zahra: You know, we can say not all the people, but some people are thinking like this. That when we are working in the methodology people say, "Because our character is not good we can do some bad behaviors." We were faced with this kind of a problem once in Bamiyan.

Bamiyan came to the attention of the world in early 2001 when colossal stone Buddhas, dating back to the 3ʳᵈ century, were destroyed. They were infamously eradicated by the Taliban because they were "UN-Islamic graven images." Zahra was part of the group that performed in Bamiyan. The troupe also presented one of AHRDO's signature week-long Participatory workshops.

Zahra: We had a Playback performance there. Then one man came to me and said, "We respect our wives, we respect our females in this area, but it is not good to participate or to attend this performance." No, we perform for the people, I said. It is important that they watch us. He had bad words for us, you know.

Sarah: How did you respond? Were you afraid?

Zahra: I was a woman with the group and there were men with me. So we stopped and gave them some information, said to them that no, we are not classical theatre actors. But in the technique that we use, we are trying to work with grassroots-level people and we use the Playback methodology. We are working to support the people. Our aim is not just to perform for the people; we want to help the people and to we want to serve the people. Then, after that, we tried to convince them that we could serve the people.

Sarah: Okay, do you think that it would have been easier for you to explain this or do this if you were a man?

Zahra: If I was a man, it'd be easier to do this methodology because they don't expect me, a woman, to come in front of the people with the men. It would be easier for me.

Sarah: When you do a performance or a workshop, can you explain some of the things that you have the group do? What is a typical exercise?

Zahra: As we start our workshop training, we have many games and exercises. At first we are trying to work on trust building, improvisation, and Image Theatre.[1] We are trying to create a game that can help them connect to leadership. How they can take the leadership position, how can they be a leader?

Sarah: Is it acceptable in Afghanistan for women to take leadership positions?

Zahra: Not mostly, because Afghanistan is a man's . . .

Zahra seems to be at a loss to describe the social construct she has been living in since birth. It's obviously, for her, an enormous concept to convey. Hjalmar-Jorge and Salim confer for a second, and then contribute "male-dominated society." Everyone agrees that Afghanistan is, indeed, a male-dominated society if ever there was one.

Zahra: Because the men do not want ladies to be a leader, an authority, or to be in a higher position.

I briefly paused to think how I can express my own feelings without being offensive. I settle for "That would make me very . . . angry." Suddenly, everyone is laughing. Whatever else may separate the four of us in language, experience, culture, or upbringing . . . apparently I'm ineffective at hiding my view on this subject.

Sarah: What is your dream for this kind of theatre, for this kind of workshop? What do you think you can do with this in Afghanistan?

Zahra: At the beginning, personally, my vision is that I can do Participatory Theatre all over Afghanistan. That in the future no one should be left out. At least once they should work in this methodology, because I believe that, when the people are working with this method, the changes will come. This is my aim, because I believe when everyone is participating in this process they will have some vision, too. They can make a vision for themselves. It is my wish that with this methodology I can go forward—we can make a movement in the society. That every woman can go back into the society and work with others. From the root of the society we can make some changes.

In the background, I can hear Hjalmar-Jorge say, in English, "Awesome."

Zahra: And I hope this day comes. I try.

Sarah: Would you like to do this outside of Afghanistan? Have you traveled outside of Afghanistan?

Zahra: I would like to. Especially with the show that we are working with, its name is *Infinite Incompleteness*. The character I was doing, I loved that character. I wanted to show this performance all over the world. There are victims, ladies, who remain with their children. To present this message to other people: Afghan ladies have moved forward. Though she is oppressed and she is a war victim, still she is trying to struggle.

Sarah: Is there anything else that you want to say about the work that you do? Is there anything that you think it's important for the world to know about this?

Zahra: I am happy that someone is going to write in a book about Afghan women.

Sarah: Do you think that people really understand what it's like to be a woman in Afghanistan? Do you think that the rest of the world understands what you're doing?

Zahra: I think for others it is really difficult to understand Afghanistan's situation. They come in Afghanistan and see, practically, a small share of the situation in Afghanistan. You know, a lady in Afghanistan faces lots of lots of problems. For example, there is a lack of education, awareness. There is poverty, domestic violence, there is no guarantee about security. And many other problems that Afghan women are facing in this society, but no one understands the situation because they see it just in media or something like this . . . they see but they do not understand deeply. I think if the people do not come in our society, it is very difficult for them to understand this bad situation.

Sarah: Would you ever consider writing a play that explains a woman's place in society in Afghanistan? Is that something that you would ever do?

Zahra: Performance itself can be a part, but doing the workshops, when we show the problems or their stories, is important. To show all of the problems is not possible because small things come together and to make bigger and bigger problems, you know. It is difficult to show full details (in a performance), every problem one by one, but at least we can show the general problems that Afghan women are facing.

Sarah: What would it take for you to stop doing this?

Zahra: I don't think that something can stop me, because we cannot guarantee our future. Maybe something will happen to us, maybe some revolutionary thing happens to us that we cannot do our Participatory Theatre . . . no one can predict that. But I think if we have a great purpose, if we believe in our activity, nothing will or can stop us. We will try. It is in the hand of our colleagues and the people who are work with us for this idea. If they support us and they work with us, we can deal with this methodology and with the world. We will never stop this method.

I think Afghan women should be introduced to others as they are. Afghan women are oppressed, but on other side they are kind also. I think that if the facilitation would be given to Afghan women they could control the world. Because they have so much power, they are strong enough, but unfortunately in this society everything was taken from them. When some people are talking about Afghanistan woman, they show only the burqa—and it's something that no one understands. I believe when they don't focus on the burqa they see a strong woman. I want to repeat that . . . they could control the world if this kind of facilitation would be given to an Afghan woman.

*   *   *

ARDHO's profile has risen steadily since this initial interview. The delegation of the European Union reported on March 10, 2012 that the group's Legislative Theatre had garnered international attention. A press release from the EU stated:

> On International Women's Day, the Chargé d Affaires of the Delegation of the European Union, Luc Vandebon, and the Ambassador of Sweden, Torbjörn Petterson, co-hosted a briefing by the Afghanistan Human Rights and Democracy Organisation (AHRDO) on its Legislative Theatre initiative on women's rights. This program (in which 4,500 women participated) was conducted in Kabul, Mazar-i-Sharif, Jalalabad, Bamiyan, and Herat. Legislative Theatre is a community-based initiative aimed at encouraging bottom-up participation in key legislative, political, and social processes. The outcomes of this initiative are written into an analytical report: "Afghan Women after the Taliban: Will History Repeat Itself?" Women's major concerns, challenges, and opportunities expressed within the framework of the legislative theatre, consultations, and referendums are reflected in this report. Legal predicaments, international scale-down, potential political deal with the insurgent groups, increasing hostility of the Afghan conservative religious elements to women's public role, and lack of systematic relations between the urbanized female elites and the masses of the women are some of the challenges that are highlighted in this report.[2]

In 2011 Zahra's story began to emerge on a global scale. Her life story, including the fact that she had been married against her will at the age of thirteen and had escaped in-laws that threatened to murder her, was published in a small newspaper article about the play Infinite Incompleteness. A letter she wrote about her life was read aloud as part of a symposium on Forum Theatre held in Hong Kong. Zahra, a woman who had worked as a therapist, cook, and manual laborer in order to support herself after leaving her husband, realized her dream of being an international actress in *Infinite Incompleteness* when the show traveled in November 2011 to Washington DC and New York City. After a lifetime of injustice Zahra got to use the theatre to express her past, present, and future as an Afghan woman.

Zahra continued to pursue her dream as an actress and theatre practitioner even after she was attacked by a group of men waiting for her outside her home in April 2012. She had been warned by a group of anti-feminists against appearing onstage but she went on anyway. Her injuries were so severe that AHRDO temporarily put her into a safe house. By February of 2013, a wire transfer account had been set up for Zahra and her children so that donors from the West could facilitate her move out of Afghanistan. She moved to a nearby country; out of respect for her privacy, I won't say which one. I will say that she must return to Afghanistan every six months to renew her visa into her new home, and this presents its own set of risks. If she were recognized, her life would be in danger again. Her key motivation in leaving Afghanistan is not her own comfort or safety but that of her children. The aggressive response of a few reactionary men, targeting a woman doing nothing but asking other women to be honest about their emotions and dreams, has put the lives of innocent children at risk. AHRDO is working towards a way for Zahra to be permanently relocated in a safe country until she may return to Kabul, but, for now, no one can guess when that may be.

I wrote Zahra to ask if she wanted to continue her participation in this book. I was concerned for her safety, remembering how reluctant she had been to even tell me her full name. But she didn't back down against the men who threatened her at the theatre and she wasn't going to back down now.

This time, Zahra told me to use her full name and include a photo.

This is Zahra Yagana.

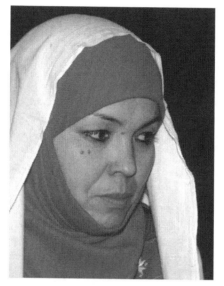

Zarha Yagana, member of AHRDO in Kabul.
Photo undated, courtesy of Hjalmar-Jorge
Joffre-Eichhorn.

9 - A Mirror of Conflict

Monirah Hashemi of Simorgh Film and Theatre in Afghanistan

"Theatre does not break family relationships; theatre wants to be a mirror of conflicts for those families, for society to see them and solve it. Theatre wants to help people to help their society and their country."

The Magdalena Project is an international network of women who are focused on supporting theatrical endeavors by, about, and for women. Founded in Wales in 1986, their website proclaims:

[We are] a dynamic cross-cultural network, providing a platform for women's performance work, a forum for critical discussion, and a source of support, inspiration, and performance training.[1]

It was through the Magdalena Project that I first learned about Simorgh Film and Theatre in Herat, Afghanistan. It turned out that Simorgh has been affiliated with the Bond Street Theatre of New York City, in the same way that FAVILEK of Haiti has been working with them. Through the information given by The Magdalena Project and the generosity of the Bond Street team, I was able to find Monirah Hashemi to request an interview with her.

Monirah Hashemi is a director for the Theatre Department and Women's Department in the Simorgh Film Association of Culture and Art (SFACA). Simorgh itself is a revolutionary entity for art in Afghanistan: It produces both theatre and film, approximately half of the staff are women, and women routinely take the helm of major projects. Monirah Hashemi herself has an unusual background. Her family has supported her decision to make high-profile art in a country that encourages women to be silent. She has directed, written and performed in film and on stage. She is also the leader of workshops for children as well as touring shows that focus on violence in the home and its impact on Afghan women and children. Perhaps most remarkably, Ms. Hashemi has been doing this since she was a teenager. In a written interview sent from Herat, she told me about her life as an artist in Afghanistan.

*   *   *

Sarah: Please tell me how you got started in theatre. How old were you? What attracted you to the arts?

Monirah: I was interested in acting since I was a very young girl, since I can remember I was interested in acting. But because of wars my family migrated to Iran and there, like every refugee, we had education problems. As refugee's rules changed, our situations changed also. So my mind was busy with acting, being in art, and how I make my way to my interest. I tried to spend my time by doing sports, Kung Fu, joining the Afghan English Institute and also to find place and groups where I could be an artist. But unfortunately, this idea that Afghan refugees have no idea about art spontaneously created obstacles in front of me.

My first step in art was singing a song by the name of "Peace in the World" while I was graduating English in an Afghan English Academy in Iran. I was 17, it was 2003. When I came back to Afghanistan with my family in 2004, I decided to go to make my way. The most important thing that attracted me to do this was to help society. As I got closer to the new society I felt that they need mirrors. They need people to take this mirror in front of them. Especially those women who forgot themselves. Forgot about their face and visage. Their beliefs and desires, their wishes of the world and of their family.

It was really painful to see women create problems for women and have the idea that women's voices should not be heard, women should stay at home. I wanted to show the social conflicts and problems through art. Of course, as a young girl it was hard for me to stand in front of a society who knows the women's voice as a taboo.

So I contacted a filmmaking company to ask if I could work with them. In 2004 I acted in a film by the name of the *Passengers for Tomorrow*. After a while, I stopped for a few months because of troubles and problems the public made for me and my family. I had to think about my family honor and also my own best interest. My mother, father and my brother were supporting me all the time and encouraged me to fight against those wrong beliefs. They did believe in me and they were not worried for noise and rumors about their daughter. The only thing that they feared for was my life. To put my life in risk as I received threatening calls and letters from different people.

After one or two months I resumed working and went to private TV stations where I met Mr. Abdul Hakim Hashemi, who established the Simorgh Film Association of Culture and Art (SFACA). My younger brother Mustafa and I decided to work with him. After a while I had my next experience in acting. A short film written and directed by Hashemi was produced for a short film festival for the Teacher Appreciation Day. I acted in that and the film was the first Simorgh product in 2005. It won second prize in the festival. I acted in two films by the names of *File* and *Black Wolf*, both written and directed by the same man.

Bio Points

- Monirah is the daughter of Afghan citizens who fled the country as refugees. She was born in Iran and moved back to Afghanistan in 2004.
- An actor, director, writer, and teacher, Monirah is one of the founders of Simorgh Film Association of Culture and Art.
- In 2013 she moved to Sweden to continue working in the arts.

Sarah: You work in both theatre and film. Can you tell me how this came about?

Monirah: After one year working in Simorgh Film I decided to do some writing and directing and improve my ability. I wrote *In the Embrace of Wind.* It's the story of a girl who is forced by her family to leave school and marry an old man who was quite rich and paid money to her father. I was quite satisfied with that, as my first experience in writing and directing. My second experience in writing and directing was a short film by the name of *Last Laugh,* a story of street children that was made in 2007.

In the same year there was a theatre festival by the name of The Educational Theatre Festival. It was a competition between girls' and boys' high schools. So Simorgh Film participated in that festival and we used participants from Jebraiel Girls' High School. I wrote and directed my first play, by the name *Cry of History.* It rehearsed for one month.

I was worried about the result because it was my first work in theatre, and all my actors were students at school and had no idea about theatre. But after one month rehearsing we had the festival, and after one week we had the results and our group won the first prize of the festival. It is really an unforgettable time and day for me where I found out that "This is theatre, it's what I want and what I was looking for." And from that time I decided to focus on theatre. After that I acted in one or two short films but I am not doing films any more. I help in film. I always like to help our students in the company in expanding their ideas and writing their stories.

Sarah: You have written and directed for theatre and film. Why do you do both? What messages are you sending in each?

Monirah: I always like to help society (especially women and children) through art, through film and theatre. I do believe that art is the Ambassador of Peace in every society so I know it's my duty to help this ambassador to expand his power all over and help oppressed people who are oppressed by governments and sometimes by themselves.

Sarah: What setbacks and triumphs did you experience with *Cry of History* and *Letter of Suffering?*

Monirah: *Cry of History* was the story of great women that are mentioned in the Holy Quran and society's belief about them. In the year 2007 I decided to write and direct it because women needed the most help. They were surrounded by taboos made by wrong customs and traditions. It was not that painful to see these taboos were made by the opposite sex, it was more painful when you feel that women also believe in these things and know them as an order by God and as statements of the Quran.

So *Cry of History* showed how women in different ages, in different religions, spoke for the people and people heard their voices and God admired those women in the Quran. We brought different examples of great women in Islam and also Mary, Asya, one of the Pharaoh's wives, and then we showed how we limit our women in the house. *Letter of Suffering* was also about women's will and desire.

After performing in the Educational Theatre Festival of Herat, *Cry of History* performed in the Fourth National Theatre Festival of Kabul in 2007. It was held in Babur Shah Garden. It was the first time in the history of the festival that nine girls performed on the stage and used some movements in front of men, who believed the presence of a woman onstage was taboo. After that, *Cry of History* was invited to Bharat Rang Mahotsav International Theatre Festival at the National School of Drama in India in 2008. It was performed in New Delhi and Mumbai. *Letter of Suffering,* written by Abdul Hakim Hashemi, performed at the 5th National Theatre Festival of Kabul and won second prize of festival. It was done again when we joined the NSD International Theatre Festival in India in 2009.

Sarah: Where does your funding comes from? Is it hard to travel outside of Afghanistan?

Monirah: I would like to mention that all actors in our company are doing voluntary work so we do not pay our performers, but all of Simorgh Film's needs are covered by our own income and we don't get support by any political groups or government. I would also like to mention here that *Cry of History* could join the festival in India because the Goethe Institute paid the travel cost of the troupe. *Letter of Suffering, Salsaal,* and *Shahmaama* have been supported by the ICCR (Indian Consul for Cultural Relations). Our "Stones and Mirrors" troupe has been supported by Bergen Theatre from Norway.

Cultural and artistic activities do not receive support from the Afghan government, so most of the time it is really hard for artistic activities to survive here, in the country where the money is just spent on military things and people are forgetting about art and culture. The most important things in society can help people to understand each other better, improve themselves, improve their society, and bring security, safety and peace to a country.

Sarah: I want to know about the theatre workshops for girls. When you began your career, was it acceptable for women to participate? Are girls encouraged in the arts now, in Afghan society?

Monirah: There have been different theatre workshops organized by Simorgh since 2005. We had acting workshops for more than fifty girls and boys who were interesting in acting. And also we had a collaboration on organizing theatre workshops, supported by the Bergen Theatre from Norway and National Theatre. We did that three times in Herat; more than thirty-five girls and twenty boys participated in these workshops from our company. There was also a program by the name of Theatre for Social Development supported by the US Embassy. We even had two filmmaking courses organized by SFACA for twenty young girls, who learned screenwriting, editing, filming and directing in 2009. At the same time we had some acting workshops implement by Bond Street in Herat.

Of course, for such a country we have had different periods of life, and especially the darkest one, Taliban period, it was not acceptable to let their young girls appear on the stage. It was something completely against what they have been fighting for. Some people believed that all these kinds of activities are against their religion and these kinds of activities will ruin their family structure. They were people who were strongly involved in wrong practices and traditions against women's rights and presence in the society. Sometimes you can find these ideas among those people who most of the time cry out for women's rights. We have an expression that says: the people who want democracy want it for their neighbor's daughter. But I believe that it depends on us—how we define and introduce the art of theatre and cinema to the people who believe it is against their morals.

It was hard to convince people that your family can be involved in art, in theatre, but at the same time can keep all those values in your culture. Theatre does not break family relationships; theatre wants to be a mirror of conflicts for those families, for society to see them and solve it. Theatre wants to help people to help their society and their country. Our company was successful in giving these messages to society, so we have more than thirty young girls working in theatre and cinema. It is unbelievable because the Faculty of Fine Art, at Kabul University, only has few girls and they are just studying writing and directing. I think we were successful in our mission because at the same time we show outdated traditions and beliefs, we also keep those values that are so important for the society.

Our theatre group has participated in the international theatre festival of Bharat Rang Mahotsav in India in 2008, 2009, and 2011, and also South Asia Women's Theatre Festival in 2010.[1] We participated in the National Theatre Festival of Kabul in 2008, 2009, and 2010. We also have been invited to the Black Sea International Theatre Festival in Turkey and we performed on May 4, 2012. We have been invited to the Women's International Playwright Conference in Sweden in August 2012. These things shows that families are going to trust that art, that theatre is going to give the most important messages to the Afghan people and also people out of Afghanistan. Who wants to know about Afghan people?

Sarah: Are the girls encouraged at home?

Monirah: There is a very famous sentence says: If you want to destroy something (religion, revolution, development) just defend it in a wrong way.

Nowadays this is the problem Afghan girls are facing. There are people who abuse women in a different way. It was much better in 2008 and 2009, you could see more girls participating in the National Theatre Festival of Kabul, but unfortunately every day that it gets better, there is something else completely reversed. I think the families will support their daughters wherever they feel it will help them to build character, to find themselves, to find their talents and make their future. It is the people who want "democracy for the neighbor's daughter" who ruin all efforts.

Every movement needs a kind of spark. I think we did it, and encouraged families to come along with us and their young girls to change families, change societies, and let theatre bring them to a new world. A world we will introduce. A world full of love, peace and safety, for both men and women, young and old, and especially for children.

Finally I would love to mention that we organized a four-month filmmaking course for more 120 young girls in Herat, supported by the US Embassy, in 2011. There were 120 girls studying screenwriting, directing, and editing. The course provided this opportunity for young girls in Herat to express themselves and experience the feeling of being a creator. Some of them went to work with TV stations in Herat and Kabul. It shows that if we support the isolated small communities, if we support talents, if we support our fields with correct definition, we can bring and donate what can to help people and society.

Sarah: What specifically did the girls learn in your workshop?

Monirah: They learned about acting basic elements, basic elements of theatre, body language, mise en scene [the staging of a production], and

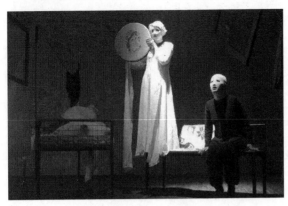

Photo from Monirah Hashemi's Masks under Burqa *performed in Turkey in 2012.*

directing. They learned how to express themselves, and different exercises that are important for a person as an actor or actress, to connect with the stage, partners, and audience.

Sarah: What are your dreams for girls and women doing theatre in Afghanistan?

Monirah: It is really hard for me to gather all my wishes for girls and women in Afghanistan doing theatre in one sentence. There are many things I wish for theatre and girls in Afghanistan. To have a suitable stage to perform, to perform what is inside them, perform what they want to say, without any shame or fear from society. I wish they will never swallow their ideas, their speeches on the stage.

My wish is that one day, we can freely perform a street theatre, and choose the most far away area in Afghanistan and go there and perform for those children who are thirsty for theatre, for drama. I think the farthest wish for me, for Afghan girls, is to perform for far away girls, women, men, and children in Afghanistan.

Sarah: What is your biggest dream for yourself?

Monirah: I think I can reach to my dreams when I do my study in theatre. Right now my biggest dream is to have a scholarship for theatre and study theatre in a university, where I can learn a lot and be the first woman who brings the most important changes in the history of theatre in Afghanistan. Right now I feel empty of knowledge about theatre and my biggest dream is to fill the emptiness with knowledge. I hope one day achieve to it.

*   *   *

Simorgh took their work to Sweden for the Women Playwrights International Conference in Stockholm in August of 2012. Monirah actually moved to Sweden in 2013, continuing her work as theatrical ambassador, playwright, director, and promoter of women's rights. She remains associated with Simorgh and reports that she is doing well in her new home.

10 - Revolution & Censorship

Dalia Basiouny of Egypt

"After the revolution I stopped taking my play texts to the censorship. I just perform and they can come and find me."

In November of 2011, I first contacted Dalia Basiouny asking if I could interview her concerning her groundbreaking work in Cairo, Egypt. Dr. Basiouny is a director, playwright, actress, and professor. Her reply to me, in its entirety, was this:

Hi Sarah,

Thank you for your email.
I can give you an interview by phone, email or skype when things settle down a bit, now we are really on the literal front lines.
Send your prayers to Egypt.
—Dalia

On January 25, 2011, over 50,000 Egyptian protesters marched into Tahrir Square demanding the end of the oppressive regime of Hosni Mubarak. By the end of that week, over 250,000 people were in the square, demanding not only the resignation of Mubarak but freedom of speech, a higher minimum wage, democratic elections, and an end to police brutality and restrictive "state of emergency" laws.[1] This protest climaxed in the resignation of President Mubarak, who had held power since 1981. The government of Egypt underwent massive changes in short succession, including the suspension of Parliament and suspension of the Constitution.

The uprising against Egyptian President Hosni Mubarak was a genuinely unscripted event. Social media and television coverage led thousands of Egyptians to protest against their government in Tahrir Square, located in downtown Cairo. Similar protests were held in Aswan, the eastern city of Ismailiya, the northern city of Mahallah, and other locations across the nation. The Egyptian people saw Mubarak, their once feared (and often hated) dictator, ousted, detained, and eventually convicted of the murder of Tahrir

Square protesters and of other crimes. Due to his failing health he has spent much of his detention in military hospitals.

At the time of this interview, the political future of Egypt was not yet clear. Elections had not been held, the Parliament had not been reinstated, and President Mohamed Morsi had yet to be elected or subsequently overthrown. Dalia Basiouny was blogging about the shifting sands of Egyptian politics and using theatre to celebrate, mourn, and record the powerful events that started January 25th.

Her words serve as a diary of conflict. Her play *Solitaire,* which she wrote, directed and performs, is about an Arab-American woman rethinking her identity and destiny. She looks at the events of 9/11 and the Egyptian uprising of January 25th in a provocative multi-media presentation, performed in her native tongue with English surtitles. It has been performed in Iraq, Morocco, Germany, and Zimbabwe, and, in the United States, it was seen in New York City, Chicago, North Carolina, and New Jersey. When our interview started, though, we didn't even begin with her work in the theatre. We talked about the days in Tahrir Square when she was actively fighting against the Mubarak regime.

*   *   *

Dalia: Activism kind of gives me hope sometimes when it's really dark outside.

Sarah: It's been very, very difficult in Egypt lately. Are you okay?

Dalia: Yes, yes, I am. I mean, I get unhappy because it gets depressing at times, but I feel like we all have a role to play and when I am doing what I am supposed to do I feel a little better.

Sarah: I just wondered if you could talk to me a little bit about how you feel about that, how you wrote *Solitaire,* what's going on with you?

Dalia: A lot, actually!

I couldn't help but laugh. This woman had been working for months in a tinder box of emotion and political outcry, and she's faced with an American offhandedly asking, "What's going on with you?" To her credit, she overlooked my momentary (and absurd) casualness.

Dalia: When you are thinking about danger, it's a matter of perspective. When we're dealing with people who are facing death and making heroic acts to fend for themselves or to rescue somebody or to deal with a tear gas bomb, doing theatre becomes a little less dangerous in a way. I don't feel I am doing something that major or heroic, because I'm seeing true heroes who are not even calling themselves heroes at all. Each of us is just doing our piece, what we can do. On the other hand I think sometimes that theatre failed us because all of art becomes paralyzed in the face of the intense atrocities we are witnessing.

I was rehearsing for a new performance called *Magic of Borolus* and I stopped rehearsals because in November we [Egyptians] were fighting. At the time I was thinking, if I'm a doctor I might have been useful, more useful or something. Art, or even teaching, felt, I'm sorry to say, it felt obscene to go and feel any sense of normalcy when we are in that situation. But, when it's not as intense an emergency, I'm back to the thing I know how to do best, which is the work in theatre and the arts. I'm back to rehearsals, and—it's crazy to be rehearsing right now! I'm rehearsing for this new project that was supposed to open in December and I couldn't open it because of the extreme violence that took place in Mohamed Mahmoud Street. I and most of my cast and crew were in the street, some were at the front line of confrontation with police and military. Luckily no one was badly injured, but we were all affected by the fresh tear gas bombs, just imported from the US.[2] Most of us are still coughing!

I'm calling people today to come tomorrow for a rehearsal because the seamstress needs to measure them, and it's all very, very obscene and odd and I don't know, I don't know how to describe it. But when it's less of an emergency, I mean, it's what we do and it's important and I would be very happy to be touring with a play, to be touring with *Solitaire*, because I was informing people about something they only see snippets of information about. Snippets in the news or wherever, and I was giving them a firsthand experience of how it felt to be part of the Egyptian Revolution. They were able to see that this is real and there are women who are doing it. When I was performing in Zimbabwe, for example, they had never thought that people of North Africa have it in them to revolt.

We are perceived as pious and docile by other Africans. Seeing a company live rather than a news flash, it's very different, the personal story does matter. At these moments I get to believe in the heart of the work I do, but sometimes it all feels so useless and so futile. So, I'm in some frustration conundrum right now. When I think long range, we are all doing important work, but when someone is bleeding I cannot do a performance, you know what I mean?

Sarah: You talked about touring with *Solitaire*. I'm really curious about this idea of 9/11 and the Arab Spring being "identifying markers" in the Arab world. Can you expound on that?

Bio Points

- Dalia, an Egyptian, holds an MA from the University of Bristol, England, and an MA and a PhD in theatre from the City University of New York.
- She trained with Augusto Boal, the creator of Theatre of the Oppressed.
- A writer, director, and performer, she teaches at the American University of Cairo.
- She created the Sabeel Group, which focuses on women in the arts.

Dalia: For me, this is partly a personal story as well. *Solitaire* was part of a bigger project that had three stories of three different women, and as we were rehearsing the revolution started, so we stopped, of course. When we went back we could not do the same story the same way anymore because we were different, the world was different—so I added a new section on the revolution. It's the story of this Arab-American woman who was dealing with changes in her life and her society, becoming more vividly aware of 9/11 as she's an Arab living in a place that considers her the enemy.

Initially, this play did not have the revolution section, because I wrote it in 2009. I added that section, and it made perfect sense because this woman is talking about marching in demonstrations in New York, for Afghanistan, against the war in Iraq, and for the Palestinians. It didn't make sense to talk about all the other wars and demonstrations and not talk about the Egyptian demonstrations which at the time seemed to be the biggest of this century, at least. So that section fit in perfectly and it felt like an integral part of the production.

The audience did not believe that we added this section later. Somehow the weaving made perfect sense, because seeing the world from an Arab perspective, these two seminal moments (9/11 and the Arab Spring) are truly defining moments, especially for an Egyptian. This woman was experiencing 9/11 and the aftermath while living in the US. Ten years later, she watched the beginning of the revolution in Egypt on television, she had to travel to Cairo to be part of that. So it's connected, it's an organic flow.

At this point, we experienced some static and call interruptions while Dalia apologized for not being "focused." It turned out that this "lack" of focus was due to talking to me while coping with the immediate fact that her workday was being rescheduled at that very moment due to demonstrations outside. I assured her anyone who has a revolution actively chanting outside the window gets a free pass on distraction.

Sarah: It's about you, as an Egyptian and Arab woman, navigating this new world. As you were doing these pieces, how was the audience reacting to this?

Dalia: The first piece I did about the revolution, *Tahrir Stories*, was actually performed during the revolution in February 2011 and it was a verbatim piece presenting sections of the testimonies of from people who were demonstrating in Tahrir Square.

Its debut performance was February 23rd, just as the revolution was kind of figuring itself out. Some of us were still out in the Square and . . . and trying to make it work and protect ourselves and stuff like that. Even then, audience members, people who were in the 18 Days in Tahrir, were saying, "We were reminded of why we suffered, why we went." So only three or four weeks after the ouster of the previous President it had its value and its meaning. We were honoring the names of the martyrs, and at the time there were only 192 names identified. Now over a thousand have been identified. We thought it's important to say their names, and this is all we did really. After the testimonies of the revolutionaries we simply said their names and had a drum beat after the name of each of them. We were the first performance to present stories from Tahrir and to honor the martyrs.

After that, there was this media madness of everybody talking about the martyrs and Egypt. But I thought it was interesting to be doing a performance about the revolution and have the revolution disrupt that performance, because things were happening in the streets and the square during the days of the performance. It was making it impossible for people to come to the show or to even come to act in the show, so—

Sarah: Your show about the revolution was disrupted by the revolution.

Dalia: It's part of living in these interesting times and hopefully being able to respond to them in an artistic or intellectual way. You cannot really plan, you just have to be on your feet, and as theatre artists we are trained to do that. So we changed the performance based on what happened that day.

The same performance *[Tahrir Stories]*, there was one day we did it on stage and the audience was in the auditorium. The next day, because most of my chorus could not come, could not attend the performance because of the fire that blocked the traffic everywhere, we did that same performance with all the audience onstage to create the intimacy of the lost chorus. We are trying to be as alive as the revolution and it's an interesting time to be alive or to be doing work, but we're trying.

Sarah: There are blogs and reports you wrote about taking supplies to the hospital. When you look back on this, what are you going to use in your theatre going forward? What types of things do you think that this revolution means for theatre in Egypt? Do you have a dream of what you want theatre to be in Egypt, or are you living that dream right now?

Dalia: No, we are in nightmare. *(We're back to that hearty, forgiving laugh).* We're still in the nightmare phase. I feel like having more voice is what most of us are dreaming of. Having more say on how we do what we want to do. Also, where are the places to perform? This is the main challenge for art, at least for independent artists like myself. Where do you rehearse? I have a new play and I don't have a place to rehearse. I don't have a place to perform, I booked a theatre for a couple of days but where do I create my visuals and things like that? It doesn't seem like much to most, but this is how we create our work—like where to perform and how to reach people. Things of that nature, if we have more autonomy, if we have access to more of the beautiful historic spaces that are available all around Cairo, like there are beautiful restored buildings that I would love to have access to work in. That's one of my dreams, it's a personal dream. I mean, I have an eye on a few of them.

We shared a good laugh over that. Apparently the dream for better venues, more space, and access to new kinds of buildings is a universal dream of practitioners.

Dalia: More freedom—there is still an official censorship office in Egypt where you should take your plays, books, films etc. to be censored before you can present them to the public. After the revolution, I stopped taking my play texts to the censorship. I just perform and they can come and find me.

I'd like for the Censorship Office to be abolished officially. They could have their job in rating the performances for PG or rated R, but they should not tell me "this scene is not appropriate for the audience" or "remove a kiss from a movie" or that kind of stupidity.

That's one important thing for me. Also, it's the way we run things and the official way in Egypt. There are many festivals all over and they have competitions, but it's not really harboring true artistic communication. There is funding for art, it might not be as much as other countries, but there is some funding for the arts. Sadly, the way it is being used is to host a few guests in a five-star hotel. It is not very helpful for a lot of the artists who need the education and exposure. I am also a professor, I teach theatre in the university, and I see my students dreaming of being able to really make a difference. While art is out there to make a difference, there is something in the way things are organized in the bureaucratic system that is blocking creativity and artistic flow. You have to have connections or know somebody to have influence or access to present your work. I feel all of this will change. We are working on changing it right now. It's a bit of a crazy time of different changes needing to occur at the same time.

Sarah: Americans have some of the same problems: finding places to perform and not having enough funding.

Dalia: Yeah, I understand. Actually, when I was planning for *Solitaire*, earlier on, I was planning to do it at the same time as a friend of mine was opening a show in New York, and I wanted to do a movie about our processes, like "A Tale of Two Theatres." We have almost the same set of problems, but they just look or feel slightly different. Like now with the revolution, it's like the flavor is quite, quite urgent here. It's not "woman or man" or "here or there," it's like if you're trying to do new art or "outside the establishment" art, it's an uphill struggle, but we'll continue to do it, I hope.

Sarah: It's worth it, it's worth it.

Dalia: It's worth it.

* * *

With that we signed off, leaving Dalia to attend a performance that night and repair her classroom schedules to accommodate the needs of protesting students. Sadly, those repairs would be the first of many stopgap solutions in the new Egypt. As of this writing, Tahrir Square is still the site of protests, as the Muslim Brotherhood continues to protest the ouster of elected President Mohamed Morsi (although protests have declined due to security crackdowns)· Dr. Basiouny continues her work on an international scale. She has toured *Solitaire* in the USA, spoken at Women in Action 2 (a convention for female artists in the Middle East), contributed to the book *Doomed by Hope: Essays on Arab Theatre,* and blogs to give current information on the state of artists within Egypt. Egypt is once again shifting away from artistic freedom. A leading figure in the Muslim Brotherhood's Freedom and Justice Party, Isam el-Iryan, called a number of Egyptian journalists, artists, and intellectuals "pro-Western atheists and secularists who have betrayed the religious creed of the Egyptian people."[4]

It is possible that Dalia will continue to perform her original works and that the Censorship Office will, indeed, decide to come find her.

11 - Rise of Fundamentalism

Madeeha Gauhar of Ajoka Theatre in Pakistan

"Burqavaganza is not really just about the burqa; it's about the rise of religious fundamentalism and the complete subservience of the Pakistani state."

In 1983, Pakistan was reeling from a series of social and political changes. The President, General Mohammed Zia-ul-Haq, had declared a state of martial law in 1977. The nation was worried about the Soviets at war in Afghanistan, fearful they could be next. Religious leaders were nervous as the President announced the country should be moving towards a hardline Sunni philosophy that would appeal to Islamic fundamentalists. In the space of a few years, alcohol was banned and stoning a person to death was officially legalized under Sharia law. How could Pakistanis cope with so much change? How could the society express their misgivings when such expression was tantamount to an insurrection?

That year, a young TV actress named Madeeha Gauhar led a group of independent, idealistic artists to create a theatre in Lahore, Pakistan. She wanted to protest the conservative and oppressive regime of General Zia-ul-Haq. That theatre, named Ajoka, has become internationally famous for producing theatre that directly confronts social issues while never losing a sense of humanity or humor. Since 1983, Ajoka has produced plays about what it means for a woman to cover herself with a burqa, the mistreatment of brides, honor killings, political freedom, even the complicated love/hate relationship Pakistan has with the United States. Ajoka also runs an independent television studio that can create high quality, unique TV movies promoting gender equality, social awareness, religious freedom, and the social benefits of family planning. As an organization Ajoka is a liberal (some would say radical) but well-respected voice in Pakistan. Their shows are frequently invited to participate in international festivals as well as festivals and retrospectives inside Pakistan's borders. In May 2012, the company was given the prestigious Otto Rene Castillo Award for Political Theatre.

Ajoka first caught my attention because they had mounted a show called *Burqavaganza.* In 2010 they mounted the satirical comedy as a "love story in the time of Jihad." Although the company did an interview with the BBC specifically stating that the play wasn't meant to be offensive towards Islam in any way, Ajoka definitely stirred up controversy. According to the *New York Times*, a senior official at the Ministry of Culture said the play "pollutes young minds" and "should not be shown anywhere in Pakistan."

Ajoka's Pakistan of 1983 was a religiously, politically and socially conservative place. I wondered what it would take for a theatre to spend the last twenty years defying a regime started by a fundamentalist Muslim general. It turns out, what it would take is a creative, no-nonsense feminist named Madeeha. She's still creative, still no-nonsense, and still on the front lines of dangerous drama.

*   *   *

Sarah: Ajoka is a theatre dedicated to peace. It was founded to fight oppression in Pakistan. What is Ajoka's history and why is it important?

Madeeha: Well, we founded Ajoka in the early '80s, and at the time there was martial law in Pakistan. The primary motivation then was to raise a voice against the dictatorship and against rioting [in support of] of fundamentalist policies of that dictator, which were particularly targeting women and minorities. This targeting was being done through changes in the constitution, bringing amendments to the constitution and changing the legislation in order to make it much more conservative and anti-woman and anti-minority. Because those days there was like a total, you know, clampdown on any freedom of expression. The media was very tightly controlled. There was only one television channel, which was again controlled by the government, and there was no freedom of expression. Censorship was really being used indiscriminately. So I was a voice of protest for theatre.

I was already a women's activist, because the women's movement in Pakistan started around the same period in the early 1980s. Again, I was a voice, as a protester against the oppressive laws of that Islamic dictator, against the Islamization of our constitution. And I think, because I was already an activist, and already doing theatre, it just happened that it was both my passions. I was a political/social activist and a cultural artist, so cultural activism was how Ajoka was founded. That was a primary motivation, the oppression of that particular dictator and sort of Islamization that he was bringing in. But one should not forget that, apart from that, our societies are extremely patriarchal and feudal in nature, and so the struggle was not just against Islamic education. It was also against any creed, laws being brought in but also against patriarchal practices which have been there for centuries now in the different parts of the country. So, it was a struggle, a two-pronged struggle against the dictatorship for democracy to spark. Ajoka has always

Bio Points

- Madeeha, a Pakistani, holds a Master's Degree in Theatre Sciences from the University of London.
- She and her husband formed Ajoka Theatre in Lahore, Pakistan in 1984.
- Madeeha has a younger sister, Feryal, who is also a well-known actress.

---

been speaking up against oppression of any kind, whether it's women, whether it's minorities, whether it's workers, whether it's children. That is what we have done through our theatre for almost twenty-eight years now.

Sarah: What do you think are the biggest challenges for women performing in Pakistan now?

Madeeha: These are two challenges, two broad categories. One is fighting against discriminatory laws because, unfortunately, even though democracy has been restored to a certain extent, we still have laws which are very discriminatory against women. They actually cause women to become a second-class citizen in this country. There have been certain improvements in the very recent past and there have been certain bills on domestic violence, other sort of crime, violence against women, but the main thing are the *Hudood* laws, which are Islamic in nature.

Hudood literally translates to "limit," or "restriction." Hudood is the word often used in Islamic social and legal literature for the bounds of acceptable behavior. Hudood laws prescribe punishment for serious crimes such as murder, adultery, and theft. In many countries, these Hudood laws and punishments contravene what the United Nations deem basic human rights.

In addition to these laws, there is a separate set of laws that deal with blasphemy. For a brief period starting in 2008, the death penalty was set aside in Pakistan, but after five years it was revived. Under the Pakistan Penal Code, a person may not declare or even imply anything negative about the prophet Mohammed, his family, or certain religious symbols. It is possible to receive a death sentence in Pakistan for saying something bad about the prophet Mohammed.[1]

*   *   *

Madeeha: Like most religious interpretations, you know, things are controversial. But anyhow, no government has been able to touch that legislation because they are afraid to revoke religious rights or to touch anything that smells of religion. We have been very passionate campaigners against the Blasphemy Law in Pakistan for twenty years now, but no one wants to change it, despite the fact that last year the governor of the Punjab, Salman Taseer, was assassinated because of his support for the removal of the blasphemy laws. His own government, the People's Party government, did not really take a stand. They sort of just shoved the whole issue under the carpet and acted quite shamefully. So, that is certainly there, and religious fundamentalism is growing in Pakistan. It's not just Talibanization, but it's also the mindset of people that has changed over the last fifty years, ever since that dictator [Zia-ul-Haq] brought it in, this whole factor of Islamization. Those challenges are still there, and again, the official abuses against women, like honor killing and other such very terrible crimes against women which are sanctioned by certain sections of society, those are very much there. They have not gone away.

I must say that there is much more of an awareness that these are issues which have to be dealt with. Changes which have to be brought about . . . and to a certain extent . . . the media's quite free now. So, these issues are taken up, but it's largely restricted to an open sort of elite who'll debate the issues. I don't think it has really and truly permeated down to the women who actually face these issues in their day-to-day life. As I said, it's better only in as much that these practices have not gone away, but people are struggling against this—women's groups and even now political parties are sort of bringing these issues on their agenda.

Sarah: There is little practical progress for the average Pakistani woman?

Madeeha: On the ground I think it's still very, very problematic. Some of these traditions are deeply entrenched in the psyche of people, particularly men. It becomes difficult to change unless there is more awareness about all this. We have tried to play a very small role in bringing about awareness regarding these issues.

Sarah: What is the audience for your work? Who comes to see this?

Madeeha: We have a varied audience. There are people from a cross-section of society. Our performances are mainly in Lahore, which is a big city, and other urban centers. We also travel to communities and perform in villages or smaller towns. We particularly perform those plays which we call our "community theatre," theatre which is issue-based: for instance, our play on honor killing. We have traveled with that. Similarly, our play on the Blasphemy Law or our play on bonded labor. Then, of course there are our other productions, full-fledged proscenium productions.

We have also performed in a lot of places in India. Again, it's a cross-section of society which comes. There's elite, there's students, there's, you know, young people there. We always invite people from the trade unions and workers' unions and the "man off the street." A huge sort of cross-section of Pakistani society sees Ajoka's plays.

Sarah: How do you feel as a woman in your field, putting yourself out there as an artist? Is this a dangerous thing for you to do?

Madeeha: Well I have actually never felt that. I think it has a lot to do with the background that one comes from. I come from a relatively liberal family, and even when I was not married, I, you know, I belonged to a privileged class, to upper-middle class. I never really felt that being a woman in any way did any . . . blockage to me. I think that is mainly because of the fact that I come from a privileged background and I have support from my family, and now my husband—we work together in the theatre. He's the playwright, he writes most of our plays, that's one reason I have not felt the fact that I'm a woman affects my work in any way.

In trying to explain her position, Madeeha came up with contemporary comparisons. She references Sharmeen Obaid-Chinoy and her groundbreaking documentary, Saving Face, *about Pakistani women who have acid thrown in their faces. Both men and women perpetrate these attacks, but the victims are always women. Obaid-Chinoy focused on the efforts of a plastic surgeon who is trying to help these victims by repairing some of the damage done by the acid. Madeeha also talked about Mukhtar Mai, a woman who spent nine years seeking justice after she was gang-raped as a punishment for her brother falling in love with a woman of a different social class. Mai's attackers were freed by the Supreme Court of Pakistan. She continues to fight for justice for herself and other Pakistani women.*

Madeeha: But that does not mean that I do not sympathize with the large majority of Pakistani women who don't have a voice and who don't have that support. I would be similar to the woman who just won the Oscar for her short documentary on acid throwing on Pakistani women. She also comes from the upper class and has a very privileged background—strong family support. And so for women like us, you know, it's not quite the same.

Women like Mukhtar Mai, this woman who was the gang-rape victim who, you know, really struggled for justice. At her level it was extremely difficult and those are the women who really have to face the consequences. If they struggle for their lives in the least, show their anger or their resentment, or that they want to bring the perpetrators of violence against them to justice, then they have to really fight hard. They live their lives in oppressive family structures, tribal structures, community structures. For them it's very difficult and to me it's very courageous of them. From my point of view, I think being a woman has not been problematic for me—

There is a long pause.

Sarah: But . . . ?

Madeeha:—but being an activist has certainly been problematic for me, because, especially during the martial law years in the '80s, I had to advocate on some occasions. I lost my job, which was a government job. But that was all happening to men and women, you know, regardless of gender, to anyone who was speaking out against what was happening in those days.

Sarah: So you were targeted more as an activist than as a woman. Can I ask, then, what was the inspiration for the *Burqavaganza*?

Madeeha: *Burqavaganza*—that was written and directed by [noted Pakistani actor, writer and activist] Shahid Nadeem, my husband. *Burqavaganza* is a comment on growing fundamentalism in Pakistan, and the inspiration is all around one, there is no particular one incident. It was the growing Talibanization, not just the Taliban, but as I said before, it's people who start thinking like the Taliban, which influences all facets of life in Pakistan. I think that was what *Burqavaganza* was. I mean, the burqa just became a metaphor for this Islamization, for this growth of religiosity in Pakistan, which has certainly happened. The seeds were sown when Pakistan came into being, because it was created in the name of religion.

Although one does understand that Jinnah (the first Governor-General of Pakistan) was a secular person, the fact is that he used religion to create a separate state.[2] It has had terrible consequences, and the secular country that he envisaged certainly never existed because, you know, how could it? It's a contradiction in terms because you cannot create a separate nation in the name of religion and then expect that everything is going to be fine and we will be able live a happy secular life after that. I mean, it's just not possible.

I think events in history, over sixty years, have shown that it's not possible. It is inevitable that the fundamentalist tribe is going to finally take over, which is what is happening in Pakistan. At the moment, we have a so-called democratic government, and there are parties which are not wildly religious in nature, but the moment any issue arises which deals with religion or this country's beliefs, they really don't want to cope with it. They can be killed for it, like [assassinated Prime Minister] Benazir Bhutto. She fought the Taliban, so she was killed for it. So no one is as brave as she was, and people don't want to speak out. I think that that is the basis of Pakistan's problems, which, unfortunately, really cannot be rectified. The unfortunate thing is that there is no recognition of this fact, it's easy to blame external factors.

A lot of hard work is dealing with these issues, not just *Burqavaganza*. *Burqavaganza* is not really just about the burqa, it's about the rise of religious fundamentalism and the complete subservience of the Pakistani state. Some people say it is burqa bashing. It is certainly not; it has many layers of meaning, and I think that's precisely why it was deemed subversive and subsequently it was not allowed to be performed. It is unofficially banned, so we don't perform it any longer.

Sarah: Wow.

Madeeha: And, yeah. So that's it.

*   *   *

Although *Burqavaganza* is (at least for now) shelved, Ajoka is still busy producing theatre pieces that challenge the fundamentalist Muslim as well as secular Pakistani ideas that keep women and minorities as second-class citizens. Their works include *Hotel Mohenjadaro*, about fundamentalists wreaking havoc in a futuristic secular state, *Amrika Chalo*, a look at Pakistanis who may hate the West but also want to settle in the United States, and *Mera Rang De Basanti Chola*. *Mera Rang De Basanti Chola* is a celebration of the life of Bhagat Singh, one of the revolutionaries that made the Indian Independence movement successful. During his lifetime India and Pakistan were one nation, and Singh actually lived and died in Lahore. Ajoka calls their play a tribute to "a great son of the Punjab."

If all goes as planned, Ajoka will gain further world-wide attention in 2014, because playwright Shahid Nadeem's *Dara* has been selected for adaptation into English by the National Theatre of UK. Shahid visited London to finalize the project and meet director Nadia Fall and NT Artistic Director Sir Nicholas Hytner. The English version will be staged by NT in 2014.

12 - The Rise of Theatre

Phionah Katushabe, founder of Rafiki Theatre

"I take that as a positive thing, when people open up and share what they feel, no matter how nasty, because then together we can always debate and find a solution—a win-win situation."

Uganda featured prominently in the Western news in 2011 and 2012. Of positive note was the fact that HIV rates among adults were lower than for other African nations, and that on the final day of the London Olympics, marathoner Stephen Kiprotich won Uganda's first gold medal in 40 years. On the flip side, Western media publicized the fact that Ugandan lawmakers were considering making homosexuality punishable by death. There was also a social networking phenomenon surrounding Joseph Kony, the leader of the guerilla group Lord's Resistance Army. For a while, the West was eager to help end the injustice that kept Ugandan children as soldiers, spies, and slaves in the LRA. Unfortunately, the furor died when the methods and motives of the man reporting on Kony were revealed to be suspect. While news on the LRA helped shed light on the plight of many Ugandans, it only told part of the story.

The Western media tends to cover Uganda from a British perspective, which is perhaps understandable since the BBC is a major source for global news, and Uganda was not freed from English rule until 1962. In fact, Uganda remains a member of the Commonwealth, the organization of countries that used to be identified as the British Commonwealth. Perhaps as a result, many native Ugandans lack the power or access to speak to the West about their own condition in their own words. There are Ugandan news outlets printed in English, but they tend to be overshadowed by the more powerful Western press. While Kony and the plight of gay Ugandans are important topics, it's unfortunate that we hear very little about other critical issues like access to education, prevention of domestic abuse, and the widespread acceptance of women as second-class citizens.

Curious about Uganda as seen by its citizens, I contacted Rafiki Theatre of Kampala. Kampala is the capital of Uganda, and home to approximately 1,659,600 of Uganda's 35,000,000 people. Rafiki states its mission as follows:

Exploring and employing the tool of 'Participatory Theatre' to conscientise communities and individuals on issues of injustice and violence, and enhancing a process where the people discover alternative non-violent ways of addressing these issues in a secured theatre setting.[1]

Can theatre make a difference in a country where illiteracy is common (particularly among women) and life expectancy at birth is 53 years of age? As we read about child soldiers, the LRA, and the plight of rural Ugandans, it's daunting to think of a theatre group arriving in communities armed only with a play and some dialogue tools. Can theatre help change the patterns of domestic violence and alcoholism that make life difficult for so many Ugandan women? Rafiki thinks it can. Rafiki member Phionah Katushabe is certain it can.

I had a Skype session with Phionah late one night so I could ask her about Rafiki and how their mission statement is applied in rural Uganda. What she had to say left me feeling certain it can, too.

*   *   *

Sarah: How many people are in Rafiki? How many people go into the field with you?

Phionah: At the moment we are like a team of 19 people, inclusive of the two directors, so the actors are roughly 17. We currently have two of our members working in Karamoja in the northern region. We sent them there to work on different projects there on behalf of Rafiki, but with partner organizations, so we are like 15 now in Kampala. Now, not all of us go to the field when we have a project. There are some projects which require like eight or ten people, so it's rare that you find all of us going on a particular project. But if possible, we all go. If not, we pave the way for some people who are on that project, or people we think can do us proud, you know, then come back and we continue.

Sarah: Rafiki is a collection of artists who go out in groups to engage the public in theatrical performances. Can you describe what you do?

Phionah: As an individual, I do acting for the group, and then PR. So when we go out there, I act, and when we are back in Kampala, I help do other work like signing documents, writing proposals and other things here and there.

Sarah: How did you get started being an actress? What's your history with acting?

Phionah: It was something! In 2010, we carried out a workshop through an institute called the East African Institute of Governance and Conflict Management, and were doing a workshop on "Theatre and Conflict Resolution." So they called artistic people out to come and join the workshop. Most of them were really music, dance, and drama graduates. I was still at campus in my second year, but I got an opportunity because one of my friends was one of the people who were given the first opportunities, so she called me and told me, "Do you like acting? Do you think you can join us for the workshop?" I was like, "Okay, let me just come since it's holiday time and I'm not doing much, I would just come and be there with you, have free lunch, and then hop my first boat back home."

So it turned out that as the week went on things were a bit amazing, the things we learned. You know, looking at the workshop, it was not a typical workshop where you go, get a book, sit down and write. We never had such a thing like books or anything, just did exercises as part of the workshop. And we sat down on the last day, it was a five-day workshop, we sat down and we decided that we can form a group. By then we were only twelve people. We all agreed, started there looking for a name for our theatre group. We suggested so many names. We came up with one—Rafiki (the Kiswahili word for friend/friendship). Then we started. Just like that. I found myself with all these people.

Sarah: What exactly is the mission of Rafiki? Why do you do theatre?

Phionah: I cannot summarize the mission statement and I'm not going to. But personally, I do theatre specifically because it can help me as an individual to deal with things, many things in my life. And to help some people's lives. Because it's not been the same, since I started doing theatre. I can better handle myself, I'm more confident, and I have become a better listener to other people's views.

Sarah: Fair enough. When Rafiki goes out and they do performances, it's like a Theatre of the Oppressed event? Is that right?

Phionah: Yeah, in fact we mix many schools of theatre. We do Theatre of the Oppressed, we improvise a lot, so we do Improvisation Theatre, and we also involve Invisible Theatre sometimes. So many forms of theatre we combine to come up with a method that is now customized to us. We do not follow one school of thought. That's why it's a little bit diverse. But at the end it's all serving the same purpose.

Bio Points

- Phionah, a Ugandan, holds a Bachelor's Degree in Mass Communication from Makerere University in Kampala.
- She started learning about theatre when a friend asked her to a workshop.
- Phionah started Rafiki Theatre with a group of friends in 2010.

Sarah: What issues are you addressing with Theatre of the Oppressed and Invisible Theatre?

Phionah: We have not fully explored Invisible Theatre; we have done it just a few times. But with the Theatre of the Oppressed, we mostly deal with issues that have to do with domestic violence and sexual abuse. We've done crazy things on the environment, prejudices, we have worked on climate change and environment, and we've tailored plays on malaria, rights, diseases, and nutrition. In all these we are really exploring Theatre of the Oppressed.

Sarah: It's my understanding that parts of northern Uganda are very poor. Is that right?

Phionah: Very. Very poor.

Many parts of the nation lack access to clean water, electricity or roads. Cattle rustling and land disputes—problems that cause genuine rebellion and violence—are common. In some places, education is virtually non-existent. Since the British school curriculum was discontinued in the 1970s, literacy has dropped. Less than half of all Ugandan women can read. The CIA lists Uganda as a country where the risk of contracting an infectious disease is very high. Thanks to a national education program about AIDS, new cases of HIV are not rising as rapidly as other African countries. This does not mean, however, that disease isn't prevalent. Malaria, Ebola, and Hepatitis A are all genuine threats. It's not surprising, since hygiene requires education as well as financial means, and many Ugandans have access to neither. Unique issues arise when it comes to educating former child soldiers. Upwards of 30,000 children were abducted to fight or serve as sex slaves in the Lord's Resistance Army (led by the now-infamous Joseph Kony).[2] Those children are now young adults facing a lifetime of poverty, inequality, and misinformation. A total of US $5 a day is considered a living wage in northern Uganda.

Sarah: Very poor. So why is theatre a good way to bring your message to them?

Phionah: I think theatre is good because in one way we do not go to communities as though we were messiahs taking solutions to them. They have seen that before, they have done it, almost every organization that comes to Uganda goes to the northern region, and they take there all these things, messages, all the time, messages. "Don't do this, do this, don't do this, do and don't and do and don't." The people just kinda look at them and just go on with their things, daily lives. If it's drinking, you take that campaign just to make them stop drinking, they'll still go and drink. So I think it is good that we are taking theatre there, because we do not go there as solution providers, but we go there to dialogue with them and hopefully they find solutions within themselves.

Sarah: From within?

Phionah: When we go to do a play and then talk to them, they kind of calm down and we discuss issues. Sometimes they tell us reasons why they do those things, and one in fact identifies with them. So we go there as people who identify with them and with their problems. When they see our plays, they see themselves in this play, so they can talk about these things simply and then find solutions to them. So they understand we are not the solution providers, but they are. In a way it's a bit easier for them.

Sarah: Very interesting. Who attends your plays?

Phionah: We usually work with communities, really the local people at the grassroots level. Depending on the project and where we go exactly, we can decide to deal with leaders or the so-called perpetrators at first—if we deem it's possible, or we think it's very right, we deal with those leaders first. We get, you know, their opinions and everything and then we go down to the local people. But sometimes, and mostly in the northern region, it's a combination—we go to a community, we go really down to that last level, the grassroots people, we talk to them. Then, most of the times during these performances when we have the grassroots, we have local leaders as well. Because, for them, traditional leaders are sometimes more important than political leaders.

We make sure we invite their traditional leaders also, so they are all around. They watch the play, they need to see it because those traditional leaders can influence decisions and people more than political leaders. So we make sure we involve everyone.

Sarah: Once you perform, do people want to talk to you about it afterwards? Are there meetings or talkbacks afterwards?

Phionah: We always have discussions at the end of every performance. Sometimes follow-ups are made with partner organizations, and the things discussed after the play are later followed up and put into action. But sometimes it is very interesting because you can never know what to expect or not to expect from an audience. They are unpredictable. Understand that sometimes we freak out, you look at people, they are looking at you like, "We are waiting for what you have to offer, and then you go away." You do a play, and at first it's challenging because they can decide to just look at you like this. And because of the language barrier, they speak a completely different language to what we speak, so it's even more difficult.

Ugandans speak many different languages. English is the official national language, taught in grade schools. It is sometimes used on the radio. Then there are Ganda or Luganda, the most widely used of the Niger-Congo languages. After that, people may speak a tribal dialect, Swahili, or even Arabic. It's easy to see how a traveling theatre group must trust that their message will get through in more than one way, since they can't count on language.

Because of the language barrier, you keep speaking English for someone to translate into their local language. Most of them in the north can hear English, though it's hard to just, you know, speak. So it's a problem, the language barrier, and when we speak sometimes it's hard to open them up. But I have never seen a time when we go and fail to open up an audience to talk. At times, when it's hard, we have to devise other means, like divide the group. Perhaps women separate and men separate, or be more provocative.

Sarah: When is that advisable?

Phionah: If it's an issue, let's say, of gender-based violence, the women can fear to talk because their husbands may be a part of the audience. So she knows, "If I say this, we'll go back home this day, he will continue slapping me, will even beat me the more." We separate them after the play to make them free to talk, and then after we have talked to both sides, we bring them together again. We tell them, "Hey, this is what has come up from this side, and this is what has come up, so can we continue like this or we need to find a solution?"

Most of the time it really works. If we find a technique that may not work, we find other techniques and we end up opening up and we talk to one another.

Sarah: What do you do when the audience doesn't respond well to you? Do they get angry with you, do they walk away, shout at you, what do they do?

Phionah: Shouting? Not really, I've not seen it before. But sometimes we greatly provoke them. There are moments when you provoke them to the extreme and they can get agitated, angry . . . there are places we've gone to, mostly with gender-based violence, and they've told us, "You've come to make our women big-headed, they are good women, they are listening women, so all these things you are bringing here, the women may end up being rebellious."

But for us, we take that to be positive, but of course before we leave we make sure we clear the message, we make them talk, and you know, we find ways of making sure they can cool down and we discuss. And I take that as a positive thing, when people open up and share what they feel no matter how nasty, because then together we can always debate and find a solution—a win-win situation. But it is fatal when you go somewhere and people just keep quiet or they just pretend to be good people who have no problem. When you bring something, they say, "Ah, no, we are good here, we do this, we know that, we are good."

So for us it's positive to go somewhere and people get agitated when you provoke them, and you see the anger in them, so that they can find ways of dealing with it because they have identified with it. If it's alcohol, and someone doesn't want to stop drinking, and you show him something that mirrors his life he will shout, he will say, "No, this, you know what, you know why I do this . . . " and he will end up sometimes saying the reasons why he drinks. Together with the other people around who are within his community, they can show him the way, not us. So, it's a bit like that. The moderator really has to be good to make sure the message does not go the wrong way.

I take a moment to look at Phionah on my screen. The passion and joy she feels are palpable. I say to her, "You have a huge smile on your face. I think you really enjoy doing this, right?" Her laugh is immediate and wonderfully unrestrained.

Phionah: I love it, hah! I love it, I don't know if it's the inquisitive journalist in me?

Sarah: What do you mean?

Phionah: I studied journalism and communication for my bachelor's degree, but I'm stuck in theatre. I have practiced journalism before and I enjoy it, talking to people, getting the story behind the story, but at the moment I feel I just need to do theatre. And again, the two fields are complementary, they can only make me better . . . than if I chose one and dropped the other.

Sarah: What are some topics that you want to address that Rafiki hasn't done yet?

Phionah: Hm. Ethnic violence. Yeah, ethnic violence. Some time back we had wanted to start a project on it, but somehow along the way the partner organization pulled out, so we could not implement it because they were the ones who had the funds. That is one of the topics we are really interested in doing. Maybe to expand on the human rights thing. There are many things we still need to do on human rights.

Sarah: Like what?

Phionah: We are considering doing something about the law. But that is still in consideration, we have not yet found the means to do it, but we were considering it last year when were in a committee meeting.

Sarah: Are there any projects that you feel are dangerous to you or that make you uncomfortable to discuss in some places?

Phionah: At first I was a bit uncomfortable with domestic violence, I should say. Because it was our first topic to deal with. That play was roughly twenty minutes when we started it. It is now over forty-five minutes. We keep adding in things, as time goes on. Recently one of the things we added in was marital rape. So at first it was a challenge to have to discuss marital rape with married people. I'm not married; in fact, most of us are not married. They sometimes look at you like "You are a little kid, you don't understand this. So don't even address it." At first it was a challenge for me, and yet I act that part.

   I'm the victim in the play. So at first it was a challenge to even act it out myself. I felt it was *(here she gave a sigh that sounded like ugggggghhhhhh)* a bit too touchy?

Sarah: I can understand that.

Phionah: But we, the players, are used to it now, and even doing discussions I think we can better handle it. You know, when we did the project on climate change, what made it a bit uncomfortable at first was the information bit of it. Because sometimes to do such a thing, you really need facts. If it's climate change, you have to know things. Facts, if it's percentages, you have to know the percentages.

Sarah: Scientific facts.

Phionah: Yeah. At times it was a challenge to have to conceptualize all these things. While you can improvise easily with other things, feelings—with climate change you have to know something or you don't know it.

Phionah began to recall a specific show that Rafiki presented concerning the citizens of Karamoja. Karamoja is a province in the Northeastern part of Uganda. The United Nations has documented many clashes over livestock and supremacy of one nomadic group over another. These fights were somewhat curtailed through efforts of the UN and other groups, but in 2011, armed conflicts were still resulting in deaths in Karamoja.

The group Human Rights Watch has reported that torture and killing of children has become a particularly distressing trend in areas where nomadic groups fight over land and cattle. The region is extremely impoverished and life is made even more difficult in years of drought and the famine that results.

Phionah: There was the project we did with one of the troupes we created in Karamoja. They came around to Kampala. We did a joint project with them. We created a play called *Full Moon over Karamoja.* We were trying to deal with perceptions that people have about the people from Karamoja, because it's really bad here. People take them to be backward and everything, so many things that are going on. You know Karamoja is that part where you don't want to even . . . *(she didn't finish that thought).*

So we called them down here, went to the streets together, we did research together in pairs—a person from Rafiki and a person from their group. And when we went to the streets, it was so hard because people would say really mean things like, "Those people don't dress, they eat people, they are primitive!" They said so many things about them and you'd be paired with this someone and you're telling them "write!" So she has to write down that she eats people, or he . . . uuugghh!

Sarah: She has to write down that she's a cannibal.

Phionah: So it was a bit hard to work on that project at first, it was a bit touchy.

Sarah: I would imagine.

Phionah: To work, to come together to form this play, because they know if someone on the streets has said this is what they think about them, they think everyone in Kampala thinks about them the same way. So in a way you are not very excluded from those Kampala people. I was ashamed at first. But when the play was ready, it was so good. They acted out those parts, asking why people refer to them as cannibals . . . we generated good discussions.

I would love to hear what some of the people from Karamoja say because we let them deal with the issues that are on the ground in their region. We do not . . . how do I explain this? Let's say in Karamoja we know one of the biggest problems is cattle rustling and raiding. We do not go there and talk about that topic as if we were experts. We can demonstrate for the new actors using other topics, and then let them work on that topic that is a problem to them in their area, and go around their region, in their language, to their people with the play and discuss it.

So, I would love to know what it is like for the members of the groups we created there, those ones who are dealing with cattle rustling and tribal differences. It must be a challenge to them too.

Sarah: This is very interesting to me because, in the United States, people usually have a singular thought about theatre. They think that theatre is entertainment. Most people don't realize that theatre is used for revolution, it's used for provoking thought, and it's used for peace building.

Phionah: I really wish you luck, because this is something interesting you're working on, to me. That is how it has been in Uganda. You know, entertainment. You talk about theatre in Kampala, people think, "Go to Theatre La Bonita, see people laugh!" I think we are the first group that has come out and been like, "We are doing this our way. Not only entertainment, but we are doing this for development, combined with fine art."

It's something interesting to know we are there. We also like it because, once in a while, we hold free performances in Kampala, for our partners and everyone around. We invite people, and the last one we did on climate change was very interesting. It was a dark night, power went off. We put on a generator, it went out in the middle of our performance! The people stayed so calm we used torches to finish the performance.

We had a discussion at the end only using torches, like two of them, if not one, and the people just did not want to stop talking up to 11:00 in the night. They wanted to stay there, and we decided, people, we have to go! But it's interesting because you realize they would rather use theatre to talk about their issues. If you've not been there, seen it, you think no, theatre stops at laughing and everything. So that's what makes me proud when I go somewhere and I realize I can make a contribution, a positive contribution. If someone can talk about something and they realize maybe they've been doing it the wrong way, they can improve or make someone better, that's what makes me proud at the end of the day.

Sarah: Is there anything else that you want to tell me right now about what you do or the hopes that you have for theatre in the future?

Phionah: Like I said, it is still a bit of a challenge in Uganda to do theatre, because we depend on projects. If you do not write a good project and maybe get funds to implement it, sometimes I don't think you can pull it off. Because most of our actors, all of us, depend on the little we get from the work we do, from the projects, so if we do not get the projects there's really nothing coming in, pocket-wise. So we depend on the little and, even though it's really little money compared to what we do sometimes, because we love it, we do it.

If we could get an opportunity, let's say in Uganda, for more people to appreciate this form of theatre, I believe it has a really long way to go and I believe it is very important, because the more steps we take, the more people we work with, the more we realize this can work here.

You work with a person or with one organization, someone sees this, they call you here, you go here, you go there, and it's so sweet to see all this work out. I hope that people can understand more of this theatre . . . because of the network we have created with more than six theatre groups around Uganda, Rwanda, and South Sudan. We only hope we can help to transform Uganda and make it a better place. Someday, of course. We cannot just do theatre and hope things are going to become fine overnight. But one step at a time. Yeah, it can work like that.

Sarah: I believe it. I believe if anything can do it, theatre can.

Phionah: Uh-huh!

*   *   *

I sign off from Skype, leaving Phionah to her morning in Kampala, laughing with delight at the thought that theatre can, indeed, change the world.

You can imagine my surprise when, in September 2012, I opened a web article on another dangerous drama, *The River and the Mountain,* to read that their producer has been jailed in Kampala for backing a play about a gay man. One of the creators of this new, divisive work? Phionah Katushabe. How was Phionah working to change the world this time . . . and was she in danger of being imprisoned?

I had to find out about *The River and the Mountain.*

13 - The River & the Mountain

The River and the Mountain, Uganda

"I knew that people would have very strong opinions about it and I knew that there were people who were very passionate about it for either side. I wasn't foreseeing violence or legal action, to be honest."

On August 18th, 2012 there was a minor revolution taking place in a cultural center in Kampala, Uganda. An actor named Okuyo Joel Atiku Prynce took the stage in a drama called *The River and the Mountain.* Towards the end of the first act, his character Samson drunkenly declared that he is gay. That's all it took: in that one sentence, he became the very first performer to ever portray an openly gay individual in Uganda.

Uganda has become notorious in the Western world for its draconian laws against gay and lesbian individuals. Ugandan laws criminalize homosexual behavior: it's punishable by up to three years in prison, and even Ugandans outside the country can be extradited and forced to face punishment for having a gay/lesbian relationship in a country where it's legal. Those are just the laws on the books now.[1] In October of 2009, Member of Parliament David Bahati proposed a bill that would make gay or lesbian sex punishable by death. Anyone found to have committed "aggravated homosexuality" could be executed. The crime of "aggravated homosexuality" was written to include having gay or lesbian sex while being HIV positive or being a parent, or having sex more than once. The original bill was never voted on, but Bahati reintroduced it in February of 2012. Again, the bill sat without a vote, prompting some outsiders to wonder if it was only introduced to cause a rift the outside world would notice, while other, more corrupt procedures were taking place behind closed doors. This has never been verified. MP Rebecca Kadaga also used the bill as a way of building political credibility while ensuring that her name was frequently mentioned in newspapers around the world. It was Kadaga who declared the bill a "Christmas present to the nation."[2] The bill was passed into law, with the death penalty revised to life in prison, in late 2013, and Uganda's president signed it into law in the spring of 2014. In August of 2014 the Constitutional Court of Uganda ruled the law invalid, as it was not passed with the necessary quorum.

Despite the fact that the law was overturned, it's no wonder that Ugandans don't write or attend plays with gay characters. Even the thought of supporting gay rights is inherently dangerous. According to Frank Mugisha, chairman of the group Sexual Minorities Uganda, private citizens have endured hate campaigns after being forcibly outed by the media. Some Ugandans consider the topic to be taboo. It's not easy to find organizations or individuals inside the country who are actively in favor of gay rights.

According to the BBC News Africa division, David Cecil, the producer of *The River and the Mountain* was put in jail from September 13-17, 2012 for "disobeying lawful orders," because the play *The River and the Mountain* was performed without authorization. Beau Hopkins, the playwright, was taken to a police station and interrogated about the meaning of his play for two hours. He eventually got off with a warning letter.[3] Cecil, who is British, faced a full trial that October. Once someone is jailed for creating a play, this most definitely qualifies it as dangerous drama! Without another set of hearings, Cecil was deported in February of 2013. He wasn't even allowed to tell his Ugandan partner, Florence, or their children goodbye.

So how did this one play, *The River and the Mountain*, get staged? What compelled director Angella Emerwon and the actresses in the production to go on with the performance, even though the National Theatre of Kampala, the original venue, violated its agreement and refused the production stage time at the last second? Was this a deliberately pro-gay play, or were they just trying to tell a story?

Meanwhile . . . how could I resist bringing some of this dangerous drama to my front door?

Here is what actress Esther Bwanika and director Angella Emerwon had to say about their roles in the creation of *The River and the Mountain*.

*   *   *

Sarah: Obviously, *The River and the Mountain* was a dangerous and controversial play in Uganda. Could you please tell me why you chose to be involved with it?

Esther: I had an audition at the National Theatre here in Uganda. I read the script, and it was very different. I knew how dangerous it might be, but the script we were given during the auditions wasn't that complete. So I didn't know how deep it was into the topic of homosexuality. Luckily enough, I was passed through the auditions, and when we got the full script it was quite different from what it had seemed. It being in Uganda, it was quite risky, but nonetheless I couldn't back out of it. Not because I was forced to, but you know, it's good doing something different. I was in love with the

Bio Points

- Angella Emurwon and Esther Bwanika are Ugandan.
- Angella got her start in amateur theatre. She went professional when her play *The Cow Needs a Wife* took third in the 2010 BBC African Performance Playwriting Competition.
- Esther Bwanika began performing in the theatre, but has become known for film acting. In 2014 she was singled out as an actress to watch at the Ugandan Pearl International Film Festival.

---

script and we had a brilliant director. I wanted to do something different. I'm not sure it was dangerous, I just took the chance. And I must say, I'm not regretting it, even one bit.

Sarah: Was there ever a time after David Cecil was arrested that you were concerned you'd be in trouble?

Esther: No. I was concerned about his safety. I don't know if I'm being naïve, or I guess, not wanting trouble, but I was an employee. I was employed to do this bit of work, it doesn't mean I'm an advocate. If you are to read the script, or watch it, there is no part in the play where the man makes a move on another man. There's no gay activity at all. He just says, "I'm gay." That's it. There has been, I mean, some negative feedback from the society, also some actors and some directors, but hey. That's what they think.

My most significant role in the play is when the mom finds out her son is gay. In Africa, we don't understand that someone can actually be born gay. She thought it was the work of the devil, like . . . she couldn't understand. So, the mom sends her son to get cured, and that doesn't work. Then she takes him to a witch doctor, and that fails to work. Finally she brings him to me. I'm a traditional dancer. Some call me a prostitute, but I'm more like a private dancer. I try to seduce him, to make him realize that I am what he wants. That was the most significant role that I had.

Sarah: How have you trained as an actress? What's your background in theatre?

Esther: I must say, I'm not that big in theatre, I have mostly done motion pictures. I am mostly in movies. But I had a brilliant time. Now I know why people say theatre is more entertaining than motion pictures. To me, I had a great character. Oh my God! And David Cecil, the producer. I'm probably being a bit racist, but to me he is the nicest white man I've met!

I couldn't help laughing here—in a play about humanizing the individual we're talking about "the nicest white man" she's ever met.

You know? Honestly. Like, he's a Black in a White man's body! I haven't met that many white people who are . . . I don't know. I'm sorry if I'm sounding a racist. Overall, it was the best crew you could ask for, you know? So, it's so sad what is happening to him. On the other hand, if he doesn't come out hurt, it is a good thing then and it means our play actually does have a message! It's working, you know? It means more than a piece of work, we did have a message. A brilliant message.

Sarah: Do you have plans after this? Do you have another project?

Esther: Yes, but both of them are motion pictures. I'm actually going to be on set tomorrow. It's good, you know, but it's not the same. I think I am more attracted to theatre now, the emotions, the connecting. So, I'm going back to my normal life. But it's weird. I'm not the only one who can't focus anymore. But it's okay, okay, you know?

Sarah: I wish I could have been there to see the show.

Esther: We hope we get a chance to show you what our play is all about. It's a good piece of work, I know you'd like it. In our play, there are pieces of comedy. He doesn't even say he's gay until towards the end of the first half. It's about a number of things: religion, culture, politics, and society. If anything, the religious community should be offended because they are not portrayed at all well in our play. But it's a platform to open dialogue about this issue in Africa. People are shy to talk about it, they are whispering about it. Because how can you not? So, let's talk about it!
 We actors showed that gay people, as much as they are gay, they are not bad people. This man is actually a nice man. When he tells his co-workers he is gay, they say, "What?! He is gay?!" And I say, "But he is a nice man." It's a message that's getting introduced in Africa: how do we react to a gay, nice man? We are saying this does exist in Africa. If you don't come into my business, who cares what you do in your bedroom? That is your problem, that is your business. Anyway, we are in a third world country, we are in Africa, we have a long way to get there.

At the moment Esther and I were talking, neither of us could have known that I would receive the script via email from playwright Beau Hopkins, the playwright, and that I would indeed like it. At the time, information surrounding the Ugandan debut was my focus. So, after talking to Esther I contacted Angella Emerwon. It was a few days before David Cecil was set to be put on trial, and her shock at the turn of events was still evident.

Sarah: It strikes me that *The River and the Mountain* is a dangerous project to take on in Uganda. Why did you agree to direct it?

Angella: I think I'm discovering later just how dangerous it was. I don't think that I thought it was dangerous going in, to be honest. I thought that it was an interesting project; it was a conversation I wanted to explore. I didn't see that there was going to be danger. I knew that people would have very strong opinions about it and I knew that there were people who were very passionate about it for either side. I wasn't foreseeing violence or legal action, to be honest.

Sarah: How did you come to the project? What's your background in theatre?

Angella: I could say I've been in theatre, in and out, for most of my life. But I got really interested three or four years ago, about pursuing it professionally. I've been in a couple of dramatic societies, done a lot of backstage things and assistant directorships. Then about two years ago I wrote a play that did really well. It was a radio play that eventually made its way to the stage. That was my first job, when I directed a piece by myself. It was called *The Cow Needs a Wife*. It placed in a BBC radio competition and then a couple of amateur dramatic societies wanted to put it on. I rewrote it as a stage play last year.

Since then I've directed some things, but I wanted to work with this playwright who was inspired by Shakespeare and Shakespearean theatre, which I've never done before. From a purely professional point of view, it was to work with a playwright who had been in theatre and a theatre-based culture and was inspired by the Shakespearean period. It was a challenge for me to see if I could get into that world and see what it would look like in a Ugandan setting. Professionally, that was it. From a personal view, I'm a Christian. Obviously, the issue of homosexuality is interesting to me. I won't get into it, but I will say I wondered what it would be like to think about it while I'm inside the world, so to speak. At the same time it was a play about corruption and about the things people do to get ahead. I felt like there were a lot of things there. There were a lot of things that went into my decision.

Sarah: One of your actresses, Esther, said that the rehearsal process was very liberating for her and that she learned a lot. How did you prepare the actors? What was your rehearsal process?

Angella: Like I said, I was steeped in the idea of Shakespeare. Shakespeare's plays take place in so many locations, so many scene changes. So the way this play was written, I had to have the scene changes in my head. That's a big part of how most theatre is done at the moment, because you need to feed the scene to your audience. Make them believe they're in such and such place with your backdrop and all that. It was an interesting challenge for me and for the actors to try and create the place using their bodies and using their points of focus in the scene. People were transported into that place even though the stage was very minimal. That was one of the things.

Another thing I should say is that theatre in Uganda is either a stand-up style comedy or it's very developmentally based. So you have your HIV-focused plays, your sanitation plays. It's very rare to find something that's in the middle. It's rare to find something that is message-based but also has some comedy. We like to say this is entertainment that makes you think.

Sarah: Some Ugandan newspapers made it sound like the first theatre you were going to perform in cancelled your play. Is that true?

Angella: Not exactly. We were slotted to perform at three spaces. We were going to be at Tilapia Center, where eventually we had six performances. Then we were going to be at the National Theatre, finally we'd be at a cultural center called MishMash. The National Theatre cancelled on us. Well, they didn't cancel on us, they made certain demands knowing that we could not meet them.

Sarah: So . . . they cancelled.

Angella: Yeah. When people say to me "are you surprised?" or "did you expect this?" I can say I didn't. When we met with the National Theatre we went in with a synopsis. They knew from the get-go what sort of story we were working on. It took them eight weeks to decide we needed permission, we needed censorship from the Ugandan Media Council. It took them eight weeks after our casting, and knowing we had set dates, for them to send this letter saying, "You need to get permission before you come here." And this happened two weeks before our performances. That makes me think they knew we were not going to get it. So, that's the story, that the National Theatre stabbed us in the back.

Sarah: Censorship is something that I am lucky to say I'm not familiar with. In the United States you can put what you want onstage and that's your right. How does it work in Uganda?

Angella: Censorship is a strange thing, I would say, in Uganda. There are some topics that are considered taboo. Homosexuality would be considered taboo. People would say to me, "Do you definitely think you'll get shut down?" And I said no, because it's not a homosexual piece per se, we just had a homosexual character. It wasn't a homosexual story. One person, a person whom I consider very levelheaded and very reasonable, came to a rehearsal and said to me, "As soon as your character says he's gay, it becomes a homosexual play." I thought that was interesting. Before that, the play is about everyday people living in Uganda, the things they go through in relationships and so forth. But the minute he comes out, you know, it becomes a homosexual play. Samson [the character] coming out definitely pushes the story forward, but it's very innocent. He's drunk. He's just trying to become more truthful with his friends. It's only later that the information is useful. At the time it's innocent.

I know for a fact that a couple of years ago [Eve Ensler's play] The *Vagina Monologues* were also squashed. I think the Uganda Media Council advised them to change the title of the play. The title was the issue, not so much the content. They didn't want them to be called the *Vagina Monologues*. We have topics like that. So that's interesting. But when you look at the law, the law does not actually require anyone to get the Media Council's permission to put up a play. However, the Minister of Ethics and Integrity can squash anything. He has the ability to squash anything.

Uganda's cabinet has a position known as the Minister for Ethics and Integrity. In 2012, Minister Simon Lokodo was repeatedly decried in Western newspapers for using his power to quell meetings organized by gay and lesbian activists. In February of 2012 he attempted to arrest prominent Uganda gay rights activist Kasha Jacqueline Nabagesera at a hotel in Entebbe. The hotel was the site of a workshop for gay activists.

Nabagesera, who is open about being lesbian, ran out the door of the hotel and was able to avoid arrest. The day of the raid Minister Lokodo was quoted in a Ugandan paper as saying, "I have closed this conference because it's illegal. We do not accept homosexuality in Uganda. So go back home."[4] Angella begins to talk about a documentary named Call Me Kuchu, *a film aimed at promoting gay rights in the region.*

Angella: There was somebody who did a documentary where they went around finding out from Ugandans what they think about homosexuality. They wanted to have people watch it and then dialogue about it afterwards. Apparently the Minister of Ethics turned up and shut it down. So a restriction, I think he has the power to do that. We are not required by law to have our play reviewed before they are put on stage, but of course the National Theatre, that's their space. They can dictate whatever it is

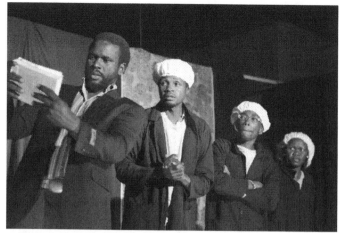

Still photo from The River and Mountain, *in Kampala in 2013. Photo credit: Jan Cattebeke, courtesy of David Cecil.*

they want done and in this case they decided to have the media consultant review it.

Sarah: Did you have a plan in place in case you were told you couldn't perform this?

Angella: Do you mean was there someplace else where we could have the show?

Sarah: Was it possible that none of the theatres would have permitted the show?

Angella: That was never a concern. The Ugandan National Theatre is a center for culture in the center of Kampala. The foot traffic alone, if someone had been walking by the theatre, would have been great. That's why it was important: a central location, and of course it is our cultural center. That's why the National Theatre was important. There are so many other places, theatre programs that go around all the time around town and no one knows what happening there. The national theatre is partly funded by the government. It was a key location.

Sarah: How did you learn that your producer David Cecil had been arrested?

Angella: I found out on TV, if you can believe that. I had just spoken to him the day before; we wanted to make plans to go on tour in the region. That was a Wednesday. On that Thursday night a friend of mine sent me a text message saying, "Isn't that your play on TV, where the producer is being arrested?" I said, "What?!" Yes, we had come up on the 9:00 news. I turned on the TV and there is David being arrested and put in a van and being sent to prison. This apparently had happened in the morning and I had no idea.

Sarah: How did you feel?

Angella: It was terrifying. I did not think that it would go that far. I mean, I didn't think . . . I didn't see anybody was winning, if that makes sense? I didn't see what use that would be to the government, what use that would be to the National Theatre, I couldn't see what capital this could increase. It was terrifying because it felt very petty and we saw that the entire thing was orchestrated by an expert hand. Honestly, I got chills.

Sarah: Were you concerned for yourself or your cast?

Angella: Not really. I hesitate to say this because obviously there are all these weird ideas about the justice system in Africa. I don't want to propagate that. I will say, if you're in trouble, on that scale, you would know. It's not something that you would wonder about or worry about. You would know you're in trouble. You would know they had something that they could hold over you. So I was never really concerned for myself or for my safety. I just think it would be the strangest thing. Unfortunately, David was in charge of publicity and marketing and doing the logistical things even though we were co-producers. Since he was in charge of that, he signed a lot of things and I think that's why they have him on the hook. Nobody came to the shows and sort of waited around to ask a question or start something or anything like that. Everyone that saw the show is completely shocked about, you know, why such measures are being taken. I guess we had been laissez-faire thinking nothing was going to happen, but when they arrested David it became very serious very quickly.

David Cecil was held for two days before being freed on bail. After his trial on October18, 2012, he was released. His sudden deportation had yet to occur. Almost immediately, plans were being made to produce readings or full-scale shows in the United States and Great Britain. As Esther had predicted, as soon as it was clear that David was not going to be permanently harmed at that time, the publicity actually helped The River and the Mountain *a great deal. Additionally, it allowed Cecil to remain in Uganda, where he has very important ties.*

Angella: David has Ugandan family, Ugandan children. A conviction would mean a circus that would follow him, something that would make it very difficult for him to remain here. That would be a shame. He's amazing. You can't believe that there are people like that left in the world.

Sarah: Do you have a project lined up now that *The River and the Mountain* has debuted?

Angella: I've had a very packed year. I worked on a musical for 17 weeks and then I jumped into a high school project for eight weeks before I did *The River and the Mountain.* So I am completely bushed. I think it would be great to go on tour with *The River and the Mountain.* That can happen next year. I think I'm going to take a couple of weeks to relax. I'm predominately a writer and I haven't written anything for about three months. I think it's time.

*   *   *

As the story of Uganda's first play with a gay character is publicized around the world, more attention is being paid to the legal system which criminalizes both homosexual behavior and the people who create art as a way to talk about it. However, the motivation to do what's right must come from within, rather than as a result of international pressure. In fact, David Cecil actually requested that people not circulate a petition in the United Kingdom in favor of his release. Although the petition had been signed by many famous Britons, such as Stephen Fry, Vanessa Redgrave, Peter Brook, and Tom Stoppard, Cecil was concerned that the petition itself would be treated as an act of colonialism. In an interview with The Guardian UK newspaper Cecil was quoted as saying, "It's amusing and gratifying to have celebs making statements that I should be freed. David Lan is a good man and the intentions behind this petition are fair enough.

However, I think it is a mistake for Europeans to be perceived as putting pressure on an African government. Colonialism is not such a distant memory."[5]

I was so intrigued by the story of *The River and the Mountain* and well as the political drama behind the scenes that I sought to bring the play to the United States. In March 2013, the US debut of *The River and the Mountain* US was seen in five locations in the US. We fought to bring Okoyu Prynce over to reprise his role as Samson, but, after months of negotiating with the visa and embassy staff of the US embassy in Uganda, our own government refused to let him leave Uganda to take part in the play. He was deemed a risk to bring over, a seemingly ridiculous decision because he was filming a TV series at that time and had every intention to return and complete his African series. Around that time, the tabloid called *The Red Pepper* ran outrageous claims against Prynce, claiming that he was involved in human trafficking and that he knew about an illegal organ donation scheme. These were huge, multi-page articles with splashy photos prominently displaying his likeness. Prynce had to get lawyers and Interpol to clear his name because of the stories. He also heard DJs on the radio lying about him and saying derogatory things, all because he played a gay man on stage.

I'll never know what happened in the consulate's office in Kampala that led to the decision forbidding him from here. He was a perfect candidate for a visiting artist, and no one could argue his historical value, since he is the only man to play a gay character ever in Ugandan history. It's tempting to assign blame to the Ugandan government, the US government, hate groups, or a nameless conspiracy—but temptation must be resisted since we may never have all the facts. Despite that casting disappointment, a professional cast presented readings of the work in and around our nation's capital, and then playwright Beau Hopkins was invited onto the stage each night for question-and-answer sessions. Hopkins always maintained that the piece itself was never about gay rights or activism—it was about using that agenda to cover up corruption and misuse of religion. The fact that a gay man is killed for being gay is not the central message of his story, he says.

As for myself, I got a firsthand chance to experience this piece of dangerous drama in a place where it was not only safe, but the play was actively encouraged. We certainly didn't hide our production, but we agreed that inviting the Ugandan envoys to the US would be a bad idea. On March 6, 2013 I asked Prynce about inviting people from the Ugandan embassy in Washington, DC. This was his response via email:

> I have my reservations about inviting the embassy given the history of government officials with the homosexuality subject. Our speaker of Parliament sometime back exchanged bitter words with a Canadian MP while she was in Canada because he brought up homosexuality in Uganda, most government officials are negative about it either for reasons of job security or something else I don't know.
>
> So it is of paramount importance to know their positions for certain (Sometimes they tell you they're liberal while you are alone with them then turn around later) before inviting them otherwise, I might be in trouble. Otherwise, I would rather NOT invite them. I know it is a good gesture and public relations and more but let's not take the risks that may come with it for granted. Thanks.

Through the bureaucracy of trying to arrange Prynce's visa and hearing him say he didn't want people in Uganda to know that's why he was traveling until we couldn't avoid it, I became grateful for the relative ease of securing venues, press, and actors in the US. Prynce's replacement went on in the role of Samson and performed superbly. Audiences quickly forgot their disappointment at not seeing the "real" Samson because the story itself is involved and compelling. We were well received by the public and the press. Astonishment that this one play caused so many legal problems was a common theme in our talkback sessions.[6]

None of my actors were the subject of malicious tabloid gossip as Prynce was, or arrested for their involvement, as Cecil was. Although the play has since left my hands and is no longer being performed in the US, I feel the process of *The River and the Mountain* remains an important episode in looking at how and why drama becomes dangerous in different ways, at different times, for different people.

Incidentally, my entire reason for following this trail was because Phionah Katushabe had been listed as someone involved with the creation of the show. It seems she suffered no discernible consequences due to her involvement. My fervent wish is that the next group to present *The River and the Mountain* finds this to be true, as well.

14 - No Longer Ashamed

Bond Street Theatre and the women of FAVILEK

"At the beginning we were ashamed to speak. When we found others who were victims of the same crimes we were no longer ashamed to speak."

There is no easy place to begin telling the extraordinary story that continues in Haiti. It is about a group called FAVILEK, the women who run it, and the mission begun with Bond Street Theatre. Before the 2010 earthquake, Haitian women were frequently subjected to violence because the government was unstable, laws were not upheld, and poverty was extreme. The United Nations Development Program reported that Haiti had one of the highest rates of women affected by violence in the world. Relying on Haitian aid organizations and self-reporting, the UNDP estimated that seventy-two percent of Haitian girls had been sexually assaulted before they reached adulthood.

A 2009 report from the Inter-American Commission on Human Rights held even more shocking statistics. They claimed ninety percent of Haitian women had experienced some form of violence in their lives. Restavek, the custom of keeping child slaves in the home where they are sometimes abused, is still permissible in Haiti.[1] As bad as it was, however, it was nothing compared to the earthquake.

On January 12, 2010 an earthquake registering a 7.0 on the Richter Scale struck near Port-au-Prince, the capital of Haiti. In the immediate aftermath of the earthquake it was estimated that 150,000 people had perished beneath the rubble. By 2011 the Disasters Emergency Committee of the UK suspected a final total of 220,000 dead. Overnight, 1.5 million terrified people were forced to start looking for loved ones, clean water, and food in a city that had been completely decimated. Civilization had disappeared overnight.

Because the infrastructure of Port-au-Prince was severely compromised (sixty percent of government/administrative buildings collapsed, about one third of all civil servants had died, and rubble blocked all possible means of getting food packages), an international effort was immediately launched to aid the survivors. Neighboring Dominican Republic began sending rescue equipment, large trucks, and food the next morning. The United Nations, reeling from the loss of 102 of their own staff in Haiti, declared an emergency and facilitated the arrival of over 20,000 aid workers from member nations. [2]

Port-au-Prince became a virtual hell on earth. Entire blocks had been leveled, there was no clean water, not enough food, over 3,000 escaped penitentiary convicts were now loose in the community, and thousands of people were trapped in collapsed buildings that couldn't be shifted. Survivors fled to other towns to escape the stench of rotting bodies, most of which were never formally identified. In some parts of Port-au-Prince, aid workers had to stack human bodies in front of intact churches and leave them there to rot in the sun. Photos of jewelry and identifying marks were taken by the gravediggers and placed near each pile of corpses to be buried. It was hoped that people could identify missing family members that way. Desperate mourners sometimes clawed through stacks of bodies to look for their dead. A census of the dead was attempted but never really completed.

The men and women who survived the quake found themselves vulnerable in many ways: disease, starvation, kidnapping, and sexual assault became the new norm. There was an outbreak of cholera in October of 2010, a direct result of people living in refugee camps and temporary shelters, where they could not access clean water. Over 200,000 people got sick, and almost 6,000 died.[3] Many younger women, unable to work and care for their children, were forced to perform sexual acts in return for food aid packages being handed out by male volunteers.[4] Women who had never turned to prostitution as a means of making money before the earthquake began having "transactional sex," meaning they had sex with men in return for shelter, clothing or other necessities.

Orphans and women were preyed upon in shelter camps. Something as simple as using the bathroom was life threatening every day. Women and children on their way to use the facilities at the edges of the camp were attacked by gangs and dragged away to endure hours and sometimes days of repeated gang rape. While gang rapes were reported to the UN, Red Cross, and journalists working for news outlets, there were few civil authorities that could respond. On June 23, 2010 the *New York Times* published the story of Rose, a young woman who was kidnapped and held for ransom in the ruins of a collapsed home. For her, being forced to crawl into the rubble was "torture" because she was so frightened of the roof falling in on her. Like thousands of other traumatized Haitians, Rose had not returned to a place with a roof since the night of the earthquake. Rose was raped repeatedly until her brother-in-law delivered the $2,000 ransom. A reporter from the Times was the one to take Rose to a medical clinic for help.[5]

Children as young as two years of age were being raped and sexually assaulted.[6] It is impossible to know the true scale of the rape epidemic because so many people chose not to report it to anyone. In the accounts of the

Bio Points

- The members of FAVILEK are Haitian.
- The name FAVILEK comes from the words Fanm Viktim Leve Kanpe, which means, "Women Victims, Get Up, Stand Up."
- Bond Street Theatre of New York City, started in 1976, facilitates theatre projects in over 40 countries around the world.

---

survivors it's common to read, "I didn't know him," and, "I have no money," which were both significant barriers to getting the support needed to make a complaint. Getting adequate police cooperation was rare for the women and girls who were willing and able to file a complaint. In some cases, rape victims were told by the police that they must bring their attackers to the station or a patrol van for questioning. On March 16, 2010, the *Huffington Post* reported that Haitian Information Minister Marie-Laurence Jocelyn Lassegue had said of the sexual assault epidemic, "We are aware of [a] problem . . . but it's not a priority."[6]

Out of this devastation came a new beginning. FAVILEK, a name comprised of the words Fanm Viktim Leve Kanpe, actually means "Women Victims, Get Up Stand Up." FAVILEK represents the thousands of Haitian women who have been assaulted, gang raped, beaten, and forced to carry their rapist's child, many left in abject poverty for three generations. Many women have been and will continue to be raped many times over the course of their lives.

FAVILEK began in response to this horrific and ongoing violence. The group started out as an ad hoc help center—women whispering stories of horrific violence to each other, then to other women, to Haitian society, and finally to the world. Through their association with the Bond Street Theatre of New York City, FAVILEK is ready to take their act to anyone and everyone who will listen. The time for silence is over. The women are using drama to help themselves, help child prostitutes, and help us understand what a life lived in fear, or a life lived with empowerment, is really all about.

One of the groups most responsible for helping the women of FAVILEK is Bond Street Theatre. Joanna Sherman, one of the founders of Bond Street, gave this account of the theatre's history and mission.

* * *

Joanna: Bond Street started as a street theatre company, like the San Francisco Mime Troupe or Bread and Puppet Theatre. We were commenting on social issues of the day locally, and then more nationally. In 1984 we did a big project with Palestinians, Jews, Yemenis and Ethiopians, all residents of Jerusalem, and that led to our realization that theatre works as a way to bring people together to address issues in a conflict area. This was a huge project, sixty people of different ethnicities working together in Jerusalem. It was an epiphany to realize this was even possible. It was a sink-or-swim situation because we were a pretty young company, but it was tremendously successful. And that company that we started, out of sixty people, about twenty-five remained to form Jerusalem's first interethnic street theatre group. In addition, we initiated a whole new style of theatre that they hadn't been doing there: site-specific work. From then on, we were just hooked on the idea that theatre can be used in all different kinds of troubled environments.

After that, we started working in Eastern Europe, and, when the Berlin Wall came down in 1989, this opened the door to working in Eastern Europe in a different kind of way. This was huge, being able to go into East Berlin before the Wall came down and after the Wall came down . . . we were the first company to perform legally in East Berlin right after the Wall came down. At first, no one know whether street theatre was legal or not. When they decided it was okay, they were so happy. It was a very gray-looking place. There wasn't a single sign anywhere because you don't need to put up a sign. You don't care if anyone comes to your restaurant or not.

Bond Street performed their show Nightmare on Wall Street *in Alexanderplatz, a central location with historical and geographic significance to Berliners. A theatre company from outside Berlin was doing a piece on the downside of capitalism in the center of a city that was just beginning to seek a clear economic path. Joanna described how the play, which used very few words, seemed appropriate for the time and place.*

Bond Street has also worked extensively in South America, performed a non-verbal Romeo and Juliet throughout the war-ravaged Balkans, and traveled to Pakistan to explore theatre in a post 9/11 world. Bond Street started working in Afghanistan and Pakistan in 2002. Joanna described the beginning of that journey and how they found their partners.

Joanna: After 9/11, we began working in Afghanistan and Pakistan and we have been focused on that region since then. We started working in the refugee camps in Pakistan in 2002. While working there, we met a theatre group that had fled during the Taliban regime. How it is that artists find other artists? It's just one of life's magical things. In one of the camps, we found a company called Exile Theatre, and they were indeed in exile. The group included some of the best playwrights, actors, and film people from Afghanistan.

In the next year, 2003, when many Afghans returned from exile, we suggested to the group, "Let's meet. Let's create, let's do a collaboration." Bond Street Theatre had been doing a kind of symbolic theatre that Exile Theatre had just heard about but had never done or experienced. We worked together at Kabul University, where the theatre building and many other buildings had been destroyed by the Taliban. We stayed in one of the buildings that were still standing and worked together every day.

*   *   *

Bond Street Theatre traded warm-ups, exercises, stylized stage combat techniques, and performance techniques with their Afghan counterparts. As the practitioners shared performance rituals and traditions, they found universal themes and expressions that brought them together, something Joanna says Bond Street has found to be true everywhere they have worked. It's a secret to the success Bond Street has had all over the world. They create plays that do not rely on language to be understood or deeply felt. In the case of Exile Theatre, the work emerged as a collection of stories that they gathered from local people who had experienced war from the 1970s until the present: the Russian invasion of Afghanistan, the civil wars between Afghan tribes, and the subsequent period of time when Afghans were ruled by the Taliban. These histories had been taken from men and women of all ages, then presented as a work called *Beyond the Mirror*. In 2005, Exile Theatre and Bond Street were able to tour the collaborative effort, and they performed their show for appreciative audiences in Kabul, the US, and Japan. Sadly, Exile Theatre would end when some of the performers were forced to emigrate to Canada for their safety, and their star actress, Anisa Wahab, passed away.

Bond Street would return to Afghanistan many more times in the following years. In 2007, it was to work with an all-female theatre group in Kunduz. That group was formed by a young woman who had no firsthand knowledge about performance. She had never even seen a TV, yet had the courage to create a theatre group as a way for the girls find their own voice. That same year Joanna took the group to collaborate with Aschiana, a Kabul-based organization working with street-working children, which wanted to use theatre to promote self-confidence and group cooperation among the children. In 2008, Aschiana and Bond Street used theatre for the education and empowerment of women and children in Mazir-i-Sharif, the fourth-largest city in Afghanistan. From 2006-2009 Bond Street Theatre conducted the US-Indian-Afghan Arts Exchange and Conflict Resolution Project, which facilitated artistic exchange between Afghan, Indian, and American theatre artists.

Three theatre groups from the three countries worked together to write and perform *A Kite's Tale*, which toured throughout India with workshops designed to serve rural women and street children. Joanna and her team have also facilitated workshops and programs through their Theatre for Social Development project. The Project, started in 2010, created four new troupes in Afghanistan to create and tour informational theatre shows in areas where illiteracy is high. Each company has a male and female team that can perform and educate people in small towns, prisons, institutions, or anywhere people may not have access to important information about human rights, health, or other topics. In the end, it is programs like these that demonstrate the ultimate mission Bond Street Theatre has pursued since their first epiphany in Jerusalem—to bring people together using theatre as a tool of empowerment and knowledge.

To get a better idea of how Bond Street came to work with FAVILEK, I talked to two of the actress-practitioners that worked in Haiti. Anna Zastrow and Christina Pinnell were two of the women helping FAVILEK through theatrical exercises, workshop development, and rehearsals.

*   *   *

Anna: We work with FAVILEK to provide them with theatre training, and that has several purposes. One would be to give them an outlet for themselves, to have a voice and a chance to express themselves. That provides a psychosocial benefit. In doing the theatrical exercises, they get a chance to work through their experiences. I asked one of the women why they choose to do theatre and she said: "To have an outlet for our feelings of what we have endured."

Then we offer them tools that they can use with others, with the girls they work with. FAVILEK works with women and young girls living in tent camps who prostitute themselves for survival. FAVILEK gives them counseling and helps these girls find an alternative means of survival.

Ultimately, they wanted to create another show about their experiences because they feel they have no voice or avenue for speaking out. They don't have access to the "powers that be" to express their circumstances, their experiences, what has happened to them. They turn to theatre to get their voice out to the community and to the world.

Bond Street Theatre and FAVILEK first came together because Bond Street had a contact at the Haitian Embassy. That contact reached out to them after the earthquake and asked them to come down to Haiti because they were "really needed." That was the start of Bond Street's research into the area and what they would need to do to create an effective piece of theatre.

Anna: Through our research, we came upon FAVILEK and we thought this is a group we should connect with. Then I found out that Maricia, one of the founders, was coming to New York on the first anniversary of the earthquake to do a talk about the abuse of women and sexual violence that was happening in the camps. So I went to that, and Maricia talked about her experience and the experiences of so many other women. She talked about the endemic levels of gender violence and how it's rapidly getting worse. She talked about how she had been raped, how her daughter had been raped, how this happens a lot, going across generations. She talked about how she had no voice and how she was trying to speak out to the world.

FAVILEK was founded by survivors of political and sexual violence. In the 1990s, under the dictatorship, these women were victimized, but they banded together as survivors to fight for justice and provide assistance to other victims. As part of this, they turned to the medium of theatre. They had no real experience with theatre but again . . . they just instinctively knew that this was a way to get heard. After the earthquake, that epidemic of violence was only getting so much worse. Maricia told us how they lacked the means to fight it. At the meeting in New York, I asked her, "What do you need?" I expected her to say money. But she said what they needed was a theatre director to help them create a piece about what's happening. That was amazing. Here is a woman who has been traumatized many times over and survived unimaginable horrors—and what she asks for is the means to create theatre. She understands the transformative power of theatre, its capacity to heal and promote social change. We said to her, "That is exactly how we can help. That's what we do. We're committed to help."

Anna and the BST team went to Haiti for the first time in February 2011. I asked her what it was like for them to go down there on short notice, armed only with their commitment to help and some research. Their local partners were able to help the team navigate the unfamiliar city, the tent camps and interactions with locals who were sometimes unwelcoming. Even their accommodations fell through, and their Haitian guide had to find them an alternate hostel.

Anna: Our local guide, Morlon Lhe Bellerice, was someone I met during another collaborative effort. I was greatly impressed with his work and his dedication, and so when we needed a partner on the ground, we hired him to be our Haitian teaching artist. He served as our translator and co-facilitator of the workshops. He also connected us logistically with what we needed. For instance, we hired a friend of his to be our driver. With his help, we were able to move around the streets safely and interact directly and closely with the local population. This is important to us. He was our all-around helper and instrumental to the project.

Bond Street Theatre has taken a hiatus to assess what they can do next for

FAVILEK. There's no doubt that everyone considered the first trips to be successful.

Anna: The collaboration we have with FAVILEK, for me it was immensely rewarding. First of all, it's difficult to come upon all this hardship and the horrible things that these women and girls are going through. Often you feel, "What can I truly do? To really make a difference?" There's so much hardship and Haiti is a mess. A complicated mess. How can we regenerate this country? Well, I can start with one person and the difference I make with this one person can have a ripple effect through the community. Central to everything for me is the human, person-to-person connection.

Joanna and Anna agreed that those connections are what make the work so important. The spontaneous moments of joy and love, expressed through performance, help everyone feel strong and empowered in the moment. For the next piece of the puzzle, I spoke to Christina Pinnell about her time as an intern at Bond Street and her involvement with the Haiti project.

Because the interviews with FAVILEK were necessarily going to be conducted in person and in Haitian Creole (Kreyòl), I had to find someone who was willing to take a chance on an unknown author for an unknown project and safely bring back the words of the entire FAVILEK group. It was Christina who carried my list of questions, by hand, to the women at FAVILEK. Then she made sure all of the answers were recorded. Without her supportive leap of faith, that interview could not have happened. Here's what Christina had to say about her involvement in the project and her early years as a practitioner.

Christina: The focus of the international program of Bond Street has really been to go into areas of conflict, post-war zones, disaster areas, and work with different populations, identify issues within a community, and create theatre around those issues. We also create informational theatre. For example, we have a team that went to Burma [Myanmar] and did a show about hand washing—the importance of washing your hands—and did that in orphanages, monasteries and in the countryside. We also do a lot to collaborate with local artists. We train local artists in our different theatre techniques. We all come from different theatre backgrounds, so we all sort of bring everything, all of our training, to the table and come up with these comprehensive workshops to do with different artists within the country.

We also give them training as far as organization and grant writing and trying to make sustainable theatre programs in those countries. So that's what's been the model program that was started in India and Afghanistan, about 10 years ago. It's a lot of cross training, cross-cultural exchange, and then, since we are all theatre artists, we do create shows that are uplifting and entertaining. We'll go into refugee camps in Haiti and perform as a service. You know, try and bring a little joy and a little laughter into an area that has been going through a difficult time.

That's usually how we make our introduction to new countries. We research, then try to come up with something that's fun that kids and adults are both going to enjoy. Something that is low budget, can be done anywhere, just go out and have a lot of fun. It usually involves stilting, juggling, clowning, acrobatics. If we have people who can speak languages we use that, but a lot of times we use gibberish and that sort of thing, so that there's languages in the show but no one knows what you're saying because it's very physically based theatre.

Sarah: I didn't know about the gibberish.

Christina: Yeah, well, sometimes it comes up that way. My Creole was at first gibberish. And then I actually learned the real words.

Sarah: What's your background and how did you come to Bond Street?

Christina: My initial foray into theatre was musical theatre. I thought I was gonna be on Broadway. That was what I wanted to do. So, all through high school, I took dance and theatre and voice classes. I'm a singer, when I got into college I was doing musicals all the time. Then, I took a workshop in mask theatre and Commedia dell'Arte the summer after my freshman year of college and I . . . I had no idea that you could create theatre without language. Theatre that wasn't text-based. I just had never really thought of that before, I mean other than mime, and I didn't want to mime. From there I got really interested in mask theatre.

I actually went and studied Commedia dell'Arte in Italy. I did a program at the Accademia dell'Arte, which is in Tuscany. I learned all sorts of mask traditions, including Commedia dell'Arte, but I also worked with a German group called Familie Floez, did some Roman masks and Balinese masks. All these different mask traditions. We also did vocal work, clowning, physical work, and acrobatics. So, that's where it all started to come together. From there I continued with the masks. I started designing masks and did a few productions. I traveled to Bali and learned how to carve Balinese masks out of wood and learned a little bit about Balinese dance while I was there. I just continued traveling, then went back to Italy after I graduated, for another round, because there were so many great artists that I got to work with. It was very different from what I had experienced at my own school.

I continued to pursue a physical sort of theatre and got into doing some acrobatics; I liked the circus. I actually toured with the Big Apple Circus for three and a half years. I worked on the administrative side of things. So it was my first job out of college. I ran away from school and—

Sarah: Joined the circus. (My groans met with delighted giggles.) Oh, God.

Christina (still having a good laugh): Which, you know, it was a lot of fun. It's really hard, but I did love that time of my life. Through working with people in the circus and getting to know the clown community in New York City, that's where I believe I had my first introduction to Bond Street Theatre. It's a very tight-knit community. The people here just do gigs around New York City. Different birthday parties, people who stilt, you know, it's tight-knit.

Christina recalled how she met Michael McGuigan and Joanna Sherman. McGuigan is an ensemble member and the Managing Director of Bond Street.

Christina: I don't remember the exact time I met [the people in] Bond Street, but I kept running into them at different places. I invited Michael and Joanna, I just emailed them one day and invited them to come to the circus. I got them tickets to come see the Big Apple Circus. From there we continued a relationship. I went into the offices and had a conversation with Joanna about what I saw myself doing, what the possibilities were, and she talked about doing an internship in the future one day, but I was on tour with the circus so I didn't know when that would happen.

When the United States fell into an economic decline, many positions in artistic organizations were cut back or eliminated. Christina was let go from the circus and she decided that the time was right to try with Bond Street.

Christina: I was no longer on the road and so I decided to stay in New York. I contacted the Communications Manager at that time and said, "I'm ready," and so I started March 2009, as an intern. I started mostly working on Marketing and Development because that was sort of my background. As far as fundraising, I had done Public Relations in college so I was trying to help the organization increase their annual budget and work on recruiting new board members. And then from there I started learning how to write grants and trying to find a position for myself within the organization.

But the Bond Street actually has workouts, usually two nights a week. I continued to work with my physical theatre skills and working with the different artists that are a part of Bond Street, because it's a huge network of artists. Not just the people who work in the office. They've been doing this for 30-plus years. So there are generations and generations of Bond Street artists that I came in contact with. Some of them are board members now. My

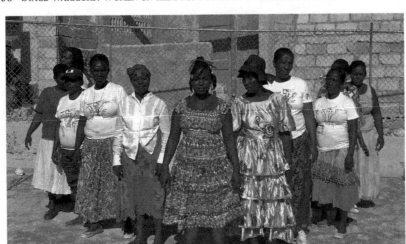

Members of FAVILEK, undated photo courtesy of Anna Zastrow.

internship ended and I just was sort of affiliated with Bond Street and then we got an invitation to come to Haiti. And Joanna asked me to work on that project. She said "I have nobody right now, just a contact, but . . . "

We didn't really have any information at the time. We just knew that there had been an earthquake there and said, "We could go." People thought it would be a good idea to go. So then we formed this Haiti team. Anna Zastrow and I really started it and then we started looking for a person to go with us. She and I just sorta dug in, started researching the situation in Haiti. We started grass-roots contacting people, seeing what we could do, we started to have fundraisers. We started that project with absolutely nothing. We put together proposals, started writing grants, then one night we went to La MaMa Theatre in New York City. It was January, so it was the one-year anniversary of the earthquake. We met Maricia Jean, who is one of the founding members of FAVILEK. She was speaking about FAVILEK. We introduced ourselves and said, "What would you need to grow? What would you need in order to make your vision of theatre happen in Haiti?" She said, "We just need more training."

We had totally expected her to say money or costumes or a place, a space, or to come to the US for classes. No, they just wanted more training. Well, okay! We know what our project is now. So we fundraised, we did not know if we were going to go until three days before we went. We bought tickets and left three days later. It was that sort of "fly by the seat of your pants," and it got delayed a couple of times, but we ended up down there in February of 2011.

Sarah: What did you find when you got there? What was it like for you?

Christina: I can't believe we did it. Like, I couldn't believe we were there. It was such a surreal experience. Because we'd been prepping and reading and preparing for so long, and I actually got to a point where I could not read any more about the sexual violence that was happening in the tent camps. I was reading article after article every day and blog entries and following reporters who were down there. I just had some major burnout from the emotional stress reading these horrible accounts and just horrific things. And to get there, it's like, "Whoa, we're really here, and, and we're gonna meet these people. They're real, they're not just names and accounts on a piece of paper."

Yes, it was a little hectic when we showed up, because our housing fell through. We were trying to figure out what we were going to do on the ground when we got there, but we had meetings set up and we just plodded through. We have a Haitian artist that is a partner of ours, his name is Morlon Lhe Bellerice. He had worked with Anna before in Haiti, when she was there with another organization. He was very instrumental in getting us settled and giving us the lay of Port-au-Prince. He was very protective of us, so we jumped into it. We met FAVILEK on the second day that we were there and it was love ever since then. We started talking and felt immediately like it was meant to be for us to work together.

Sarah: Where did you end up staying?

Christina: We ended up staying in a hotel in Port-au-Prince for the first trip. We had been looking at some hostels, but the situation was still so . . . it had only been a year and a half, I guess, from the earthquake. So it was still in pretty bad shape. Port-au-Prince was in pretty bad shape. Electricity was out most of the time, rubble everywhere. We ended up staying at a hotel that was very near to where we were working.

Sarah: Were you ever concerned for your own safety while you were there?

Christina: I have never felt unsafe in Haiti, but I've also never been by my-self. I was always with Haitians and the Haitians I was with were always very protective. You know, we never took any unnecessary risks. We were inside before dark. We did go out in public areas and we were a part of Carnivale, we were in crowded with the public, but, no, we were never, never by ourselves.[8]

One of the artists on the team, Josh Wynter, is African-American so every-body thought he was Haitian even though he wasn't. It looked like there were these two American girls and two Haitian guys. People thought we were these white girls down from America who were on vacation and picked up two guys! That's what people thought on the street a lot. They would say things like that to us. But I never felt unsafe.

Sarah: What kind of training did you provide for FAVILEK and what did they ask for? How did that develop as you were there?

Christina: FAVILEK had created and produced a show of its own. I believe it was ten years ago that they did this show. They did a show about their rape account from the coup d'etat.[9]

In 1991 President Jean-Bertrand Aristide, elected in the Haitian general election of 1990, was deposed by the Haitian army. This caused massive civil upheaval and left people who were considered Aristide supporters vulnerable to rape and attack. In 2004 the Washington Post *recounted many of the survivors' tales, including the story of Immacula Deluce. She had been gang raped, beaten, and temporarily blinded. When she was taken off the streets and given medical care, she was suffering physically and mentally. Like many women, she was unable to identify her attackers because they wore hoods. She was looking for a way to find peace and stand up for her rights, even if she couldn't face her attackers in court. Deluce helped found FAVILEK. That first show was called* Ochan Pou Tout Fanm Yo Bliye *(Tribute to All Forgotten Women). Immacula Deluce is still involved in raising funds and running the Facebook page for the group.*

Christina: They wanted to create a new show with a current group of artists that was reflective of the situation in Haiti since the earthquake.

Sarah: The reports coming from *CNN,* the *New York Times,* and the *Washington Post* were terrifying. It was an epidemic of rape. This was part of your work?

Christina: On that first trip we focused on working with them from an ensemble basis, because we had all these different artists with different levels of training. Some had no training. We wanted to fuse them together as a group so that they felt strong and like they could support each other, especially because we're dealing with such heavy subject matter. We wanted to make them feel unified and also bring back a sense of play.

Christina had seen a video of that first show FAVILEK produced. The play was militant and angry, which was absolutely appropriate to the situation and understandable. However, the Bond Street team wondered if FAVILEK might benefit from adding more elements to their show. There was a place for the very real (and warranted) anger, but perhaps there was also a place for varied responses and other theatrical elements.

Christina: We felt that we wanted to give FAVILEK training in different levels of intensity, so there would be texture to whatever they created. Just more tools.

Sarah: For themselves as well as the audience? How?

Christina: We worked on basic theatre exercises. Some movement, you know, working with their bodies. We did ensemble exercises. I come from a background where I use a lot of Viewpoints.[10] That's one way that we work. We did exercises from Jacques Lecoq's "Seven Energies of Man" technique: walking as an ensemble, stopping together and starting together.[11] That was the real basis of our training with them, was to get them to move as one and to create as one. We explored presence and exits and entrances, really basic things as well so we'd all have a common vocabulary. We also played a lot of games. You know, to have that sense of play and that willingness to go to that silly place. To find that spirit of joy within yourself so that you can portray it on stage. We did a lot of mime and passing energy. It's very typical of the Bond Street curriculum. Mostly it was to instill that sense of play and the ensemble.

Sarah: What would you say was your biggest success with FAVILEK?

Christina: My biggest success? I think the progression. We went in 2011, and then we went again in 2012 and to see how quickly they progressed from where they originally started. They are a group that is fired up and passionate and very strong. We're encouraging them, but you know, they are fighters and they have been fighting for a long time. I was really proud of being able to channel that energy into a show that that they wrote. It's their own words.

It's a message of hope and a message of what the possibility of the future is, and a message to encourage other Haitians to come alongside them to fight. I think the biggest accomplishment, the freshest in my mind, is this show's creation on this past trip. It's only fifteen minutes long but it's sort of a calling-card piece. They wrote a song that is their theme song but it deals with heavy stuff. There are three rapes in this show, but it's done in a way that makes it accessible to the audience. It invites them into the experience instead of being militant or preachy. I think it's really encouraging. And it doesn't alienate men, which I, which we, thought a lot about—how men fit into the equation here.

Sarah: That must be a difficult balance to find.

Christina: You can't walk into a tent camp and assume that every man is a rapist or potential rapist. You need men in this fight against sexual violence, to be a part of that dialogue. The new show that we created pokes some fun at men; there's a little bit of a clowning scene with all the different types of men sort of portrayed in maybe less than flattering light, but sorta tongue in cheek. The play is still entertaining enough that men would not walk away and feel bad.

We hope they would feel encouraged to be a part of this, of what FAVILEK is fighting for. I would say this fifteen-minute show is a really well-run piece. Plus it's very interesting to me, to see the theatre come out of the workshops.

Sarah: Is there anything about your experience that you want to add? Is there something that we've missed?

Christina: There's so much. I believe even more in the universality and the necessity of theatre and the arts in the international sphere. Everywhere that I've been with Bond Street (and everywhere that I've travelled not with Bond Street but doing theatre), I always have this same conversation about how there are no barriers in theatre. There are no barriers in the arts. We're able to communicate with each other, with our bodies and voices, and talk about really awful and hard things but also really great things. I have been encouraged to see this from being on the ground myself. The need is there and things are happening when we go into these communities and present this type of training. It lasts.

One of the women we trained in the first workshop was not able to participate in the second workshop. She was a FAVILEK member and she found out that we were in Haiti again. She came to our apartment and told us that even though she wasn't still with FAVILEK, she had started her own group and was continuing to do all these different exercises with women in her community. That was telling to me. It was important enough for her to not only continue but to take the opportunity and come find us and tell us that what we did mattered.

The most important thing that I've taken from getting to go on these trips (not just preparing in the office for them and writing grants) is that there is real proof in the experiences that the women are having. They want to continue even without us being there. They're currently trying to secure funding to do a ten-city tour of their show and that was their idea. We introduced them to different Haitian artists and they contacted those artists to help them continue working. There's a huge something there now that wasn't there before. That's what art is, creating something out of nothing.

In March of 2012, when Bond Street returned to Haiti, Christina carried with her a list of questions for this book. There were no other options for an interview: there was a language barrier, electricity and phone service couldn't be guaranteed, Skyping was technically difficult (if not impossible), and there wasn't an e-mail address I could use to address the entire company. Therefore, Christina did so on my behalf. [12]

Although some of the members did provide a first and last name, others provided only a first name or declined to be named at all. For everyone's security we decided to use only first names or the designation "FAVILEK member."

Christina: What are your names?

Françoise: My name is Françoise, and I am the joint secretary of FAVILEK. I have been a member of FAVILEK since 1991. I have four sisters.

Bazelais: I'm Bazelais, I have been a member of FAVILEK since 2003. I'm responsible for the agents working in the field. That's what I've been doing since 2003, working with the field agents. Pursuing the plays to see how we can make it work, to see how we can make it progress.

Maricia: I am Maricia, I was a founder of FAVILEK and then became treasurer. I am a person who was a victim of violence in 1991, in 2005, and in 2010. In 1991, I lost a child. I lost my son. In 2005 I lost another—he was killed in my house.

FAVILEK Member: I have been in FAVILEK from the beginning. In 1994 many of us were victims of sexual violence. I lost my child also, in that time we came together. The legal papers were drawn up for FAVILEK in 1994. We have been together since then. We've collaborated and worked together in the same venues where we have been victimized. We started to look for others who were victims of the same crimes.

At the beginning, we were ashamed to talk about it, and when we found others who were victims of the same crimes we were no longer ashamed to speak. We also encountered people who told us not to be ashamed to address it, so others will not be ashamed to speak. They said we must be bold to speak to do the job well, because if we are afraid and ashamed to speak out the others will be the same. We then decided to have our say and started working.

We started speaking out to advance the work.

Crysta: My name is Crysta. I am a delegate of FAVILEK. I joined in 2010. I first got together with another member and was telling her my story when she said she would "take me to FAVILEK where they will understand you. They will convey your message." That's how I became part of FAVILEK. Since I came in they've welcomed me. They put me in the committee.

Christina: Bazelais or Crysta, had you acted before you were working with the Bond Street Theatre?

Bazelais: Yes. I have an older brother who lives in Canada, who took part in plays. I used to take part in the play with him, in these theatre pieces. I was about twelve or thirteen years old. He no longer does plays. His theatre name was "ti epingue." It means "little pin." He played in *Alcibiades*. You may have heard of Alcibiades. That is how I started—a small child playing in the theatre.

Crysta: I used to play in school theatres. I had a cousin who was responsible for a scout troop. They used to put together big scenes. I did that when I was younger.

Christina: Maricia has already told us the story of FAVILEK. So, as for the rest of you, how did you start in FAVILEK?

FAVILEK Member: How did we start? I could say we had a common fear. There's an office called Pirraide, we used to go there for help when we had problems, and that is where we encountered the other women. There was a woman who was interested in us, who had therapy for us, and said she was putting together a group. Well, this group, what name shall we give it? And Sylvie chose the name FAVILEK. We formed "Fanm Viktim Leve Kanpe." That means "women victims, get up stand up!" That's how we have the group.

Christina: Where did you have your first show? In the field?

FAVILEK Member: Yes. Not all of the shows, but the first. The first show we put together with all of us was on September 30, 1993. The first big show that was known worldwide was myself, Françoise, Sylvie, Suzette, Raymonde, Immacula, Edime, Fannie, Deloude and Adeline.

Christina: Bazelais? Was that your start?

Bazelais: No, I did not participate in that show.

Françoise: She was not in FAVILEK then.

Christina: Then how did you start with FAVILEK?

Bazelais: There was a group member, Fannie. She was one of the founding members who knew my story. She knew a bit about my life and she encouraged me. She was taking a trip in 2003. She encouraged me to take part in the group, introduced me to the women. We shared a common problem. I had gone through the same situation, violence. I was raped in 1987. Since 1987, I have had a child on my hands without a father. I went through the same violence, and being part of the group helped relieve some stress. So I became part of FAVILEK and started working together with them. I came to realize I am not the only one that was subjected to this problem. There are a lot of others who were subjected to the same. We came together and they have accepted us the way we are.

Christina: Crysta, how did you become part of the group?

Crysta: It was due to what I was subjected to, the violence. I was telling Jacqueline and she said she would take me to a group, because "every time you ponder this it could have an effect on you." So I became part of the group. That was why I joined FAVILEK.

Christina: Cool. So Françoise and Maricia, did you ever act in theatre before FAVILEK?

Françoise: Did I? No, the September show was my first. We played for the people, whole families in a field. We presented *Ochan Pou Tout Famn Yo Bliye.*

Christina: Who said, "We need to do theatre?"

FAVILEK Members: We all decided!

Christina: What were the rehearsals like?

FAVILEK Member: There was a woman named Anne Daphne Lemoine, she was the first one to sit with us and put together the theatre pieces. [Ms. Lemoine is a broadcaster from the local radio station and a public figure]. The piece was put together according to our testimonies. We told her about what we were subjected to, our testimony of what we went through. She wrote our testimonies and then put together the scenes. We did this for four to six months. We rehearsed two or three hours every day for six months.

Christina: Wow, so, the process was different than at Bond Street?

FAVILEK Member: Yes, it was not the same thing. By then, we were already professionals in the six months that we spent. When we started with Bond Street, our fire had already slightly subsided. The task was smaller. That's also why we could learn this one so quickly because we had the theatre experience, so we didn't struggle as much.

FAVILEK Member: And there's another thing, this piece is not the same. In our piece it was our testimony and before we started to rehearse the show they passed out the text to everyone. We took it, read it to determine who could play which part. There were some of us that started and did not make the cut.

The initial FAVILEK shows were extremely honest, gut-wrenching pieces using the testimonies of rape survivors. Each woman who spoke of her experiences had at least part of her testimony make it into the script of the finished piece. While the message was powerful and immediate, the show itself wasn't mature as a piece of theatre. It was long, sometimes hard to understand, and didn't effectively reach as many audience members as they would have liked. That's why the collaboration with Bond Street Theatre was so crucial. The testimonial aspect needed to stay, but the performance itself could grow into an experience that spoke to a variety of audience members.

Christina: Bazelais, tell us about the process with Bond Street Theatre from FAVILEK's point of view.

Bazelais: We started with Bond Street in February of 2011. The collaboration was about three weeks. Everything went very well, we already had experience so when we started with Bond Street we just took off. The process was not difficult.

FAVILEK Member: Bond Street is leaving now, otherwise we would take off even more! We are waiting to do more, very quickly. We are waiting for you, next month, next year. We are waiting for Bond Street so we can instantly take off again!

The Bond Street team wrote and arranged material for FAVILEK to perform. Then the piece was rehearsed and technical elements were added. Christina asked about the technical aspects of the play and their overall level of satisfaction with the Bond Street experience.

Christina: Were you happy with the most recent show?

FAVILEK Members: Oh yes. We were very happy with the show. It was important. Each person had a text, a story, and Bond Street put it all together. We wrote together then we read, we sang, we spoke.

Christina: Where have you played?

FAVILEK Member: We played in Port-Au-Prince first, then Cap Haitien, Pétionville, Bois Monquette, Leogane, Jacquemel, Les Cay, and Gonaive.

Christina: It was a grand tour!

The women enjoyed that idea, complaining, "Only in the US did they not play." Calling it a grand tour wasn't an exaggeration. Jacquemel is as far south as you can go in Haiti, Cap-Haitien is far north, and Port-Au-Prince sits between the two. Les Cay is in the West and Gonaive is actually an island to the west of the Haitian mainland. The country itself is about 10,000 square miles, making it roughly the size of Maryland. Therefore, even though the travel between cities only took a few hours, on the scale of the country it was properly defined as a national tour.

Because this tour was large by Haitian standards, the set for their tour was quite mobile, using a tapestry that had been modeled after the background from their first show. This time, the tapestry was sturdier and more professional looking. There were also logistical concerns such as transport of the performers and their safety while traveling. As Christina continued her line of questioning, it was clear the safety of the performers became an issue in a way not frequently seen in the developed world.

Christina: On the tour, who do you perform for?

FAVILEK Member: For everyone, for the Haitians and sometimes visitors. We have people who visit us and would come to see us. They would ask us a lot of questions about the scenes, what happened, we would tell them what happened to us. The words are so poignant. They would ask a lot of questions, they watched with great care. Some would even cry and ask how can we play this when we went through it?

Christina: How does your audience respond to the play? To you? Is the response good?

FAVILEK Member: When we played Pétionville it was a rehearsal and we weren't good, but everyone liked it and applauded. Just like with Bond Street, everyone liked it. It was the same with *Fanm Yo Di Ase! (The Women Say Enough!).* People always clapped.

Christina: I know violence against women is a threat in Haiti right now. Do you feel secure performing this play about violence against women?

Once the subject of security came up, it was clear that some of the places suggested for the tour were eliminated because the safety of the actresses could not be guaranteed. One of these places is the Cité Soleil, a slum in Port-Au-Prince. After the 2010 earthquake, it became an exceedingly dangerous place as gangs and drug lords overtook the streets.[13] The police were virtually powerless to protect citizens as criminals set up operations in the shanty town and began recruiting orphans to commit crime. As of this writing, it is still a volatile place, though certain parts of the Cité have embraced anti-violence and anti-crime initiatives.[14]

FAVILEK Member: When Bond Street wanted us to play Cité Soleil, we did not accept. I refused. I was already a victim. Look, when we played in the camp, near the airport, in Benameze, we had a lot of pressure, the men said, "Listen to them, listen to how they are talking badly. We need to kill them after we rape them." Then they said, "We see them, we will remember their faces, we will recognize them." We felt a lot of pressure. That's why we said we will not play Cité Soleil. Cité Soleil is a place where they could block the car, take the car over, then kidnap the whole troupe. It's dangerous there.

Christina: We understand the situation with Cité Soleil. Although the subject matter is important for Cité Soleil, we need the security before we go there.

FAVILEK Member: If we have the security, we don't mind going, but we need the security.

Christina: Agreed, agreed. We'd need security for all of us.

FAVILEK Member: If we had security, we'd have no problem going.

Christina: In the fields do you have enough security for the show?

FAVILEK Member: Yes, we have security, we don't play just anywhere. [Troupe member] Paula picks us up, she has a car for us to take us there and to return us home. We don't walk there. We always have security.

Christina: One day FAVILEK will have its own car for a grand tour.

All of the women murmured their agreement, saying things like "God is good" and "Yes, God is able."

Christina: For all of you: how did FAVILEK change your lives?

FAVILEK Member: FAVILEK changed our lives because, when we got together, we understood each other. We understood what we had gone through. When we all sit and exchange ideas, at times one of us gets discouraged, so we support one another. It's a group of people with the same problem. When we get together, we are a force.

Christina: Yes, a force.

In 1991, FAVILEK provided emotional support for the women in a way that other post-rape and trauma assistance could not. Sometimes there was medical assistance, sometimes there was limited legal counsel, but in the end, it was talking to each other that helped them the most. Many of the women marched at the Place des Martyrs near the President's house in Port-Au-Prince. A weekly march was held on Wednesdays for people to protest against the violence and terrorism Haitians suffered under the brutal military regime that controlled Haiti from 1991 to 1994. That march was to demand legal reparations and acknowledgement that women were being tortured and raped as a part of everyday life.

After the earthquake of 2010, a tent city sprung up in the Place des Martyrs virtually overnight. Over 10,000 people camped there for nearly two years. The nightmare of the earthquake meant the FAVILEK members relived their worst feelings of insecurity and fear. How could they make things different from 1991? Could they avoid reliving some of the worst horrors?

FAVILEK Member: In the 1990s, there was a tent for medical assistance. We received medical assistance. We got help from lawyers present under the tent. We did not receive political exile when we asked for it, but we found assistance under the tent. There were four of us who had the AIDS virus, they were sent to the doctors, some of those women are now dead.

What changed our lives was that we got together and formed this organization. We didn't regret talking, we revealed ourselves, and we marched. We marched near the Capitol Building at the Place des Martyrs every Wednesday.

We got together with Lo, who was with us on Sept 30th for the foundation show. We asked for justice and reparation, we received neither. But we stand firm and will continue to fight until the end. We know that we will not get compensation or justice in Haiti, but even if it's from another country we are hoping to get help for some of us.

Christina: Françoise?

Françoise: When we say it changes lives, we mean that when we get together to share our ideas, we start to speak of our different struggles and we support each other. We say we are still alive, we are not dead, and life is not over. We will continue, moving forward.

Christina: Bazelais?

Bazelais: Yes, what changed my life was coming to hear what everyone else suffered. How I suffered and then I see when you suffered this kind of violence—there are people, so-called "friends" when you are with them, they can make you feel humiliated. But when I come here I see that it is different, there is no humiliation here. We group ourselves together—we get strength from each other to fight against what happened to us. That has helped to release some stress. When we get together we joke, we sing, we exchange ideas, and that is what changed our lives. We haven't received justice or reparation, but banding together helped us to be okay psychologically.

FAVILEK Member: I rejoice because I found FAVILEK. We all have the same problems. When I got together with them and explained what happened to me, I felt like nothing had happened to me compared to what they went through. We want FAVILEK to continue. We will continue with FAVILEK until the end.

Christina: After the earthquake what did FAVILEK do for everyone?

Maricia: Bazelais, Yolande, Jasmine, and Yanie were taking census, looking for the victims. Especially for the children who had lost their parents and the people out on the streets that were victims. I was also a victim—I spent two and a half months in the hospital. The house I was in had 11 deaths. God showed me grace. Even though I am handicapped in one arm, it's not grave. There are others who are worse off than I. Two of our members walked around in all of Port-au-Prince, taking head count. They were under the directions of the foreigners. The foreigners placed them and directed them to take the census. They didn't know to do it themselves. I was there and didn't know to do it, either. We looked for survivors. Those who were violated also were supported by FAVILEK. FAVILEK made documents for them—the recently attacked and those that were known to have been violated, Bazelais made sure they got legal aid. We would like to do everything possible for them.

Almost daily we have new victims here. The agents find them and bring them here to prepare documents for them in the office. When Bond Street leaves here, the place will open up and all of us will work hard.

The members of FAVILEK never had the luxury of being a full time theatre group. As soon as the earthquake ended, each of the women tried to help others in the best way she knew how. Some, like Bazelais, were taking census. Others were helping victims report the sexual assaults, battery, and other crimes that they had endured while displaced. One year after the earthquake, Doctors Without Borders noted that Haitians continued to live in "appalling conditions" and that cholera was causing another wave of death and misery in Haiti.[15] During this time, the members of FAVILEK were collecting experiences from survivors with horrific stories to tell but no real way to express them. Françoise recalled meeting children who were prostituting themselves in order to eat.

Françoise: Since the earthquake, most of the homeless are children who lost their parents. They've been abandoned. They're selling themselves for a plate of food. They are hungry, they need to eat, and they can't continue to suffer. Hunger is not sweet. They go to these people who will give them 25 gourde or 50 gourde ($0.59 - $1.19) for food, afterwards they sleep with them, sometimes they will even beat them or give them counterfeit money.[16] So, we judge it necessary to help these kids, even though we have no money ourselves. We planned to start out rescuing fifty kids from the streets, the ones prostituting themselves. We will school them, teach them painting, sewing, play acting to prepare them. If what they make can be sold, it will benefit them and FAVILEK. We would want to have housing for them, it wouldn't do any good to try to help them just to have them go back out on the street at the end of the day.

FAVILEK Member: Just last Friday there was a fourteen-year-old girl who lost both of her parents.

Christina: Fourteen years old?

FAVILEK Member: Yes, she was here the day before yesterday. She lost her parents. I asked her where was she during the quake. She said she was in school, that's how she is still alive. She was living in a tent, but now all the tents have been removed. So, she went to live with this woman. The woman went to work, to return at 8:00 PM. While the girl was sitting in front of the house waiting for the woman to return, five men took her and gang raped her. Those men told her if she talked they would shoot her. The girl told the woman with whom she was living, the woman kicked the girl out. She had no place to live, so she was still sneaking/hiding around the woman's home. The day before yesterday she came here with all of these draining boils, she was feverish.

She asks the other women if they have seen this young woman when she arrived. "Didn't you see her? Oh you were not here. Well, the test revealed that she is pregnant. She doesn't know yet."

The women being interviewed continued along this line of conversation for a moment, leaving behind the conversation about the theatrical work. One woman asks about "a lavage." Had the girl come earlier, it might have been possible for a man they call Father Betie to do "a lavage." One of the FAVILEK members suggests this may have helped. The literal meaning of the word lavage is "to wash." It's unclear whether this particular participant is suggesting that a douche solution may have helped avoid pregnancy or if she was suggesting something for the boils the young woman has developed. Like many of the situations that arise in this group of women, everyone is just doing the best they can to provide aid, comfort, and care in the absence of adequate income or training.

FAVILEK Member: She came here, all those things draining, feverish, I gave her bread and coffee. You know, the girl I told you I gave $20.00 to, she doesn't know she is pregnant.[17] I don't know what we can do to help her. Someone was pondering how she could help this girl, but she lives so far away. FAVILEK would like to help her, but we don't have any funds to help. It's a problem, we would like to help. My heart breaks for her. Whenever I look at her, she always has her head bent. Did you see her? We kept telling her to lift her head up. When she was leaving, I gave her 100 gourde ($2.38) to pay for transportation. I have an appointment with her on the 18th to come back here in the office.

Christina: So, what do you hope to happen or what do you dream of happening with FAVILEK theatre?

FAVILEK Member: The dream that we have for this show? Well, we have played in several places now. We would like to see the dream become a reality where FAVILEK would be able to help us help the homeless kids, the ones with no parents. If we become very visible and achieve something, we have to help these kids. That is the dream that we have for this theatre. The theatre is our commerce—it is all we have to work with, so we can help these kids.

FAVILEK Member: We would like to see the violence eradicated, not diminished but finished. When they hear the message, it would penetrate them and that would help them stop the violence. The message would change their mentality.

FAVILEK Member: Yes, I would like the theatre to become a weapon to help FAVILEK, because while playing in different places, hopefully get contracts to get funds that could help FAVILEK and also us. We, who have no jobs, we can help the kids who are out on the street prostituting themselves. It's hard when the kids are on the streets, no parents, living badly, it's hard. Apart from the theatre as a weapon, I would like us to be more zealous and for Bond Street to help us even more, so we can play more, find more sponsors so we can raise more funds for the organization. That is what I would hope.

Christina: Christa?

Christa: My dream, FAVILEK's dream for the theatre . . . alas. It's more so for the children prostituting themselves. We want to teach them things like painting, so they can grow up to become ladies, women. With the theatre we could accumulate funds for us and to help them also. We can teach them how to live better, how to be better guardians of their lives. Because the things we are teaching them can be a way for them to make money. The theatre is a big dream, it's my dream, the dream of FAVILEK. The message needs to be heard by the violators, when they hear what happened, they can replace violence by love. That is our message: to replace violence with love. To stop mistreating women and girls. That is our dream.

Marie: There is another dream, I specially would like to be a big artist in the theatre and for FAVILEK to be called to Hollywood to make a film.

Elvie: What I would like, just like Bond Street saw us on Facebook, I would like others to see us and for them to ask Bond Street to tell them about the organization and how they could join us.

My final question got to the heart of the matter: What does FAVILEK want us, the non-Haitians, the outsiders, to know about them? Who they are? What they do? The answer was simple and stunning.

FAVILEK member: We want all good things, to get together. We want everything that would be good for us. I would like FAVILEK to be represented in the US. For Bond Street to get all of the women to play in the US. I think if we expand the theatre, it would help with the reconstruction of the country.

The theatre is a great tool for what they're doing and we need more women to participate. The program is an extraordinary program that will enable the men to see what devastating result violence against women has. It would assist the men in feeling the pain, it will calm their fury. They should see all women as their mothers, sisters, and hopefully one day we can live without the violence. Instead of violence from the men, they can be our protectors. We need to stand together. After all, God made woman from the rib of man. It will also help the women realize they need to take better care of themselves, to maintain their dignity. We want to say, "Down with violence." We want to say, all together, "Down with violence."

*   *   *

FAVILEK continues to work with Bond Street to educate Haitians on the subject of rape and violence. In 2013 they are continuing to organize workshops and appearances designed to help survivors of the violence epidemic in Haiti. Christina Pinnell has accepted a posting to the Philippines, where she works with anti-human trafficking advocacy for the human rights agency International Justice Mission. Eventually, her group will use theatre to help counsel, heal, and integrate survivors back into their communities.

If you go to the website FAVILEK maintains for their group, you will discover a T-shirt available for purchase. The slogan on the shirt reads:

Ti tak! Ti Gout! Ti tak nan vwa wak ti tak nan vwa pam, Nou ka konbat vyolans kont fanm yo.

A little bit here, a little drop there. A little bit of your voice and a little drop of my voice together can fight violence against women.

Epilogue

I never intended for this book to have an epilogue. It was my belief that each of the stories, each of these women, stood alone as testament to her own resourcefulness, artistry and integrity. But then, I never intended to leave the final chapter unwritten.

The final chapter should have been the story of celebrated Syrian actress and dancer Mumassila. Mumassila is not her actual name; it's the Arabic word for "actress."

Mumassila and I first met in June 2010. She was a co-founder of a critically acclaimed group in Syria that used theatre to explore feminism, death, celebration, and symbolism. Their performances blended dance, movement work, instruments, singing, and modern technology. Her troupe had been supported by backers from both the Arab world and Western countries. They were very prolific in recent years and had done high-profile performances in front of large audiences. Mumassila was passionate about her work and the people that came to see it. Reviewers admired her, audiences loved her.

In February 2012, I was watching the news when an item came on about armed conflict in Syria. The report didn't use the word "war." The footage showed a different story; you could see armed men, faces covered, running through city streets that looked like they had been bombed. I sent Mumassila this email.

> February 7, 2012
> Dear Mumassila,
> I hope this finds you well. I'm working on a book about women who do dangerous theatre. We read every day that the situation in Syria is quite serious . . . please let me know how you are, and what's going on there.

> February 12, 2012
> Dear Sarah.
> I'm sorry to tell you that the situation here is more serious than you read or hear . . . we are facing a real war!!! I'm happy to hear [about Stage Warriors]. Right now nobody is doing theatre,

there's only some work in "National theatre," they
are doing it just to prove that nothing happen
here. Unfortunately most of the independent
artists are left the country . . . A very little group
of female actresses and dancers are here now.
Waiting to hear from you
Peace

Into April and May we thought it might be possible to talk about what
was happening to the arts in Syria. When I sent a list of questions, however, I
didn't get an answer. I realized I had been naïve and foolish. How did I know
if emailing was safe for her? How did I know for sure that a list of questions
wouldn't be read by someone who was against theatre as a form of free expression? I'm fortunate to know nothing about civil war firsthand. Maybe I
was stupid to imagine anyone would be watching these emails. Maybe I was
stupid to imagine they weren't.

June 11, 2012
Mumassila,
We're seeing every day on the news that Syria is in
all-out civil war. If you're able, please let me know
that you are OK. We're thinking of you.

June 11, 2012
Hello Sarah.
I'm fine and my family too.
What you see on the news is nothing but 40% of
what happens here . . . the situation is SO BAD
Hope is the only thing we have
Thank you for thinking about me
We'll keep in touch
Peace

With that, I left well enough alone. In the US, the war was now being
covered by every major news outlet. It had taken over a year for the people
of my country to appreciate the truth of the devastation Mumassila had been
living through.

August 13, 2013
Hi Mumassila,
The book that I have written about people who
do theatre in dangerous circumstances is headed to

the publishing house very soon! In my conclusion,
I would like to state that I wanted to talk to a
particular artist in Syria but that her situation
was so dangerous that it couldn't safely be done. I
would not say your name or your theatre. I won't
give any information that would identify you.
Would you be OK with me writing this? Please
let me know. I hope you're doing as well as can be
expected. Please be safe.
Sarah

August 16, 2013
Dear Sarah.
I'm glad to hear that you finish your book and it'll
be published. Congratulations in advance Sure it's
OK for me, but I just want to ask you one favor.
Please don't exaggerate about my situation here .
. . compared to other Syrian citizens who are still
living in really dangerous places I'm really fine.
Staying home was my choice but I don't want
to exaggerate with it, or use it in any way . .
. there's other artist who still work in [cities
redacted] so I'm not the only one . . .
I'll appreciate if you introduce me and my work in
a real way, no more, no less
Many thanks to not give any information that
would identify me.
Good luck
Peace

So, to comply with her wish, Mumassila has been presented here exactly
as she is, no more and no less. She is a talented, respected practitioner surviv-
ing a war that may determine how and when women like her are allowed
to make their art and without fear. Today that war is in Syria, Mumasilla's
home. Tomorrow it will be in another woman's home. It will be in the homes
of women all over the world who will turn to live theatre to find their voices,
warn neighbors, heal communities, and search for friends. They will tell their
truth onstage and we will be there to witness it.

Resources

Notes

Introduction
1. Theatre Without Borders, "history," http://theatrewithoutborders.com/history (Accessed July 23, 2013).

Chapter 1
1. Sudetic, Chuck "Slovenia's Scheme is a Cautious One" *New York Times*, February 24, 1991
2. *New York Times*, "Carving Out a Greater Serbia," http://www.nytimes.com/1991/09/01/magazine/carving-out-a-greater-serbia.html?pagewanted=all&src=pm (accessed July 16, 2013).
3. Slovenia was invaded June 27, 1991 just two days after declaring independence.

Chapter 2
1. http://news.BBC.co.UK/2/hi/middle_east/3694350.stm (accessed July 11, 2014)
2. United Nations, "Intifada: The Uprising," http://www.UN.org/depts/dpi/palestine/ch6.pdf (accessed August 6, 2013)
3. WBEZ. http://www.wbez.org/story/culture/theater/gaza-monologues. (Accessed December 15, 2013).

Chapter 3
1. In 2010 a property developer called SoHo properties announced that an interfaith center would be built near the site Ground Zero, where the Twin Towers stood until September 11, 2001. A mosque would be featured at the center, and this mosque became known as the Ground Zero Mosque although it was not actually on the site. The site is now open under the name Park 51 although construction has not finished. It calls itself a space for prayer and is open to people of all backgrounds.

Chapter 4
1. Human Rights Watch, "The Genocide," http://www.hrw.org/legacy/reports/1999/rwanda/Geno1-3-02.htm#P21_7273 (accessed January 12, 2013).
2. Non-governmental organizations are required to have a registration number and meet many Rwandan guidelines before they are considered legitimate. If the NGO is based in another country, designed to aid Rwandans using foreign money, the organization must also adhere to the NGO formation laws of their homeland. Generally speaking, "having a number" means that the NGO is certified to meet a specific need and is legitimately funded.

Chapter 5
1. *The Santiago Times,* "Chile's Prison Conditions Getting Worse." http://santiagotimes.cl/death-and-degradation-in-chiles-troubled-prisons/

Chapter 6
1. World Without Genocide, "Cambodian Genocide," http://worldwithoutgenocide.org/genocides-and-conflicts/cambodian-genocide (Accessed February 2, 2013).
2. English is a second language for Rithisal Kang. As such, occasionally the past and present tense of verbs were hard for him to translate. I have changed the grammar concerning past events to aid reader understanding. For example, speaking of Sina's late father will use "he was" or "he had" rather than "he is." The language remains largely faithful to Kang's

interpretation of Sina's words.

3. April 17th people were citizens that were swept up in the revolution Pol Pot started in Phnom Penh on that date in 1975. One of Pol Pot's most famous quotes on the Cambodian executions was "To spare you is no profit, to destroy you is no loss."

Chapter 7

1. http://english.al-akhbar.com/node/19535 (accessed July 11, 2014)
2. This study was quoted to me in an email sent by Zeina Daccache on Mar 19, 2011.

Chapter 8

1. Image Theatre uses still images or tableaus to explore abstract concepts like relationship, power and emotion.
2. Delegation of the European Union to Afghanistan, "On the occasion of International Women's Day the EU Delegation and Swedish Embassy co-host a briefing on AHRDO 's Legislative Theatre initiative on women's rights," http://eeas.europa.EU/delegations/afghanistan/press_corner/all_news/news/2012/20120306_01_en.htm (Accessed August 7, 2013).

Chapter 9

1. The Magdelena Project, http://www.themagdalenaproject.org/en/content/magdalena-project (Accessed August 7, 2013).
2. When Simorgh went to India for the first time in 2007, they had about 25 actresses. One of those actresses left the company after returning from Bharat Rang; she was attacked in her native Afghan province for being an actress. The April 2010 issue of *Civil Society Online* detailed this event.

Chapter 10

1. *Time*, "Egypt's Uprising: How One Young Man Found the Revolution," http://www.time.com/time/world/article/0,8599,2045571,00.html (Accessed August 2, 2013).
2. In September 2012, the news agency Reuters reported that tear gas had been fired by police in an attempt to scatter about 100 protesters and activists. The AP reported more tear gas attacks against protestors in various areas of Egypt that September although none of the articles I could find referenced the original manufacturer of the tear gas containers. http://rt.com/news/cairo-clashes-us-embassy-013/ cached July 17, 2013
3. YNet News, "3 Killed in Gunfire Exchanges in Cairo Mass Protests," http://www.ynet-news.com/articles/0,7340,L-4401241,00.html (Accessed July 18, 2013).
4. TCG Circle, "Trouble for Artists in Egypt" (*al-Akhbar Daily*, 7 June 2013, p. 2) http://www.tcgcircle.org/2013/06/trouble-for-artists-in-egypt/ (Accessed July 18, 2013).

Chapter 11

1. *The Independent*, "Return of Death Penalty in Pakistan Condemned" http://www.independent.co.UK/news/world/asia/return-of-death-penalty-in-pakistan-con-demned-8691187.html (Accessed August 8, 2013).
2. Governor-General Muhammed Ali Jinnah created Pakistan in 1947 as a nation for Muslims that did not want to remain citizens of India.

Chapter 12

1. Rafiki Theatre, "Our Mission," http://www.rafiki-theatre.org/about.htm, (Accessed August 7, 2013).
2. *IRIN*, "Peace Restored, but Northern Uganda's Children Still Struggle" http://www.irinnews.org/report/97206/peace-restored-but-northern-uganda-s-children-still-struggle (Accessed August 1, 2013).

Chapter 13

1. *The Guardian*, "Anti-gay bigots plunge Africa into new era of hate crimes" http://www.guardian.co.UK/world/2009/dec/13/death-penalty-uganda-homosexuals (Accessed Janu-

ary 2, 2013).

2. *The Examiner*, "Ugandan leader: Passing the 'Kill the Gays' Bill Will be 'Christmas Gift'." http://www.examiner.com/article/ugandan-leader-passing-kill-the-gays-bill-will-be-christmas-gift (Accessed November 15, 2012); Advocate, "Ugandan Parliament reconvenes, with Lingering 'Kill the Gays' Bill," http://www.advocate.com/news/world-news/2013/02/07/ugandan-parliament-reconvenes-lingering-kill-gays-bill (Accessed April 2, 2013).

3. Beau Hopkins, in discussion with author, March 22, 2013.

4. *The Africa Report*, "Ugandan Gays Outraged by Minister," http://www.theafricareport.com/Society-and-Culture/ugandan-gays-outraged-by-minister.html, (Accessed August 7, 2013).

5. *The Guardian*, "British Theatre producer Says Gay Uganda Play 'Was supposed to be Funny'," http://www.guardian.co.UK/world/2012/oct/18/david-cecil-gay-play-uganda (Accessed November 20, 2012).

6. *Metro Weekly*, "Updated: Uganda in the Spotlight," http://www.metroweekly.com/news/?ak=8200 (Accessed April 2, 2013).

Chapter 14

1. V-Day, "Gender based Violence in Haiti," http://www.vday.org/spotlight2012/gender-based-violence (Accessed August 7, 2013).

2. United Nations, "Report of the Secretary-General on the United Nations Stabilization Mission in Haiti," www.UN.org/ga/search/view_doc.asp?symbol=S/2010/200 (Accessed August 7, 2013).

3. Disasters Emergency Committee, "Haiti Earthquake facts and Figures," http://www.dec.org.UK/haiti-earthquake-facts-and-figures (Accessed August 7, 2013).

4. *Huffington Post*, "Rape In Haiti: Women, Girls Detail Violent Attacks In Aftermath Of Haiti Earthquake" http://www.huffingtonpost.com/2010/03/16/rape-in-haiti-women-girls_n_501588.html (Accessed August 7, 2013).

5. *The New York Times*, "Sexual Assaults Add to Miseries of Haiti's Ruins," http://www.nytimes.com/2010/06/24/world/americas/24haiti.html?pagewanted=1&partner=rss&emc=rss&adxnnlx=1277380851-k107YtUeC6lX0FpfFfsPHA&_r=0 (Accessed August 7, 2013).

6. *Huffington Post*, "Rape in Haiti: Women, Girls Detail Violent Attacks in Aftermath of Haiti Earthquake," http://www.huffingtonpost.com/2010/03/16/rape-in-haiti-women-girls_n_501588.html (Accessed August 7, 2013).

7. Ibid.

8. Carnivale, the celebration preceding Lent, is held annually in Port-au-Prince, with other cities having smaller celebrations around Haiti.

9. *The Washington Post*, "'Political Rapes' of 1991 Still Haunt Haitian Democracy Advocates," http://www.latinamericanstudies.org/haiti/haunt.htm (Accessed July 22, 2013).

10. The idea of Viewpoints, a way to break down problems of time and space on stage, was created from the modern dance movement and expanded by American director Anne Bogart (1951-).

11. Jacques Lecoq (1921-1999) was a French actor and teacher. His background in mime and physical theatre led him to create several theories on how to create vibrant, interesting characters that could be taken on through physical work.

12. These questions were written by myself, posed by Christina and then translated from Haitian Creole by a Haitian-American volunteer named Mrs. Gilberte Napoleon-Bock. Any errors or omission of fact are mine.

13. Streetgangs.com, "Gang Members in Haitian Slum Profit from Disaster," http://www.streetgangs.com/news/011910_haitiangang (Accessed July 4, 2013).

14. Dying in Haiti, "Violence in Soleil," http://dyinginhaiti.blogspot.com/2012/03/violence-

in-soleil-march-5-2012.html (Accessed July 5, 2013).

15. Doctors Without Borders, "Haiti: One Year After," http://www.msf.ie/haiti-one-year-after (Accessed July 22, 2013.

16. The Gourde (or Goud in Kreyol) is the standard unit of money in Haiti.

17. Although the Haitians use the Gourde as their official currency, 5 Gourdes is often referred to as a Haitian Dollar. http://www.financialcrisis2009.org/financial_dictionary/index.php?l=H. (Accessed December 15, 2013).

Acknowledgements

This book has been an extraordinary journey through history, politics, art, storytelling and diplomatic relations. I have many people to thank for their kindness as well as their willingness to share their expertise with me.

Catherine Filloux, Roberta Levitow, Bond Street Theatre, and everyone at Theatre Without Borders made it possible for me to begin my research and find people to talk to. During their workshops I met Hjalmar Jorge Joffre-Eichhorn and am grateful to him for opening a door into the complex lives of the men and women doing theatre in Afghanistan. Thanks to Ben Hanig, Becca Nelms, Alex Houchin, Calandra Daby, Brittni Nowicki, Bryan Howard, and 395H students for typing, feedback, suggestions, and general encouragement.

Lisa Suhair Majaj edited and Amy Menge assisted. Gilberte Napoleon-Bock translated in the FAVILEK chapter for which I'm truly grateful. Dr. Ian M. Borden provided insight and toast. This book could never have happened without them. Any inconsistencies are mine alone.

Finally, the Stage Warriors themselves have my personal thanks for trusting this project. From the very beginning the deal was always that they present their work in their own words to create a historical document of how theatre has been used in this time, in these places, to change the world. Thanks for letting me capture it.

Bibliography

Barfield, Thomas J. *Afghanistan: a cultural and political history*. Princeton: Princeton University Press, 2010.

Bennoune, Karima. *Your fatwa does not apply here: untold stories from the fight against Muslim fundamentalism*. none: W. W. Norton & Company, 2013.

Bergin, Sean. *The Khmer Rouge and the Cambodian genocide*. New York: Rosen Pub. Group, 2009.

Cohen, Cynthia. *Acting together: performance and the creative transformation of conflict*. Oakland, CA: New Village Press, 2011.

Cohen, Cynthia. *Acting together: performance and the creative transformation of conflict*. Oakland, CA: New Village Press, 2011.

Dallaire, Roméo, and Brent Beardsley. *Shake hands with the devil: the failure of humanity in Rwanda*. New York, NY: Carroll & Graf ;, 2005.

Dubois, Laurent. *Haiti: the aftershocks of history*. New York: Picador / Metropolitan Books, 20132012.

Farmer, Paul. *Haiti after the earthquake*. Rev. and updated. ed. New York: PublicAffairs, 2012.

Gelvin, James L.. *The Arab uprisings: what everyone needs to know*. New York: Oxford University Press, 2012.

Hall, Brian. *The impossible country: a journey through the last days of Yugoslavia*. New York: Penguin Books, 1995.

Harel, Amos, and Ora Cummings. *34 days: Israel, Hezbollah, and the war in Lebanon*. Basingstoke: Palgrave Macmillan, 20092008.

Hatzfeld, Jean. *Life laid bare: the survivors in Rwanda speak*. New York: Other Press, 2006.

Kamrava, Mehran. *The modern Middle East: a political history since the Second World War*. Third ed. Berkeley: University of California Press, 2013.

Smith, Charles D.. *Palestine and the Arab-Israeli conflict*. 8th ed. Boston, MA: Bedford/St. Martins, 2013.

Stewart, Colin. *From wrongs to gay rights: cruelty and change for LGBT people in an uncertain world*. none: P.C. Haddiwiggle Publishing Company, 2013.

Sultan, Cathy. *Tragedy in South Lebanon the Israeli-Hezbollah war of 2006*. Minneapolis: Scarletta Press, 2008.

Tanner, Stephen. *Afghanistan: a military history from Alexander the Great to the war against the Taliban*. Updated version. ed. Philadelphia: Da Capo, 2009.

Wieland, Carsten. *Syria--a decade of lost chances: repression and revolution from Damascus Spring to Arab Spring*. Seattle: Cune Press, 2012.

Index

2006 Israel-Hezbollah War, 86
Abbas, Mahmoud, 30
Actualidad Now, 72
Afghanistan Human Rights and Democracy Organization, 9, 12, 90-91, 96, 99-101, 179
Ajoka, 116-118, 120, 122
Alexanderplatz, 149
Andelic, Jadranka'Jadranka, 17-18
Aoun, Iman, 7, 9, 15, 29-30, 33, 41, 44
Arab Spring, 6, 111-112, 182
Aristide, Jean-Bertrand, 158
Aristizabal, Hector, 95
Aschiana, 150
ASHTAR Theatre, 9, 29-31, 33, 38, 41, 43-45
Azeda, Hope, 10, 20, 44, 48, 50, 66, 68, 74, 79, 87-88, 90, 97, 108, 110, 115, 133, 137, 160, 170-171, 173-175
Baabda Prison, 88-89
Babur Shah Garden, 105
Bahati, David, 134
Bamiyan, 95-96, 99
Basiouny, Dalia, 8, 16, 109-110, 115
Bellerice, Morlon Lhe, 152, 157
Bergen Theatre, 105-106
Bharat Rang Mahotsav, 105, 107
Bharat Rang Mahotsav International Theatre Festival, 105
Bhutto, Benazir, 121
Big Apple Circus, 155
Black Sea International Theatre Festival, 107

Boal, Augusto, 11-12, 31, 90, 112
Bond Street Theatre, 8, 102, 106, 146, 148-151, 153-156, 159-162, 164-166, 169, 171-172, 181
Bread and Puppet Theatre, 24, 28, 37, 148, 170
Brecht, Bertolt, 21, 43
Breed, Ananda, 50
Brevoort, Deborah, 15
BST, 152
Burqavaganza, 116, 121-122
Bwanika, Esther, 8, 135-136
Cancino, Claudio, 71
Catani, Diane, 72
Catharsis/Lebanese center for Drama Therapy, 27, 48, 61, 79, 81, 86, 88-90
Cecil, David, 9, 135-136, 138, 141-143, 145
Chhon, Sina, 7, 9, 15, 73-74, 77-78
Colina One Prison, 62, 64, 66, 68
Commedia dell'Arte, 154
Daccache, Zeina, 7, 9, 79, 85, 179
Dah Teatar, 14-15, 17-23, 27-28
Deluce, Immacula, 158
Disasters Emergency Committee of the UK, 146
Documents Center of Cambodia, 76
Domestic Violence, 88
drama therapy, 79-82, 84-88
Dubai Film Festival, 86
East African Institute of Governance and Conflict Management, 125
Educational Theatre Festival of Herat, 99, 102, 105-107
Egyptian Uprising, 16, 110
Ehn, Eric, 15
El Hakawati Theatre Company, 30
Emerwon, Angella, 8, 135, 138
Ensler, Eve, 140
ENTEPOLA, 68-69, 72
Exile Theatre, 149-150
Fall, Nadia, 12, 50, 122

Familie Floez, 154
FAVILEK, 8-9, 102, 146, 148, 151-153, 156-172, 181
Fénix, 66, 69-70, 72
Filloux, Catherine, 15, 74, 181
Forum Theatre, 12-13, 37, 91, 99
Freedom Theatre of Jenin, 38
Gauhar, Madeeha, 8, 116
Gaulier, Phillipe, 80
Gaza Monologues, 9, 33, 38, 44
George Soros Foundation, 22
Glass, Penelope, 7, 62, 66
Gisler, Karin, 95
Goethe Institute, 105
Gurik, Robert, 87
Habyarimana, Juvenal, 46
Haigazian University, 81-82
Hashemi, Abdul Hakim, 103, 105
Hashemi, Monirah, 8-9, 102, 108
Hernández, Rodrigo, 72
Hopkins, Beau, 135, 137, 144, 180
Hudood Laws, 118
Human Rights Watch, 46, 131, 178
Hytner, Sir Nicholas, 122
Ilusiones, 66, 68-70, 72
Indian Consul for Cultural Relations, 105
Inter-American Commission on Human Rights, 146
International Criminal Tribunal for the Former Yugoslavia, 17
International Justice Mission, 172
Invisible Theatre, 12, 36, 125-126
Iparraguirre, Iván, 65, 71
Jean, Maricia, 156
Joffre-Eichorn, Hjalmar-Jorge, 9, 15, 90-91, 101, 181
July War, 86-87
Kabera, Eric, 48
Kadaga, Rebecca, 134
Kahana, 34
Kang, Rithisal, 74, 178

Katushabe, Phionah, 8, 123-124, 133, 145
Khmer Rouge, 73-76, 182
Kiprotich, Stephen, 123
Kony, Joseph, 123, 126
La MaMa Theatre, 9, 15, 28, 39, 74, 77, 156
Lakhaon Kamnap/Poetry Theatre, 74
Lan, David, 143
Lassegue Marie-Laurence, Jocelyn, 148
Ledesma, Paulina, 72
Legislative Theatre, 12, 91, 99, 179
Lemoine, Anne Daphne, 164
Levitow, Roberta, 15, 181
Lokodo, Simon, 140
Lord's Resistance Army, 123-124, 126
Magdalena Project, 102
McGuigan, Michael, 155
Milosevic, Slobodan, 20-21
Milosevic, Dijana, 17-19, 21
Minister of Ethics and Integrity (Uganda), 140
Mouawad, Wajdi, 56
Mubarak, Hosni, 109
Mugisha, Frank, 135
Muslim Brotherhood, 115
Nabagesera, Kasha Jacqueline, 140
Nadeem, Shahid, 121-122
Nastasijevic, Momocilo, 21
National Theatre Festival of Kabul, 105, 107
National Theatre of Kampala, 135
Newspaper Theatre, 11-12, 92
NGO, 51, 56-57, 59-60, 178
Obaid-Chinoy, Sharmeen, 120
Open Society, 22
Oum El Nour / Rehabilitation Center from Drug Addiction, 80
Participatory Theatre, 92-93, 95, 97-98, 124
Pinnell, Christina, 151, 153, 172
Playback Theatre, 90-92

Pot, Pol, 73-74, 179
Prins, Annemarie, 76
Prison Service Art Education, 66
Prynce, Okuyo Joel Atiku, 134, 143-145
Punzo, Armando, 82
Rafiki Theatre of Kampala, 123
Restavek, 146
Revolution (San Miguel Prison Theater Group), 6, 8, 72, 107, 109, 111-115, 132, 134, 179, 182
Robles, Victor, 72
Rose, Reginald, 84, 147
Roumieh Prison, 9, 79, 82, 84-85, 88
Rwandan Patriotic Front / Rwandese Patriotic Front, 46
Rwandan Defense Forces / RDF, 53
Saito, Dawn, 78
San Francisco Mime Troupe, 148
San Miguel Prison / San Miguel Preventive Detention, 64-65, 69
Second Lebanon War, 86
Sexual Minorities Uganda, 135
SFACA, 102-103, 106
Sherman, Joanna, 148, 155
Simorgh Film Association of Culture and Art, 102-106, 108, 179
Sithuland, Ieng, 74
Sophy, Him, 74
South Asia Women's Theatre Festival, 107
Spect-Actors, 11-13
Squella, Sebastián, 71-72
Srebrenica, 24-25, 27
Sueños de Libertad, 72
Tahrir Square, 109-110, 113, 115
Taseer, Salman, 119
Tasic, Sanja Krsmanovic, 7, 17
Teatro PASMI, 62-63, 65, 70-72
The Hague, 17
The Red Pepper, 144
Theatre for Social Development, 106,

151
Theatre of the Oppressed, 1, 6-8, 10-100, 102-175, 178-182, 181
Theatre Without Borders, 15-17, 74, 90-91, 178, 181
Ugandan Media Council, 139
Ugandan National Theatre, 141
Umubyeyi, Jaqueline, 51
Umuhire, Solange Liza, 51
United Nations, 17, 29-30, 33, 38, 44, 48, 118, 131, 146-147, 178, 180
United Nations Development Program, 146
US-Indian-Afghan Arts Exchange and Conflict Resolution Project, 150
Uwayezu, Jean-Paul, 51
Uwimbabazi, Sonia, 51
Viewpoints, 159, 180
VOICETheatre, 39, 41
Volterra Prison, 82
Volterra Theatre Festival, 82
Vujovic (ex Mitic), Maja, 7, 14, 17
Wagner, Colleen, 47-49, 52, 55
Wahab, Anisa, 150
Weinblatt, Marc, 95
Women in Action, 115
Women in Black / Zene u Crnom, 22-25
Women Playwrights International Conference, 108
Women's International Playwright Conference, 107
Women's Side of War, 23
Wynter, Josh, 158
Yagana, Zahra, 9, 100-101
Zambello, Francesca, 78
Zastrow, Anna, 9, 151, 156
Zia-ul-Haq, Mohammed, 116, 119

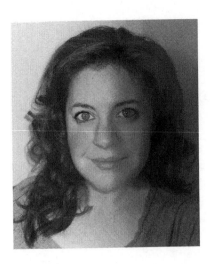

Sarah Imes Borden received her MFA in acting from the California State University, Fullerton and works as an actress, activist, and lecturer. She currently teaches about theatrical practices around the world for the University of Nebraska-Lincoln. When she's not teaching or in the theatre Sarah enjoys British television, murder mysteries and traveling with her husband Ian.

Made in the USA
Charleston, SC
16 December 2015